What We Carry With Us

Karen J. Hasley

Karen J. Hasley

To my friends ~ Ann, with her eye for detail and Paula, who gives vision to ideas ~ straight from the heart: thank you.

Cover design by Paula Buermele

ISBN: 1542851084
ISBN-13: 978-1542851084

"Memory is the diary we all carry about with us."

Oscar Wilde, Irish playwright, 1854-1900

New Hope, Nebraska, in 1878

N

<u>Railroad/Train Station</u>   <u>RR stock pens</u>

Freight office   Livery
<u>alley</u>
Telegraph/Post Office   Variety & Groc
<u>alley</u>   Carpentry &

Feed & Grain   **Main**   Undertaker
                           Jail

Leather Goods   **Street**

                        Bliss House &
Dry Goods & Notions   Music Hall
Gooseneck Hotel & Billiards
Hardware   Meeting -
United Bank of Nebraska   Entertainment Hall

W ←School]   alley/"Church Street"
     alley   [Church→ **E**

←Laundry] Dress Shop   Barber Shop
     Nebraska Café   Law Office
     Hart's Boarding House   MD/Drug Store

River

S

to Fort Cottonwood↓

What We Carry With Us

Karen J. Hasley

1

At first, it was nothing but a case of someone gone missing. No one could find Eddie Barts, the young man who worked in the telegraph office, which to start with didn't seem all that unusual. Eddie was a lanky young fellow with a love for fishing, and it had happened more often than I could count that Eddie had turned the sign to closed and taken off for his favorite spot along the river. Inconvenient, yes, but not surprising. Not at first, anyway.

I didn't even know he had disappeared until Harold Sellers stepped into the barber shop and said Eddie's name, looking at me as he did so. I heard the question mark in Harold's voice and shook my head. The man sitting in the chair with his face wrapped in a warm towel wasn't Eddie Barts.

"He's not here," I said.

"Have you seen him around lately, Ruth?" Harold asked. I shook my head again as I reached for the straightedge.

"No. Not since – oh, I couldn't say, really." I thought a moment. "A couple days, at least. Maybe Tuesday? He's down by the river, I wouldn't be surprised. You know how he is when the weather warms up."

Harold nodded. "I know how he is, all right, but he's not there. At least, not where I can find him."

"He'll show up. He always does." I unwrapped the towel and began to lather my customer's face.

"I guess you're right," Harold said, but there was a touch of something in his voice, worry or doubt or some similar emotion, that made me look over at him.

Joe Chandler, the man in the chair, heard it, too, and turned his head in Harold's direction.

"You sound worried," I said. "How's this different from other sunny days when Eddie can't be found?"

"Don't know exactly, just a feeling. Maybe it isn't different. It's just that the office was closed yesterday, too, and I've never known the boy to be gone two days running."

"Spring fever hits some folks like that," Joe volunteered. I thought Joe was right and smiled my agreement.

"Especially young men," I said. "It's either fish or girls for them." Both men laughed, but even then, Harold didn't lose his look of concern.

"That's true enough, Ruth, but I believe I'll check a few other places the boy might be. Maybe he discovered whiskey and needs a day to put his head back together."

That last part didn't sound a bit like young Eddie Barts, but I returned my attention to my customer as soon as the door closed behind Harold. I never gave Eddie Barts another thought all that working day, which goes to show you, I suppose, how easy it is to overlook an omen and miss the moment your life turns upside down. Because Eddie Barts was my omen and that was my moment, and I missed them both entirely.

I was born twenty-eight years ago in a soddy in the general vicinity of what is now called North Platte. Back then, the place didn't have a name or even a presence because it was before the Union Pacific Railroad arrived in Nebraska. Back then, it was just miles and miles of grazing land, which suited my father very well. I was eleven when he left home for good but can remember that he was an industrious man, a former schoolteacher from Pennsylvania with enough ambition for ten men. If Papa hadn't gone to fight for the Union in the war, I have no doubt he would have ended up with cattle over a thousand hills, as the Bible says, but he did go – "pure foolishness," I recall my mother grumbling, though not without a touch of pride because she was the closest thing to an abolitionist western Nebraska would ever see – and he never came home. Much later, after the war ended and men began to straggle home, we found out that he was killed outside Vicksburg, Mississippi, in 1863. When we stopped hearing from Papa, we convinced ourselves it was the war getting in the way of civil communication and we tried, Mama, my two sisters, and I, to keep the ranch going while we waited for our beloved father to come home. Eventually, Calvin Waterman brought us the bad news, and I suppose he could have given us details since he fought at Vicksburg himself, but Mama didn't want details, and I can't blame her. Calvin was a different person from the cheerful man who had left expecting the war to be a great adventure. He came home sullen and worn and easily startled, and I believe reliving the details of Vicksburg would have been bad for both him and Mama. It was enough to know that Papa slept under Mississippi mud and would never realize any of his grand ambitions.

We lasted another two years until, all the men home that were going to come home, Mama found a buyer for the land and what was left of the herd and we moved to a town called New Hope. She used the money from the sale to buy a house she immediately turned into boarding rooms. I was seventeen. My older sister married that same year and moved to Omaha with her husband. My younger sister waited two years and did the same, only moved farther, all the way to Texas, and suddenly – or so it seemed – it was just Mama and me. Running the boarding house was hard work the same as ranching was, but it was considerably more lucrative because New Hope was laid out with intent along the Union Pacific rail line, which eventually became part of the nation's first trans-continental railroad.

I've never minded hard work and I had my father's share of ambition, besides, so at nineteen and busy with the common drudgery commensurate with offering quality accommodations to boarders and travelers, I could still envision several boarding houses strung along the railroad line. Each would have a sign over the door that bore our name, Hart's, and perhaps some kind of pretty red heart painted on the sign, besides. That way, even if you couldn't read, you would still be able to recognize us. That could have happened, too – look at Mr. Harvey and his fine establishments – except the next year Mama died, and then Duncan Churchill stepped off the train in New Hope, and that was that. I missed my mother something awful and meeting Duncan brought much needed comfort. He was a big, hearty, generous man, come all the way from England, with a manner about him that made people take to him from the start. I fell in love with him practically from the first moment I saw him. My heart felt pretty bruised from losing Mama, and it seemed right to marry him. In the short time we had together, we never exchanged a cross word.

I hired someone to help me with the boarding house and used some of my hard-earned cash to set up a barber's shop. Duncan, with his English accent, good looks, and love of conversation, had a flair for barbering, and we enjoyed a happy life for a time until consumption took him three years into our marriage, and that was that. Again.

That was my story up to the moment Eddie Barts disappeared, taking over for my mother at the boarding house and for Duncan at the barber shop, living their dreams because I felt I owed them both something, loving them as I did and missing them. But then everything changed. Fear came into my life, and suspicion, and shock, and the kind of misery that accompanies those emotions. But love came, too, along with hope and a measure of happiness I thought I'd never have again, so while in a way my life was up-ended, it wasn't all bad. Like life in general, I suppose, full of both good and bad balanced against each other, God's good way of tempering the years He gives us on the earth. The Almighty is a lot of things, but predictable is not one of them.

Silas Carpenter arrived in New Hope the same day I heard that Eddie Barts was missing. I was finishing up at the shop, returning the cleaned mugs and brushes and razors to their places by the mirror when the door opened. I turned and faced what I presumed was a customer looking for a quick cut or shave and saw Si Carpenter standing in the doorway. Of course, I didn't know him then. Because New Hope was on the railroad line, we saw a lot of strangers passing through and that's all I saw: a lean, dark-haired stranger a smidge above average height wearing several days' stubble. I can't help having a barber's inclination to fix on a man's facial hair before I meet his eyes.

"I'm sorry," I said, untying my apron as I spoke, "but I'm closed. I open tomorrow at nine o'clock sharp, though, and I'll be happy to put you first on the list."

He removed his hat quickly at the sight of me and looked a bit taken aback by my words, though I thought he had a gambler's face, which would not display emotion unless he chose to let it show. His stance had not relaxed with his smile, but the smile was pleasant, nevertheless, and gave warmth to his face. I would find out later that he had slate gray eyes, but at the distance we stood and with the late afternoon sun behind him, I couldn't see that at the time.

"I appreciate that, ma'am." He raised a hand, rubbed his cheek, and said with a rueful tone to his voice, "I imagine I could use some sprucing, but that's not why I'm here. You're the barber?"

My turn to smile. "Yes. I'm told I'm the only female barber along the Platte so you can get a shave and take in a local oddity all at the same time." We stood there a moment without saying a word until I added, "Why are you here, then, if not for some sprucing? Your words, not mine."

"The telegraph office is closed."

"So I heard. And you thought—" I let my sentence drift off and waited.

"I thought maybe the operator was getting a haircut at the end of his work day, and I could convince him to open up for me, but maybe I was wrong on more than one count. Maybe the telegraph operator's a woman, too." For some reason, his dry comment made me laugh.

"No, Eddie Barts sends all our telegrams, and Eddie's definitely not a woman. And as you can tell, he's also not here."

"Yes, I see that. Would you know where I could find him?" I thought he must have an urgent message to send to someone if he couldn't wait until regular hours in the morning.

"It's funny, that," I said, "because I just heard Eddie's been missing for a couple of days now."

I didn't imagine that the man became very still, but I wouldn't have been able to say what exactly changed about him. There was a noticeable difference, though, even in the tone of his voice. I was reminded of how you wake in the night at a sound and lie very still trying to figure out where the sound came from and if you should be worried about it.

"Has he?" the man said.

"Yes, but Eddie goes missing occasionally because he loves to fish and sometimes the river beckons. We tolerate it. He's a good young man, and I suspect he'll be behind the counter bright and early tomorrow morning." But even to my ears, my voice lacked confidence.

"That's all right, then. I'll get to Eddie in the morning." He paused. "Does New Hope offer accommodations for the night?"

I grinned inwardly but said with as much innocence as I could muster, "Yes, indeed, a very fine boarding house across the street. The sign over the front steps says Hart's"

"And just the one livery across from the telegraph office?"

"On the other end of town from here, more's the pity. The city fathers' planning may have lacked a little foresight."

The man smiled again but not with warmth this time. Still mulling over the closed telegraph office and Eddie Barts' absence, I thought, and his mood suddenly made me worried about Eddie's absence, too. I hadn't given the young man a thought since Harold's visit earlier in the day but wondered if that was an oversight on my part. The stranger's reaction to the closed telegraph office left me with an uncomfortable feeling, like I had missed something important. Despite the warm spring day, a chill moved up my spine.

"Thank you." He rubbed his cheek again. "I probably will take advantage of your services in the morning. Do you offer baths, too?"

"Not at the barber shop, but for a dime you can get one at the boarding house."

"Is it too much to hope I can get a spot of supper at the boarding house?"

"It is, I'm afraid. Hart's offers feather beds, clean linens, and hot baths, but no meals." Yet, anyway, I thought to myself, having had that idea simmering in the back of my mind for over a year. "But there's a fine café right next door to the boarding house and a real sit-down restaurant called Bliss House midway down the street on the other side. You can take your pick with eating establishments, and you won't be disappointed whatever you decide."

"Sounds like New Hope has it all," the man said.

"We try."

"Well, I appreciate the information, Mrs.—"

"Churchill," I supplied. "Ruth Churchill, and you would be–?" He settled his hat, still dusty from travel, back on his head and reached for the door handle.

"My name's Si Carpenter, Mrs. Churchill. I'm pleased to make your acquaintance." I could tell he was more interested in making Eddie Barts' acquaintance than mine, but I approved of his manners. "Good afternoon." He pulled the door closed behind him, and I followed him out not long afterward, stopping on the boardwalk long enough to take a last look at the back of Mr. Carpenter as he led his mount down New Hope's broad main street north toward the livery. Something more there than he let on, I told myself, but didn't have time for more introspection just then. I turned south toward Hart's and headed home.

When my mother bought the house that would become Hart's, it was in a state of disrepair. A man named Wooster, I never knew if that was his first or last name, was employed by the railroad and expected to settle in as king of the hill, king of the New Hope hill, at least, but the Union Pacific had other plans for him and cut him loose from their employ when the house was almost but not quite finished. The separation must have come as a surprise to him. I know it surprised the fledgling New Hope bank, which had loaned the phantom Wooster money for the house, considering any railroad man to be a reliable customer. When the man and all his worldly goods absconded into the night, the bank president realized he would never see that particular investment returned. No wonder that Mr. Talamine welcomed my mother's offer to buy the house, even if the money he received came in at a smaller rate than initially anticipated. At least, money came in. Until the day she died, my mother never missed a payment and neither had I, even after using some of the boarding house profits to set up the barber shop for Duncan. I owned both enterprises outright now, with special thanks to the Union Pacific Railroad and a mystery man named Wooster.

I entered through the front door and smiled at Danny Lake where he stood behind the tall butler's desk we used for checking in new boarders. Danny was my right arm when it came to the boarding house, right arm and right leg, heart and brain sometimes, too. I couldn't imagine what I would do without him. Danny came to New Hope five years earlier, a freckle-faced lad of ten, beaten down, sun-burned, and so weak he did not make it past the boarding house into town but could only sink down against my front gate and sit there, exhausted and mute. He had walked off the prairie, the lone survivor of cholera that had taken the rest of his family south of the river. A search party found the wagon and the bodies later and because of the fear of disease, buried the folks on the spot and burned the wagon with all its contents. We never found the livestock Danny said should have been there, two yoke of oxen and a milk cow. Stolen by prairie scavengers, I shouldn't wonder. He had started out on a pony to find help but somewhere along the way the boy and the pony got separated, and Danny walked the last miles to town. I had just lost Duncan and recognized the look on the boy's face, saw my own grief and loneliness reflected in his eyes, and I took him under my wing from that moment. There was some complaint about it, fearing Danny would bring the same disease that had killed his family into New Hope, but I can be fierce when I set my mind on something, and I would not tolerate any talk of sending the boy away or even of isolating him outside of town for a while. Danny had just lost his entire family. He was isolated enough. I forfeited a little boarding house business for a while, but neither Danny nor I sickened. Life resumed, almost as if there was no interruption, as if I had not recently watched my husband die gasping for air and Danny had not tended his parents and siblings until there was no one left for him to tend. That was five years ago. Now, looking at his shock of orange hair, his freckles, and his grin, I could only be thankful that his family tragedy had occurred south of New Hope, so that it was at my gate Danny lost his strength and crumpled to the ground. Otherwise, I had no doubt that if he had come into town from the opposite end, he'd have collapsed outside the livery and would today be mucking out the stables for Cap Sherman, the old reprobate rebel who ran the livery. The good Lord must have known what I needed because back then I felt as lost as I had ever been, with no idea how to run both a boarding house and a barber shop all on my own, so He sent the boy to my front door knowing we'd be good for each other. Taking and giving, my mother once told me, is what God does best.

"Are we booked up, Danny?" I asked as I stepped beside him.

"No, ma'am, not yet, but maybe when the six o'clock from Kearney gets in, we'll fill up."

I reached for the check-in book that lay on the desk top and turned it so I could read the signatures. "I see Mr. Franks is back."

"Yes'm. Took his usual room. You just missed him. He went to find supper."

"Well, save a single room for a man named Carpenter. I expect he'll walk through the door eventually."

I went down the back hallway and turned right to enter what we called The Addition, an attached three rooms where Danny and I lived. It never failed to make me think of the railroad man Wooster because what in the world had he intended The Addition for? Servants' quarters, someone once suggested, the idea of which still had the ability to make me giggle. Servants' quarters in New Hope, Nebraska? Well, maybe the man had southern roots and was used to being waited on hand and foot on some big plantation. Otherwise, I couldn't explain the need or intention for a small, separate addition to an already huge house. Whatever Wooster's original plan, it ended up working well for Mama and me, and then for Danny and me. We had a good-size kitchen, plus each of us had a room of our own for sleeping. Not a big addition, but big enough. The arrangement allowed us to use all the other rooms in the house for paying customers, having turned what was intended for the kitchen into a bath room, with two bathtubs separated by a curtain the length of the room. All in all, my mother had shown foresight and the house was recommended as a fine boarding house. Our competition was a so-called hotel, noticeably smaller than Hart's, attached to the billiards parlor and a few available rooms over the local music hall. Considering the alternatives, Hart's was always first choice among respectable travelers.

I built a fire in the cook stove, put a pot of stew on the burner to warm, set the table, and took butter and milk from our newest acquisition: an icebox ordered from the Montgomery Ward catalog and a marvel of modern invention. In a surprising way, one of the things I missed most about my husband was cooking for him. Duncan had praised even my worst cookery mistakes, and on more than one occasion his attempts to find something kind to say had set us both to laughing. The consumption had weakened him

almost from our wedding day, but until the end we managed
to find something, no matter how minor, that made us laugh
together. I missed both the cooking and the laughter but
found a measure of comfort in cooking for Danny. He was
fifteen with an appetite twice his size and watching him eat
was a pleasure.

Supper in place, I went back to the front desk because I
wanted to be there when Mr. Carpenter came to claim a
room. There weren't many amusements in New Hope, and I
would enjoy the look on his face when he saw me.

I wasn't disappointed. I had sent Danny to the back
room to be sure water was heating and available for baths and
stood behind the big desk intent on a bill of lading when the
jingle of the bell on the front door told me I had a customer.
Looking up, I faced Mr. Carpenter himself. He stopped
abruptly at the sight of me, tilted his head ever so slightly –
much the way Othello, our boarding house dog, does when
he cannot figure out what I'm saying – and allowed himself a
slow smile.

"Mrs. Churchill." He righted both his posture and his
expression, adjusted the saddle bag draped over his shoulder,
removed his hat, and walked toward me.

"I know," I said, smiling. "It's a cheap trick, but I can
never resist. There's something gratifying about putting a
look of surprise on a man's face."

He responded with a nice, low laugh. "Then I'm happy
to oblige you, ma'am."

As Mr. Carpenter took a leisurely look around him at the
area in which we stood, I tried to see it through his eyes. The
two comfortable upholstered chairs, the rose-colored glass
lamp with its fringed brocade shade on a table between the
chairs, Miss Fenway's fine landscape painting that showed the
Platte River in summer with diamond sparkles of sunlight
dancing on the water hanging in a place of honor over the
hearth, the crisp lace curtains at the front window, the
papered walls all pleased me and made me proud. Which was
probably a sin if I believed everything our old circuit

preacher, a fire and brimstone man, used to say about mankind's frailties, but I couldn't help myself. The foyer of the house was as warm and welcoming to visitors as I could make it. I wanted a traveler to feel comfortable at Hart's at first sight, willing, even grateful, to hand over money without a doubt or second thought. The boarding house ledgers showed that moneys on the debit side disbursed to ensure clean and attractive accommodations were returned several times over on the credit side. After a long, jolting, cramped, and dirty train trip, travelers couldn't help but give a sigh of relief when they stepped across Hart's threshold. I believe I could have doubled my prices and no one would have batted an eye, but I'm not one to take advantage of people.

"This looks like a fine establishment, Mrs. Churchill. I take it you and your husband run both the barber shop and the boarding house."

"I'm a widow, Mr. Carpenter, and I own both places." I did not enjoy being patronized, and I thought I caught a vague chiding with the words *and your husband*, as if he doubted that a woman on her own could maintain two profitable businesses. Sometimes I am overly sensitive on that subject.

He must have caught the prickly edge to my reply because he looked slightly discomfited for a moment. I recognized the look of a man who accepted that he had said something wrong but had no idea what it was. The eternal mystery of women, Duncan had called it, always with a smile.

"I'm sorry for your loss," he said, "and I meant no offense by my words." As I had observed before, the man had very cordial manners.

I said, "No offense taken, Mr. Carpenter. I can hardly blame you for being taken aback when it was my plan from the start to surprise you. Both my mother and my husband often pointed out that perhaps I took too much pleasure in having the upper hand."

Carpenter laughed outright at my words. "I can't say I blame you. It appeals to me, as well." I laughed, too, back in charity with the man.

I turned the book on the desk toward him and pushed the pen and inkwell in his direction. "If you'd sign here, please. How long do you plan to stay in New Hope, Mr. Carpenter?"

He spoke as he wrote and did not meet my gaze. "That remains to be seen, Mrs. Churchill." He looked up. "Is there a limit on the number of nights you have available for me?"

"No, indeed. It's seventy-five cents a night for as long as you choose to stay. I don't allow alcohol or tobacco on the premises, but otherwise we try to make it as homelike as we can with a comfortable mattress, clean linens, and a fire on cold nights. You'll have to fetch your own water from the bath room at the end of the hallway," I gestured behind me, "and the facility is out back." Carpenter gave me his full attention and when I finished talking, he took three brand-new, shiny Morgan silver dollars, the first I had ever received from a customer, from his vest pocket and set them on the desk top.

"That sounds more than fair, Mrs. Churchill. I'll give you this on account to start with."

I never pocketed a customer's money in his presence. It gave the appearance that I feared the person would snatch it back if I didn't get to it first, which seemed both undignified and inhospitable, so I only smiled.

"That will be fine, Mr. Carpenter. Let me get Danny." I went to the last door at the end of the hallway and pushed it open. "Danny, I need your help, please." He looked up from stoking the stove.

"Yes, ma'am," he said and followed me back to the entry area.

"Danny, this is Mr. Carpenter. It appears that he'll be spending several nights with us. Give him the room upstairs with the window overlooking the street."

Danny stared at me a moment. "The front room, you mean?"

"Yes." I knew he was surprised because we usually saved the spacious front room for important people, railroad bigwigs and the like, but I thought there should be some kind of reward for good manners, and I liked Mr. Carpenter, besides. I couldn't have said why exactly but knew it was more than his manners.

"Mr. Carpenter, let Danny know when you want to have a hot bath. He'll get everything ready for you. We provide clean towels and a very pleasant lavender soap that's made at a farm just outside New Hope. Lavender can be very relaxing, especially if you've been traveling for a while."

Hart's newest guest eyed me for a moment, his gray eyes giving nothing away, until he finally spoke with gravity. "Mrs. Churchill, there's not a man alive who can resist lavender soap." His words caused me to give a gurgle of laughter; I know when I'm being teased. To Danny, he said, "Lead on, young man, and then get that bath ready. I'll make myself presentable before I go in search of supper." When Carpenter reached the foot of the stairs, he turned back to ask, "Do you own the café, too, Mrs. Churchill?"

I shook my head. "No, "I said, the regret clear in my voice, "not yet, anyway."

"Only a matter of time, I imagine," he responded as he turned and followed Danny up the steps. With those words, I decided I liked Mr. Carpenter even more than I had first thought. I have always appreciated a man with the ability to recognize the inevitable.

2

"Do you know if Eddie's come home yet?" I asked Danny over supper.

He shook his head. "I ain't heard—" He caught himself and started again. "I haven't heard anything, but I bet the fish were biting and that's where he's been. He doesn't stay away from home very long 'cause he knows it worries his mother." I was so caught up in myself that I hadn't given Cora Barts a thought. She knew Eddie better than anybody. I didn't think she'd be worried, and yet he was her youngest and the only child left at home. She might be feeling some small apprehension at his absence.

"Will you watch the desk tonight long enough for me to go see Mrs. Barts?" I asked. "I don't like the idea of her sitting there all by herself worrying." I knew Danny would be more than willing to do as I asked. He was a boy that put great store by mothers, having nursed his own until she died in his arms.

Eddie and his mother lived in a little house behind the telegraph office. When my mother, sisters, and I first moved to New Hope eleven years earlier, the Barts family had lived on a not very profitable farm a few miles outside of town, but over time Mr. Barts passed and all the Barts children except for Eddie and his oldest brother moved away. Clayton, the oldest boy, took over the farm and when he married, old Mrs. Barts moved into town to live with Eddie, who was smart enough to learn the telegraphy trade and get off the farm as quickly as possible. Not a lazy boy by any stretch but bright enough to prefer a job sitting at a desk in a heated room to early morning one-sided conversations with milk cows. I knew Eddie since he was seven years old, had watched him grow into an ambitious young man, who took good care of his mother. He always seemed a bit of an innocent to me, not given to alcohol and so shy around girls his own age that he could barely stammer out a greeting. Fishing was Eddie's Achilles' heel, the only Achilles' heel of which I was aware, and I hoped that he had lost track of time – but days? would he lose track of days? – and when I got to his house, I would find his mother frying up a pan of catfish for their supper.

Unfortunately, that was not the case. I knew from the look on Cora Barts' face when she opened the door to my knock that I should have paid more attention to Harold Sellers when he stopped in at the barber shop earlier that day. Eddie's mother was old enough to be my mother but four decades of farming had aged her even more. She had a brown, lined, usually impassive face, but at first sight of her, I felt my stomach twist. The emotion lurking in her dark eyes alarmed me, and I realized before she said a word that something was very wrong.

"Mrs. Barts," I said, "I brought you some johnny cake. I don't know what I was thinking, but there's no way Danny and I could eat it all and it'll just dry out." She pushed open the door by way of invitation, and I stepped inside. It was a neat front room, plain except for a bright afghan puddled on the seat of her rocking chair. She had been sitting there alone in the darkening evening, I thought, worrying about her son, and my stomach gave another lurch.

She took the towel-wrapped offering from my hands. "Thank you, Ruth," she said. "That was thoughtful of you. I'm partial to johnny cake myself."

"I remember that Eddie is, too," I said. "My father always said that johnny cake paired with fried catfish was a marriage made in heaven." After a pause, I asked as gently as I could, "Has he come home yet, Mrs. Barts?"

To my horror, it seemed for a moment that she was going to weep. The face of this aging woman, a woman who had faced down prairie fires and windstorms and had buried two children and a husband without ever shedding a public tear, collapsed for an imperceptible moment. The idea of it made me realize for the first time that something awful might well have happened to her Eddie. Mothers have an instinct about their children, and her instinct was giving her bad news. The moment passed.

"No," the word unadorned with further information. "Sit down, won't you? I been sitting here worrying and praying, praying and worrying. I'm glad to have the company."

I pulled a straight-backed chair away from the table and perched on the edge of its seat. "How long has Eddie been gone? I didn't know a thing about it until Harold stopped by the barber shop to ask if I knew where Eddie was."

"He left yesterday morning for the telegraph office like usual. Didn't say a word about anything, just his usual, 'Bye, Ma,' and he was off. Took a bite with him for lunch 'cause he's not one to leave his post in the middle of the day. My Eddie takes his job serious, Ruth."

"I know he does, and he's good at it. You can always trust Eddie not to miss anything important coming in or going out." She nodded but didn't speak. "Did he say anything about special plans when he left?"

"Fishing, you mean? No, he didn't, and he always tells me when he's going to head down to the river. So I can plan supper, you understand. Get the frying pan hot and the like. We like our catfish." She smiled slightly. "But he's never stayed out like this before, overnight, I mean, and without a word to me. He just wouldn't do it. I sent word to Clayton. Asked him to check his brother's favorite spots along the river. When I heard your knock, I thought maybe you were Clayton come to give me bad news."

"Mrs. Barts, there may not be any bad news. Eddie might have—" but I was unable to think of one reason Eddie Barts would have been gone without a word for at least twenty-four hours and maybe longer.

She caught my pause and nodded. "Yes," she said, "there's no way to finish that thought except to say he might've had an accident." Fallen into the river and drowned, was what she meant, or been accosted by renegades off the reservation, though we hadn't heard of any such occurrence recently, or met up with a bad man who did her boy some unnamed but deadly harm. Her mother's imagination would not let her stop with simply a bad fall or a broken bone. She must think the worst so that if the worst was how it turned out, the grief would not take her by surprise and be all the more painful because of disappointment and shock. All too often, hope can be unwise, deceitful, and cruel.

I didn't know what to say because by then some instinct of my own had convinced me that Eddie Barts, if not dead, was in grave danger. She and I both jumped in our chairs at the sudden loud knock on the door.

"Ma!" a man's voice called and for a moment I thought with relief, Eddie! but it was Clayton who pushed open the door before his mother could rise from her rocker. He stood in the doorway brandishing what at first appeared to be a long, pale, skinny stick. Until I looked more closely and with sinking heart saw it was a fishing pole.

"Found this along the river bank, Ma," Clayton said. He was a big, strapping man, the oldest of seven living Barts children and a father three times over himself, but I saw that his hand holding the pole trembled ever so slightly, "but I didn't see Eddie. We'd better get hold of the county sheriff. I don't like this." I looked from his face to his mother's stricken expression and thought, I don't like this, either, not one little bit.

Clayton left to round up a few men to head back to the river for a search. It was almost dark but the night was clear, and I understood that Clayton just needed to be doing something, that he couldn't go back to the family farm and crawl into bed as if nothing was wrong. I felt much the same.

When I got back to Hart's, I sent Danny along to help with the search. Before he left, I made a pretense of patting down his jacket collar and said, "You be careful, Danny. Take Othello with you. Maybe his nose will come in handy, and be sure to watch your step."

Puzzled at my words, he was wise enough to say only, "Yes, ma'am," instead of, "Well, that's a darned fool thing to say. I'll be safe enough. Why wouldn't I be, when I'm surrounded by good and solid men we've both known and trusted for years?" I couldn't have answered the question or said why I had such a strong foreboding of calamity or how I knew that this day was the beginning of something awful, something that would have a lasting effect on our little community. I just knew it was the case, knew we would not see Eddie Barts alive again and that nothing I loved, not my town or my livelihood or my friends or even Danny, would ever be the same again.

I waited until Danny came home before getting ready for bed because, I told myself, he might bring good news with him and I didn't want to wait until morning to celebrate it, but in reality, I waited up to be sure his freckled face got home safe and sound. I am not a worrier by nature, at least not more so than anyone else, but if there was one thing I had learned the last few years, it was that a person should not take for granted that the people she loves will be at her side tomorrow. Once Danny returned, giving a dejected shake of his head to my query about Eddie, I scooted him off to bed, fiddled with this and that, and then headed off to bed myself. The day's newest paying customers were two traveling drummers who had made quick one-night stays at Hart's on previous occasions, and the other regular boarders had already proven themselves to be a peaceful lot. Except for Mr. Carpenter, of course, and for some reason I could not picture him causing a ruckus in the middle of the night. I've experienced my share of ruckuses, but picturing Mr. Carpenter in my mind's eye, I decided he was more a person to quell a ruckus than cause one.

I didn't sleep as well as I might have wished, waking periodically to lie in the darkness and remember the look on

Mrs. Barts' face at the sight of that fishing pole, hearing the emotion behind her words: "worrying and praying, praying and worrying." I did my own praying into the still, black room, the same as I had done when Duncan took his last bad turn, repeating, "Let him be well. Let him live." Yet for all my pleading, I didn't get what I asked, and I feared it would be the same with Eddie Barts. Then why bother praying at all, a person might ask, but what else is there to do when everything is taken out of your hands and things look their blackest? Worrying and praying. Praying and worrying. I have done more than my share of both.

I woke up earlier than usual, dressed, readied bacon on the griddle, the smell of which had been known to rouse Danny from the deepest sleep, reheated last night's coffee on the stove top, and took a full cup with me out to the front room. I had a few paid bills to record in the ledger and other sundry business to finish and went to sit in one of the foyer chairs that faced the front window and looked out at the drug store directly across the street. Behind the store, the brightening eastern sky announced the sun. It was a pretty morning, cool because it was April but not so cool that we had to have a fire lit in the foyer's fireplace. The evening before, Danny had lit the stoves in the rooms of our paying guests, but we would not keep those fires going all day. This year's spring was warmer than usual so far, and the day's cheerful morning sun promised continuing comfort. How pleasant a spring morning can be, I thought contentedly, and then remembered Eddie Barts, which took all the cheerfulness out of the moment.

When the bell on the front door jingled, I lifted my head and was not surprised to see Si Carpenter enter. I thought he was the kind of man not to waste much of the day, not with those intelligent gray eyes that missed very little, if anything at all.

"Good morning, Mrs. Churchill," his words mild and courteous as usual. He removed his hat and came closer.

"May I?" he asked, indicating the chair on the other side of the small table at my left.

"Yes, of course." I closed the ledger and laid it on my lap. "I hope you slept well."

"I did. Everything was exactly as you promised, comfortable and clean."

I smiled. "Good. We aim to please." I eyed him and added, "The barber shop opens at nine. I know that's late, but I need to get everything in order here before I start snipping."

He acknowledged my words with a return smile. "I'll be first in line. I know I've let myself get a bit shaggy." I wanted to say something about the telegraph office, but he beat me to it. "I understand the telegraph clerk must still be fishing." As if reading my thoughts about how he could possibly know such a thing, he added, "Ezzie, at the café next door, was kind enough to open early so I could get a cup of coffee. She mentioned last night's search."

The man was a stranger, and I thought I should probably make light of the situation with a person new to our community, but when I opened my mouth, I said the opposite of what I intended. "I don't think he's fishing. Eddie would never worry his mother like that. He's a good son. It's true he likes to fish, but this isn't about fishing."

Si Carpenter had a disconcerting way of fixing his eyes on me as I spoke, as if he were listening with more than his ears, listening with his whole being. He doesn't miss much, I thought for the second time that morning, and realized that could be a two-edged sword, depending on what a person was trying to hide.

"No? What is it about, then?"

"I don't know." I heard the worry in my voice, even caught a small tremble, so I cleared my throat to steady myself before I continued. "But I think something's wrong, and I don't know what to do about it."

"What do you mean, *wrong?*"

"I can't say exactly," I said. "It's just a feeling I have, but I don't like it."

"Ezzie said last night's search for your missing Eddie came up empty."

"Except for the fishing pole," I said and went on to relate how Clayton Barts had showed up at his mother's door after finding the pole. "It was tossed behind a clump of bushes, for goodness' sake," I concluded. "That doesn't make sense. Eddie would never do that. He carved that pole himself to fit his own hand and he showed it off any chance he got. He acted like it was the Holy Grail."

"Eddie Barts is a Galahad then?" I suppose I should have been surprised that Mr. Carpenter knew what I meant by the Holy Grail, let alone the name of its knight champion, but several minutes ago, I had decided that Si Carpenter was deeper water than I was used to, and I should not be surprised by anything he said or did.

"Eddie's no Galahad, Mr. Carpenter. Not even close. He looks like what he is: a young man without a speck of wickedness in him, who takes care of his mother and likes to fish."

Carpenter moved his gaze away from me to stare out the big front window where the sun was now beginning to show clearly over the top of the drug store. I knew, however, that he wasn't interested in the building or its fancy sign. He contemplated something of which only he was aware. I felt a spurt of feeling that mixed equal parts resentment and curiosity, hardly becoming for a woman my age, a widowed business owner, who should be able to rise above petty feelings. It bothered me that Si Carpenter seemed to know more about my hometown than I did, but I realized without asking that he wasn't about to share his secret store of information – whatever that information was - with me.

"Well," I said, standing and hefting the ledger books into my arms, "I'm glad you and Esmerelda have become such fine and immediate friends. It's always wise to stay on the good side of the woman who makes the best coffee in town." He stood when I did, ever courteous.

"Can't hurt," he said with a small smile.

"No." I paused. "If your telegram's that important, Mr. Carpenter, the closest telegraph office is at Fort Cottonwood. It's closer than the county seat by a few miles. Clayton Barts left for the fort last night to report Eddie's absence and see if we could get any help from the Army to look for him. The poor man was desperate, and he made the point that the Army's been quiet for a good two years, ever since War Bonnet Creek, and maybe they'd be looking for something to do. I doubt they'll think searching for a missing telegraph agent is good use of their time, but you never know." I paused again after my wordy speech before I ended with a half-hearted, "Ten miles give or take to the fort and an easy ride."

"Thank you."

"You're welcome."

"I'll see you at nine o'clock, then, and Mrs. Churchill–?"

"Yes?"

"I think you're right to be worried about Eddie Barts."

I tried to find additional information in his expression but gave up. Nothing showed there but a distant kindness, though I'd have bet the boarding house that Carpenter knew more than he was saying. The day was getting away from me, however, and I had to get about my business with no time to waste trying to wring water from stone, so to speak.

I nodded instead, as if he had said something I understood, turned and walked over to the desk where I set down my books, and then headed for The Addition where I put flame to the griddle, cracked four eggs next to the bacon, and went to wake Danny. Eddie Barts might be missing, a man of mystery might be renting a room upstairs, and life in New Hope, Nebraska, might be changing, but hungry boys still needed to eat, and I still had to see to the day's business.

At fifteen minutes past eight every morning except Sunday, Lizbeth Ericson appeared in the foyer of Hart's, always with the appearance of a girl who got up too late and didn't have enough time to put her appearance in proper order. It might be a shawl tied crooked and sliding off one shoulder or a shirtwaist collar wrinkled up on one side. That particular morning it was Lizbeth's hair: two stubborn curls stuck out of the side of her head as if she'd decided to create a new hairstyle using Mr. Glidden's barbed wire. But regardless of her disarray, Lizbeth was bright as sunshine, a fair, clear-eyed girl, intelligent and cheerful and eager to please. She never said an unkind word, and out of all the people I knew, Lizbeth Ericson would have had the strongest excuse for doing so.

"You're not late," I said, looking at her from where I stood behind the big desk, "so slow down. What on earth have you done to your hair, Lizbeth?" I can never help noticing such things since I barber for a living. The girl's hand went immediately to the two stubborn curls.

"Oh, fudge," she said. "Little Paulie got something nasty in my hair last night and I washed it out, and then I fell asleep and I guess I slept on it wrong. Is it awful?" She stepped forward close enough for me to reach over the desk and try to tuck both curls behind her ear. That made it worse, however, so without answering her question directly, I stepped around the desk, positioned myself behind her, untied the limp ribbon she had used to pull back all her fine, yellow hair into a single haphazard braid, undid the plait, and finally slid the ribbon under her hair so that it caught all of it up off her neck.

"Turn around," I said, which she did like an obedient and patient child, while I tied the ribbon on the top of her head in as pretty a bow as I could manage. Stepping back, I pretended to eye her critically and finally declared, "It's much better now. You look like a girl ready to break hearts." She was thirteen and did not get compliments at home so my words made her giggle.

"Thank you, Miss Ruth."

"You're welcome, Miss Lizbeth," I replied, smiling, and turned around. "You'll see six paying customers in the book, but one is leaving on the 11:10 today. I forget who that is, but he's paid in full, so all you have to do is wish him a pleasant journey on his way out the door. The others are with us for at least another night. I put the newest guest, a man named Mr. Carpenter, in the front room. He'll be with us at least three nights, and I wouldn't be surprised to have him stay a lot longer."

Lizbeth hung her shawl on a peg of the foyer coat tree. "The front room?" she repeated in exactly the same tone Danny had used the day before.

"Well, I might decide to move him to the roof tonight, but for the time being yes, the front room." The tone I used to quell impertinent children never worked with Lizbeth, but that didn't mean I stopped trying.

"All right," she said. "My name was never Lizbeth Hart, after all. It's your name on the sign." She could have been a younger sister, I thought, because I held her in that much affection. Lizbeth had a way about her that could make me smile, had done so even in the darkest days when she was just a little girl I would see in town with her mother and Duncan still held on to breath through sheer determination. My husband was a man who loved life and refused to hurry its departure.

I reached for my shawl from the same coat tree and said as I hurried toward the front door, "Danny's already left for school. Mr. Stenton asked him to come in early to recite his parts for the closing program. He'll be home at his usual time, though, so don't do the heavy work. Danny can bring in wood for the fires and carry the dirty linen over to Ruby's."

"I can do that, Miss Ruth. I don't mind." Her words stopped me with one foot over the front threshold.

"I know that, Lizbeth, but do what I say and let Danny earn his keep. You watch the desk and our customers and tidy their rooms if they give you the chance. Oh, and I thought the picture glass looked streaked in the sunshine this morning, so give the front room a little cleaning, too, please." The foyer was neat as a pin and scrupulously clean, but I knew the words would please her. Lizbeth liked to keep busy and had the same aversion to charity that I had.

"Oh, yes, ma'am, I surely will." Her satisfied expression said I had been right to add the part about the entry area. She'd probably have a nice little snack waiting for me in The Addition's kitchen when I popped in from the barber shop over lunch, too. She often did, sometimes with a flower she picked sitting proudly in an old bottle on the table or a pretty stone she found and polished resting beside my tea cup. On my birthday last summer, Lizbeth had rooted a geranium stem and planted it in a piece of broken crockery and placed it in the center of the table with a hand-written note next to it. That geranium continues to hold place of honor at the kitchen's front window and her note is tucked into my Bible. If I think about it too much, how hard she tried to make her letters straight and uniform, that small piece of paper still has the power to make me teary. How she must have worked on her penmanship! And where did she ever find the time to do so? Her parents, who kept their eldest child busy running after rapscallion brothers along with sundry household chores that I knew from experience never truly got done, did not approve of school for girls and any reading and writing Lizbeth could do today was because I took time to teach her. Not enough time, truth be told, but there are only so many hours in the day, for me and Lizbeth both.

Outside, Othello pushed himself up from where he lay at the top step and lumbered over to receive his usual morning scratch behind his ears. Othello is a big, coal-black, flop-eared mongrel with a taste for bacon. I suppose that's one of the reasons he and Danny are often inseparable and if it weren't for the fact that I enforced the rule of the house with firm resolve – no animals inside when the temperature rose above freezing – he would drape himself over the foot of Danny's bed year-round so as not to miss out on any breakfast bacon. The mutt has soulful brown eyes and a mournful expression that might give one the impression he is ignored or abused except for the crumbs of bacon and bread hanging from his heavy jowls. It is useless and hypocritical of me to scold Danny for spoiling Othello when I am as guilty as he is of throwing the dog table-scrap treats. Othello was a puppy in Duncan's last year and gave my husband many light moments, so I imagine I will always spoil the dog. I feel a debt to him.

We crossed the street just as Dr. Danford opened the drug store for business, propping open the door with a wooden door stop shaped like a mortar and pestle.

"'Morning, Ruth." Tom Danford is my elder by at least fifteen years, tall and bespectacled with a growing bald spot on the top of his head and not enough hair left to promise me any business. Not that his wife, Margery, would have allowed me to set either razor or scissors on her husband. She took care of that on his behalf, and I managed to keep any critical comments about her tonsorial abilities to myself. She is a woman of strong opinions, devoted to her husband, and as good a nurse for her husband's doctor's office as he could have found anywhere. New Hope was fortunate to have its own doctor and its own nurse and far be it from me to offend either of them.

"Good morning, Tom. Nice to be able to let in some spring air, isn't it?" Instead of answering, he stepped outside onto the boardwalk.

"Troubling news about Eddie Barts."

"Yes. Were you along on the search last night?"

He shook his head. "No. I was bringing another Bucher into the world."

"Well, that's good to hear. Boy or girl?"

"Another boy."

"What does that make it, then, five boys?"

"Six."

"Good help for their father on the farm."

"Yes." A pause. "I don't like this business about Eddie Barts, Ruth. I don't like it, at all."

One boy brought into the world, I thought, and had one boy left it at about the same time?

"No," I agreed, "I don't like it either." We both thought our own private thoughts until Margery Danford called her husband's name from inside the store. "Let's hope for the best," I said, "that there's a perfectly innocent explanation for Eddie being gone." Tom nodded and I walked away, Othello plodding along behind me. We passed the still shuttered law office that stood between my shop and the drug store – there was no way Morton Lewis, our resident attorney, would ever be up at this hour – and I pushed open the door to the barber shop.

Sometimes I am running so late that there's a customer waiting and I must get right to business, or I push open the door and notice something I left out of order the night before and realize I don't have much time to make it right before business picks up. But other times, like that morning, with no one waiting and an extra moment from my early start, I couldn't help but stop in the doorway and remember what it was like when Duncan was alive and running the shop. Even when he had customers in both chairs, he would turn whenever I stopped for a visit and flash me a grin beneath his well-groomed mustache. He was a handsome, gregarious man, and he encouraged conversation for its own sake.

"There's always something new to be learned, Ruthie," he told me more than once, "if you let people talk." My Duncan could be a charmer when he chose to be! But it was five years since I lost him, and the memories grew fainter with time, a slow fading, the same as consumption. Losing him twice. Soon, I feared with a desperate pull at my heart, I will push open the door to the barber shop and not give Duncan Churchill a thought. I will remember him only when I wake from a bad dream and reach out for comfort or look over at our wedding picture on the bureau. The knowledge grieved me, but there was nothing I could do about passing time or fading memory. I had to make a living, take care of Danny, feed Othello his favorite bacon, pay Lizbeth Ericson too much money for the work she did for me, help put a new roof on the church, and contribute to the school teacher's salary. Life goes on. For all its lonely nights and yearning memories and unshared happy moments, life still goes on.

Othello sniffed around the shop and then apparently exhausted from the inspection, went outside and flopped down by the old bench next to the door. The dog usually kept me company until Danny came home from school, and then in the way animals sometimes have, he would lift his head as if hearing the back door of the rooming house slam with Danny's arrival – although that was impossible considering the distance and town hubbub going on around him – push himself up and lumber across the street toward Hart's. Dog and boy were devoted to each other. As he was for Duncan, Othello had been a comfort for Danny, too, in those early days of grief, and it's no wonder the mutt was growing fat on unearned treats with both Danny and me feeling in his debt.

The morning started with Si Carpenter, as I had expected. He showed up, removed his hat, and gave me a questioning look that did not need interpretation.

"Yes," I said. "There's no reason for you to wait." He placed his hat on a wall hook and came to sit in the chair in front of me. I seldom talk of inconsequential matters when I am shaving or trimming or cutting because I need to concentrate, and he was of that same practice. More of a listener than a talker.

"Shave and a haircut," he said.

"I should hope so," I agreed, which made him laugh a little. He had thick, dark brown hair with a slight curl to it. I thought the curls were probably more noticeable when he was a boy and that his mother might have found them difficult to cut that very first time. I didn't say anything, but his hair held the slightest hint of lavender, which I found gratifying because although he teased about it, in the end, he had trusted my advice. That counted for something in my book.

When I was done and Mr. Carpenter stood up, I used a small brush to remove a few hairs from the shoulders of his shirt and stepped back from him. He looked at himself in the mirror over my shoulder.

"Except for my mother when I was a boy," he said, "you're the first woman I've ever had barber my hair."

"I hope you approve."

"I do. How much do I owe you?"

"I can take it out of the money you gave me for your room," I told him, but he shook his head at the idea.

"No, I'd rather pay you now. The laborer is worth of her hire."

That was the second time he surprised me. First, the remark about the Holy Grail and now words from the Bible. An educated man, then. I told him what he owed and he stacked the coins on the counter in front of the mirror.

"Any word from the Army about them organizing a search for the missing Mr. Barts?" Carpenter asked.

"I haven't heard anything."

"Then I think I'll take a ride over to the fort. Ten miles, you said?"

"Yes. Due south out of New Hope and follow the road. It's well traveled, and the river crossing is shallow. There's a fork midway and you'll want to jog to the west."

"Thank you." Carpenter took his hat off the hook and turned to face me. He looked poised to say something, and I felt suddenly anxious about whatever that might be, as if he would tell me something I'd wish I had never heard, but before he could follow through, the shop door opened. Two bedraggled cowpokes entered.

"We heard there was a woman barber," one fellow said.

"You heard right. Here I am," I said, accustomed to being a novelty.

"Meaning no disrespect, ma'am. My brother and I would like a shave and haircut, if it's not too much trouble."

They brought with them the smells of the cattle trail: smoke and cows, sweat and tobacco. Both could have used a bath, as well. A shaggy pair, but for some reason their boyishly expectant expressions made me smile.

"It's not too much trouble, at all. Hang up your hats and then you can each have a seat." I motioned to the barber chairs.

"Well, damn—beg your pardon, ma'am, I meant dang— Bobby, look at that. Two chairs, even. You sure have a fine establishment, ma'am."

As they walked toward the wall hooks, Si Carpenter gave me a quick nod and left the shop, pulling the door quietly shut behind him. I would never know what he had been going to tell me and couldn't decide if what I felt was relief or disappointment.

3

To my surprise, a small delegation of soldiers from the Army showed up in New Hope in the early afternoon. I stopped where I was, at the front gate of Hart's on my way back to the barber shop, shielded my eyes, and waited for the riders to get as far as the boarding house.

The lead rider pulled up in front of me, held up a hand to the men behind him, and called out something unintelligible to anyone except a member of the U.S. Army. Everyone stopped.

"Good afternoon, Mrs. Churchill."

"Good afternoon, Captain." We had known each other for over three years and in private were on a first name basis, but Captain Jeffrey McGruder put great store in public proprieties. Calling each other by our Christian names in front of his troops was not proper military form. "Are you here because of Eddie Barts?"

"Yes."

"Well, that was kind of you. We're all worried."

"The Major ordered it," Jeff said. "He likes to keep on good terms with our civilian neighbors."

"You don't sound like you approve."

Jeffrey McGruder was a big, broad-shouldered man, with fair hair, stylishly long sideburns, and a neat blonde mustache, good-looking and aware of it. He was my age, maybe even a year or two younger, and destined for Army greatness one day, I didn't doubt, unless he was tripped up by his belief that he usually knew better than anyone else, including (I would say *especially* but that would be uncharitable) his commanding officer, Major Prentiss. The captain shrugged off my comment.

"It's not my business to approve or disapprove of an order, Mrs. Churchill."

"Of course, not," I agreed, "and I hope you'll thank the Major on New Hope's behalf. It's a worry and a mystery and we appreciate the help." I looked down the street and saw a group of men and horses gradually congregating outside the livery. "It looks like you're just in time."

"Major Prentiss told Mr. Barts to gather as many men as he could and to meet us at the stables at half past one."

I checked the time on the watch I kept pinned to my shirtwaist. "I'm not surprised that you're right on time, Captain."

Behind him the riders and their mounts began to shift restlessly, soldiers impatient for action, eager to be put to use. Clayton Barts' speculation that the Army might be bored with the prolonged peace appeared to be right.

Jeff smiled at that. "It's the Army, Mrs. Churchill. We're on time unless we're not." He lifted the reins, ready to continue down the street. "If I may be allowed, I'll stop by the boarding house later. No doubt searching for a missing telegraph boy will prove thirsty work for us, and the men will need to stop for refreshment before we head back to the fort."

"Of course, you're allowed. It's always a pleasure to see you, Captain, and I hope you'll be able to report some good news about Eddie when you come."

He touched the brim of his hat. "I hope so, too. Good day, Mrs. Churchill." He waved his hand in a forward motion to the six men behind him, and they all passed in front of me, each of the soldiers giving me the same respectful nod he might have given a national monument. When they were all well past, I crossed the street toward the barber shop, feeling almost hopeful. Jeffrey McGruder preened a bit more than was becoming for a man, but he was a capable soldier, well-organized and experienced. If Eddie Barts lay injured

Karen J. Hasley

somewhere along the river or for a reason I could not
imagine wandered lost on the vast prairie that surrounded
New Hope, McGruder was just the man to find him. I knew
for a fact that the captain was not one to recognize, let alone
accept, defeat.

At the end of that day, Mr. Carpenter reappeared at
Hart's at the same time I did. Danny sat next to the desk with
a book open on his lap and his lips moving in silent
memorization. He was assigned Mr. Longfellow's poem, "My
Lost Youth," perhaps not what I would have selected for an
active lad of fifteen, but he would be expected to recite it
from memory at the school's closing program, regardless of
my opinion of Mr. Stenton's choice. I never criticized the
teacher aloud for fear of eroding his authority with his
students, but at times I wondered privately just how familiar
Mr. Stenton was with children. He had answered an
advertisement New Hope placed in the Lincoln and Denver
newspapers three years earlier, and he came with fine
references and credentials, but he was not a man of warmth. I
know that is not considered an essential quality of a teacher,
but from my viewpoint, it couldn't hurt. Still, while Mr.
Stenton was not especially liked by the children, they learned
under his tutelage, which was why we had hired him, and to
his credit, the final program of the year was always
impressive, with lots of recitations and songs, and attended
by the entire population of the town and its environs. We're
always at the ready for anything celebratory. Last year, for the
first time the children reenacted the signing of the
Declaration of Independence, costumed in wigs and
flourishing pens with quills the length of canoe paddles. The
program was quite grand by New Hope standards and left
both parents and town citizens in charity with Mr. Stenton.
Perhaps that was his ultimate intention because he then
disappeared east to spend time with family for six weeks
before returning to prepare for the next school year.

When Danny caught sight of me, he closed the book and
stood, saying aloud, "'The drum-beat repeated o'er and o'er, /

42

And the bugle wild and shrill. / And the music of that old song'—" He stopped abruptly with squinting eyes and furrowed brows until I put him out of his misery by continuing, "'Throbs in my memory still.'"

At my words, his expression cleared and we finished in tandem, "'A boy's will is the wind's will / And the thoughts of youth are long, long thoughts.'"

"I'm never going to learn it," he said. "I'm going to stand up in front of everyone like a telegraph pole and that'll be that."

I patted his shoulder as I passed him. "Nonsense. You know most of it already, and you've still got time. Besides, I'll sit right up front and whisper any parts you forget to get you started again."

"Mr. Stenton won't like that."

"Mr. Stenton doesn't need to know anything about it. It's our secret, Danny, yours and mine." Danny grinned at that, which lightened my heart. He has an irresistible grin, and I'm awfully fond of the boy.

Mr. Carpenter chose that moment to push open the door, removing his hat as he did so. That gave me the opportunity to examine his haircut, nodding to myself with satisfaction when I did so. Even the press of his hat over a long ride had not spoiled the cut. After a moment, I realized he had paused when he entered, as if he knew that I was scrutinizing my handiwork and had purposefully given me the time to do so. Catching his glance, I became quite certain that was the case, although neither of us said a word about the matter, and I flushed, more self-conscious than I had been in a long while. A lady did not stare at a gentleman, even if it was only because she was proud of the results of her barbering skills.

Danny called a casual greeting to the newcomer and said to me, "I have to take the laundry basket over to Ruby's. I was studying my poem, and time got away from me. I'm sorry."

"Scoot, then," I told him and after he left said to Mr. Carpenter, "Did you find Fort Cottonwood without too much of a problem?"

"Without any problem, at all. It was an easy ride, just like you said." He stopped at the corner of the desk to talk.

Standing closer to him than I had previously, I was conscious that while he was not much taller than I and there was not a lot of breadth to the man, he carried a look and feel of authority, of someone powerful and steady. I recognized in his character the same determined quality that I possess when I set my mind on something and will not be dissuaded by any obstacle until I reach my goal. I have always considered it an admirable feature, but for the first time I thought that it could also be frightening. I would not want to step between Si Carpenter and anything he set his mind on.

I backed up from him a pace and asked, "If you were at the livery, did you happen to notice if the Army's search party had returned yet?"

"There appeared to be a crowd milling about at the stables. So the Army was able to offer some help, after all?"

"Yes." Over his shoulder, I saw Jeff McGruder push open the door. The jingle of the bell and my shifted gaze caused Mr. Carpenter to turn to face the captain.

I watched Jeff give Carpenter a serious perusal before he turned his attention to me. "Ruth," he said, by way of greeting. His use of my first name made me sigh because I could read the captain as well as I could read a Longfellow poem. I had no doubt that in Captain McGruder's opinion, Mr. Carpenter and I stood too close together, and he wanted to make it known to this stranger that he was on a first-name basis with me, and any other man would be wise to keep his distance. While it was true that Jeff McGruder and I were indeed on a first-name basis, it was only because we were friends and nothing more, despite Jeff's obvious efforts to imply more. The captain refused to accept that I was not interested in him as a suitor regardless of the many attempts I had made to explain it to him in words and phrases he could not misunderstand.

"Captain." I pronounced the word with prim inflection. "Did you find any trace of Eddie?"

He shook his head. "No."

"I can't imagine where he'd have gone." I was really worried now, almost certain there was no good news waiting at the end of this story, and Jeff heard the concern in my voice.

"Now don't go getting all upset. We'll start again in the morning and push farther south. We'll find him." I thought he was right, but that the finding would not make anyone happy.

Next to me, Si Carpenter replaced his hat and moved his saddle bag from one shoulder to another, getting ready to move past me to the stairs that led to his room. The reminder of his presence made me remember my manners.

"Mr. Carpenter, this is Captain McGruder. Captain, this is Mr. Si Carpenter. He's staying at Hart's for a few days."

"Si Carpenter," Jeff repeated the name, emphasizing *Si* as if my knowing my paying guest's first name was suspicious.

"I directed Mr. Carpenter to the fort today because he wanted to send a telegram. Maybe you saw him there before you left, or you passed each other on the road."

"No," the captain said, "I didn't see him at all today, not at the fort and not on the road." He managed to imbue the words with even more suspicion.

"But I saw you, Captain. I was coming out of the major's quarters just as you were mounting up to depart." There was a prolonged silence as the two men studied each other until Carpenter nodded at me, said, "Mrs. Churchill," and headed for the staircase.

After Carpenter was gone, I almost said something sharp to Jeff because I had found his lack of cordiality to Mr. Carpenter annoying, but I had said sharp things to the man before with little effect and did not want to resume a discussion that always ended with me longing to hit him over the head with a flat iron.

"That's a man I don't believe you should be fraternizing with, Ruth. He's got a look about him I don't like."

I took a deep breath before I said, "He's a paying guest, is all, Captain, and as I have mentioned on previous occasions, I would appreciate it very much if you would mind your own business. That said, there appear to be some soldiers waiting for you outside by the rail so it must be time for you to get back to the fort. Be sure to let Major Prentiss know how grateful the citizens of New Hope are for his allowing you to assist in the search for Eddie. I'll no doubt see you in the morning."

"Ruth—"

"Good afternoon, Captain McGruder," I said in the same tone I would have used with a room full of six-year-old boys. He scowled at me, at that moment looking much like a six-year-old boy himself, said "Good afternoon," in return, pivoted with fine military precision, yanked open the door, and exited. I heard him bark something at the waiting soldiers and then I turned away, being interested in Jeffrey McGruder only because he would help look for Eddie Barts. Truth be told, there were times I did not even like the man but when he returned in the morning, I would be friendly and speak in a pleasant tone because we needed his help. And if, in fact, the Army brought Eddie home safe and sound, I would be tempted to give the captain a big, grateful kiss, which was an indication of how very, very worried I was about our young telegraph agent.

As it turned out, we did not need the Army's assistance the next day. Very early the following morning, before full sunrise, when the sun was only just beginning to crack the horizon, I heard the rattle of a wagon on the hardpacked street outside the boarding house. I was somewhere between sleep and wakefulness, and when I heard the sounds, I rose, threw a wrapper over my night dress, and went to peer out the window of the sitting room. The wagon stopped across the street at the drug store and the driver hopped off the front seat, hurried to the door, and began to pound on it for all he was worth. If I could hear the noise from across the street, I had no doubt Dr. Danford could hear it, too, and was not surprised when I saw the door open. The driver didn't look familiar, but it was still too dark to make out his personal details and thanks to the railroad, the county was filling up with many new faces that had come west to stake out land and a new life along with it. From my place at the window, I saw Tom, a lit lantern in his hand, follow the newcomer off the boardwalk and over to the back of the wagon. As he lifted the lantern high over something in the back of the wagon, I had a sudden, dreadful premonition that I knew what lay there. Tightening the belt of my wrapper and throwing a shawl over my shoulders, I hurried out of The Addition into the boarding house foyer, pulled open the front door, wincing a bit at the surprisingly loud jingle the small bell made in the still morning, and quickly crossed the street to stand next to the doctor. All I could do was stare.

"Oh, Tom," I said. "Oh, no." The doctor turned to me with a serious expression made all the more grim because part of his face was in shadow.

"Yes," he said in response. What else was there to say, after all, at the sight of young Eddie Barts' body stretched out in the back of the wagon? The boy was covered with a blanket that had been pulled down to reveal his misshapen head with part of its forehead and one eye gone completely and what was left of his face that waxy, pale cast that can't be mistaken. There is no way to misinterpret death. I had seen it more than once and would know it anywhere. "Help me get him inside," the doctor directed the still anonymous driver. The words surprised me.

"But if he's—" I said.

"I want to take a closer look at the boy, Ruth, before we hand him over to Harold. This doesn't look like an accident to me. Will you go ask Joe Chandler to meet me here?"

"Yes." I pulled my shawl more tightly around my shoulders.

Margery Danford appeared at the open doorway of the drug store holding a second lantern. How many times had she joined her husband to assist with the unexpected arrival of a person who needed a doctor's services? Countless, I supposed. She was a woman of remarkable self-possession, seldom swayed by emotion, and a perfect helpmeet for a physician. I admired Margery Danford; there was not a woman I would rather see appear in my doorway if I or someone I loved needed nursing. She helped make Duncan comfortable in his last days, and I would always be grateful.

I hurried north along Main Street, passed the barber shop, crossed the large alley that led out of town to the church, and now nearly running, rushed across Main Street to Joe Chandler's hardware and signage store. Lifting my fist to pound, I was nearly thrown off balance when the door opened before I had a chance to connect in a knock.

Joe Chandler, New Hope's mayor and the head of the town's Merchants' Association, stepped outside and closed the door quietly behind him.

"Just got the babies to sleep after a long night, Ruth. Ellie won't thank us if we wake either of them up. I saw the wagon. Is it Eddie?" He had suspected the worst, same as I.

"Yes. He's dead." My voice cracked. "Tom wants you to join him. He said it doesn't look like an accident."

As we walked, Joe made a few inadequate passes at his hair that had no effect, and I resisted the impulse to halt long enough to calm the curls that sprang all helter-skelter against his collar. He was a young man whose hair was his best feature. I always looked forward to him appearing at the barber shop's door, but with newborn twin boys and a thriving hardware store, such visits were not often enough. The momentary inclination made me instantly ashamed of myself. What was I doing, considering a man's haircut when another young man lay dead just down the street? I have moments when I'm not very proud of my behavior.

I waited in the front of the drug store when the doctor and Joe disappeared into the back room where Margery stood next to poor Eddie's body. The door's firm, closing click made me turn to the driver, who stood hat in hand beside me.

"I'm Ruth Churchill. I don't believe we've met."

"No ma'am. I'm Charles Peltier and I farm over by Gothenberg. Do most of my business there, but I heard about your missing telegraph agent and when I spied the body I just knew that's who it was. Thought I should bring him home."

Home, I thought, and had the sudden wrenching memory of Eddie's mother worrying and praying, praying and worrying.

"That was good of you. How did you come to find him, Mr. Peltier?"

"It was an odd thing, Miz Churchill. Real odd. Two of my mules had got loose – they're a smart animal for all their stubbornness and I can't keep 'em to home – and I went to get 'em. They don't usually go far and usually to the same spot. Just being the ornery critters they are, I figure. Anyway, I started off on foot—"

"You were up early."

"I farm, Miz Churchill and I got milk cows. I'm up way ahead of the sun every day and last night I never went to bed because our prize milker was calving."

"I see. Of course."

"So after the calf got born, I started off to find the mules. Found 'em and bridled 'em and I was bringing them home when all of a sudden, we got to a patch of heavy brush and they spooked like I never seen. I almost lost both of them again, and when I went to see what it was that spooked 'em, I saw the body. In the brush covered up by dirt and dried branches and such, like somebody tried to hide it. It took me a while to get back home and hitch up the wagon and load up the boy. I could tell he was dead straight off. His

Karen J. Hasley

head—" Mr. Peltier's pronounced Adam's apple bobbed in a gulp. "It was an awful mess, ma'am. Just awful."

His words made me feel sick at my stomach for more than one reason. Eddie's ruined head was bad enough, but from the farmer's story, it was clear someone had killed Eddie and then tried, however unsuccessfully, to hide the body. Would a passing bad man, and we still had our share of them despite the rapid approach of civilization, kill Eddie Barts and then hide his body? I couldn't see why such a man would do that. And why kill Eddie to start with? He wouldn't have had anything of value on him, unless you counted that handmade fishing pole. Which made me wonder why the pole was found close to New Hope but Eddie had been found miles away. None of it made sense. The only sure thing was that young Eddie Barts, no fool and a smart boy, had allowed himself to get killed. Had he been so enrapt in fishing that he missed the killer's approach? I couldn't see it.

"Well, thank you, Mr. Peltier. Your taking the time to bring Eddie back to New Hope was a kindness to his mother and his brother."

"Got kids of my own, ma'am. I'd want the same done for mine." Something in his simple but sincere words made me tear up briefly. Whenever I think I cannot feel new grief, something happens to make me see how foolish I am. If we care for people, we are always going to grieve, one way or another. Mr. Peltier and I stood in the drug store as morning light began to stretch in the windows, both caught up in our own private thoughts, until the door of the back clinic opened and the three people who had gathered around Eddie Barts' body came out to join us.

Joe Chandler looked pale, Margery impassive, and Tom Danford as serious as I had ever seen him, even remembering the moment he looked at me across Duncan's bed and told me my husband was gone.

"What?" I asked. "What is it? What happened to Eddie?"

Doctor Danford said, "One precise shot to the back of the boy's head. It hit him high over his left ear. He would have died instantly."

I stared at him, at first not able to take in what Tom's words implied. "I don't understand," I said at last.

"If I had to guess from what I saw, I'd say Eddie was bending over, bending way over looking at something, something on the ground, let's say, and a person standing next to the boy on his left side put the bore of a pistol to his head and pulled the trigger."

"But that doesn't make any sense," I said. "Eddie was a smart boy. He wouldn't have let down his guard like that if he was surprised by some murderous villain passing through. You know that, Tom. Joe?" Both men were quiet as I worked out what the words suggested. The idea that it hadn't been a murderous stranger who caught Eddie unawares, that instead it had been someone Eddie knew and trusted, literally took my breath away. I couldn't say any more.

Finally, mercifully, Margery Danford spoke to me. "Someone needs to tell his mother, and I think it should be you, Ruth, but it might be better if you went home and changed out of your night clothes first."

I had forgotten about everything except poor Eddie Barts, but Margery's words brought me to my senses.

"Thank you for the reminder, Margery, but I don't think I can face Mrs. Barts. I just don't think I can."

Margery came forward, took me by the upper arm, and propelled me toward the door. "Of course, you can, Ruth. I know it's hard, but there's not a person in New Hope with a kinder heart than you, and you always know the right words to say. Go change into something presentable, then go tell Cora Barts her boy is dead before she hears rumors about it from somebody that won't care about her feelings the same way you will. Go on now." Margery and Tom had one grown son, studying to be a doctor back east, so I knew she understood what a heavy message she had assigned me to deliver. "Go on now," she repeated.

I left without a backward glance and crossed the street to Hart's. It was still early morning, but it felt to me that half the day must have passed. When I pushed open the door to the boarding house, Silas Carpenter rose from the chair where he sat. I suppose I should have been self-conscious that I wore my shift and wrapper with my hair plaited into one loose and undignified braid down the middle of my back, but I wasn't. I had no room for anything in my head except the picture of Eddie being shot from behind by someone he trusted. That idea seemed a lot more indecent than my parading around town in my nightdress.

"Mrs. Churchill, what is it?" Carpenter asked, not giving a look at anything but my face, night clothes be damned. His gray eyes fixed on me with intensity and concern.

"A farmer up by Gothenberg brought in Eddie Barts' body early this morning. Someone shot him in the head and killed him. Doctor Danford believes someone murdered Eddie, and that it was probably someone Eddie knew and trusted." Oddly enough, saying the words steadied me.

Mr. Carpenter did not look horrified or shocked or even surprised. I couldn't detect any kind of emotion on his face, but his voice was kind. "I'm sorry for your loss."

I shook my head. "Not mine, not really. I liked Eddie and I cut his hair now and again, but he didn't have a place in my heart. It's his mother that'll grieve. Losing a child is out of the natural order of things, and it won't be easy to accept."

He said nothing, and I went past him, down the hallway, and into The Addition, headed straight for Danny's room. At my knock and raised voice, the boy sat up, rubbing his eyes.

"Is it late, Ruth? Am I late for school?" He'd just awakened and had not quite left his dreams behind.

"No, you're not late, but it's time to get up."

I closed the door on him and leaned against it for a restful moment. What if it were Danny lying over on the doctor's table? I was not his mother, I knew that, but he had turned up on my doorstep when I was heart sore and needy. I had three nieces in Omaha and two nephews in Texas, but

Danny was right here in New Hope. I had taken him on willingly and the idea of someone he knew and trusted killing him made me so angry and so frightened that I couldn't find words for the feelings. Well, I didn't need the words for me because Danny Lake was alive and well and rubbing the sleep from his eyes. Instead, I needed the words for Cora Barts. I dressed quickly, combed out my hair and wrapped it at the back of my neck in a proper knot, set johnny cake and syrup on the table for Danny's breakfast, and slipped out the back door to make my way to the Barts' little house.

In one way, it wasn't nearly as awful as I had expected and in another way, it was much, much worse. Mrs. Barts answered my knock, took one look at my face, and inhaled sharply. She knew right away why I was there.

"I have very bad news, Mrs. Barts," I said. There was no use beating around the bush. She backed up and with a gesture invited me in.

"I can see that." We stood just inside the door facing each other.

"You might want to sit down," I said. She went to her rocker and sat without a word, folded her hands in her lap and like Mr. Carpenter earlier, did not take her attention from my face.

"Tell me now," she said, her voice steady. "Is it my Eddie?"

"Yes. I don't have any easy words for it. Eddie's dead. I'm so very sorry, Mrs. Barts."

"Tell me what happened," still staring at my face as if she feared she would miss some crucial message in my expression if she looked away for even a second.

I told her with the fewest words possible that a farmer had found Eddie's body over by Gothenberg.

"Gothenberg? What would my boy be doing there?"

"I don't know. Did he have a friend in the area or a girl around there that he was sweet on?"

"No." She closed her eyes with the word and two large tears squeezed out and trickled down her weathered cheeks. I thought my heart would break at the sight. "How'd he die?"

"He was shot." The words made her open her eyes again.

"Somebody shot my boy?"

"Yes, ma'am."

She shook her head at the words. "He was such a good-natured boy. Smart as a whip, too, but with never a bad word for anybody. You know that."

"Yes," I said, "I do." We sat in silence for what seemed a long while. "Would you like a cup of tea, Mrs. Barts?"

"No, thank you," her voice low. She had shifted her gaze from my face and in a way hard to explain seemed to be somewhere far away.

"What can I do for you?" I asked.

"I would appreciate it if you would arrange for word to be sent out to Clayton."

"Yes, ma'am."

"And I would like to speak to the reverend. We'll need to make arrangements."

"I'll ask him to come right over."

She rested her hand on the cover of the big, black Bible that lay on the small wooden table next to her rocker. "And then I believe I'd like to spend some time alone, if you don't mind, Ruth. The worrying is done, but the praying ain't."

"I understand, Mrs. Barts."

She nodded at me. "I know you do, Ruth. We've all carried our share of burdens on this earth, haven't we?"

My throat tightened so that I couldn't answer with words, could only return her nod before I left. I heard the whistle of the first train of the day as I crossed to the livery to ask Cap Sherman if he would ride out to Clayton Barts' with the sad news. Then I hurried down Main Street and turned east onto the wide side alley, more of a street really, that led to the church and to the nearby house where our preacher lived with his family. He was a good man, faithful to his duties, with a wife and three children. Reverend Shulte had been a comfort to me after Duncan died, and I liked him, liked all the Shultes.

Lydia, a baby cradled in one arm, answered my knock. "Ruth! My goodness, what brings you—" My face must have been as transparent as window glass that morning because she didn't bother finishing her sentence but turned and called, "Jerry, come quick! You're needed!" He was there in an instant, still pulling up his suspenders over his shirt.

"What is it, Ruth?" The reverend was in his mid-thirties, clear-eyed and not given to wasteful speech, even in his sermons, which was a welcome relief from the circuit preacher he had replaced. I told Reverend Shulte the bare facts, that someone had killed Eddie Barts and his mother was asking for the minister's company.

"I'll get my coat and my Bible and go right over," he said and disappeared back into the house.

I shook my head when Lydia invited me in. "I can't," I said, "Not now. I have things to do."

"You always have things to do, Ruth," she said, but gently. "It wouldn't hurt for you to stay long enough to take a breath and have a cup of coffee." The baby started fussing as she spoke, however, and I had to smile.

"Gerald Junior disagrees," I said. "I'll take you up on your offer another time." Lydia began to rock the baby with the involuntary motion I had often noted in mothers, as if they had suddenly become human cradles.

"He's got teeth coming in," Lydia said as explanation and then added, "It's awful news about Eddie."

"Yes," I responded, stepping away from the door and turning to leave, "it is awful, Lydia. You don't know the half of it."

But she would know soon enough, I thought on the way home. By lunch time, everyone would know what happened to Eddie Barts, and then what would the citizens of New Hope, Nebraska, do about it?

I didn't have the heart to open the barber shop that morning, although it was Saturday, which was usually the busiest day of the week. Maybe I would later in the day, but for the morning, I kept the closed sign on the door and hoped the touch of black crepe I draped over the door handles would explain why.

Danny was shocked when I told him about Eddie, but he still managed to eat a hearty breakfast before he left for school. Maybe it was his youth, or maybe he had seen so much of death that it no longer held the power to shake him to his core. At fifteen, he was close to being a man and he'd had to grow up fast. This was Danny's last year at the New Hope school, and then I didn't know what he would do. I could surely use his full time help with the rooming house and the barber shop, but if he was inclined to continue his education, then I would support that, too. When you're that age and the future stretches out in front of you like a ribbon, it's either feast or famine. One day you feel things deeply, and the next there's nothing with the power to quash your dreams. I could remember being fifteen and feeling the same way, even when we knew for sure that our father wouldn't be coming home from the war. My future hadn't gone the way I had imagined; now I was almost twice that age and unable to erase the image of Eddie's ruined head from my mind's eye. I wanted more for Danny.

Lizbeth arrived at her regular time sounding slightly breathless when she asked, "What's happened? People are buzzing in the streets." She wore a dress of pink calico that was too small for a thirteen-year-old girl beginning to bud, but I knew she had little choice for clothes and I was never critical. Before I answered, I stepped quickly down to the kitchen and grabbed a plain muslin pinafore off its hook and came back to where Lizbeth waited for me. I found the unspoken ritual we shared – her hasty arrival followed by me fussing over her until I deemed her presentable – to be especially soothing that morning. Neither of us spoke until I pulled the pinafore over her head, tied it at the back, and rearranged her dress's collar to suit.

Finished, I stepped back and said, "A man over by Gothenberg brought in Eddie Barts' body this morning. I'd guess that's what people are talking about."

"Oh, poor Mrs. Barts." Lizbeth had a tender heart. "What happened?"

I wasn't sure she needed to hear all the awful details, but then she walked nearly a mile on her own six mornings a week, and she should at least know enough to be put on her guard. I told her about the shooting the best I could and at the very end of my story said, "Until we find out who did that awful thing, Lizbeth, you need to watch your step. Have you noticed any strangers on the road lately?"

Lizbeth thought a moment. "Only that Mr. Carpenter."

"When was that?"

She thought further. "Day before yesterday, I think." She thought another moment. "Yes, Thursday morning. I noticed him because he wasn't on the road. You know I cut across the open field when I'm really late, like I was that morning, and he was doing the same. He was up ahead, but I know it was him because I recognized that big roan horse he rides."

"Did he see you?"

"He might have. I don't know. I don't think so. He didn't act like he did, but that was funny now that you mention it."

"What was funny?"

"The way he was riding, slow and careful, and how he was looking all which ways. It was like he was studying everything around him and trying to memorize it."

The knowledge that Mr. Carpenter had been in the area of New Hope the whole day before he showed up at my barber shop made me uneasy, but I couldn't have said why. No doubt knowing what had happened to Eddie would make me uneasy about a lot of otherwise innocent occurrences. Steps on the stairs behind us interrupted our conversation.

"Good morning, Mrs. Churchill. Good morning, Miss Ericson." Mr. Franks worked for the railroad in a capacity that brought him to New Hope and to Hart's at least two weeks out of every month. A pleasant, quiet man who paid in advance, he spent most of his time holed up in his room with stacks of receipts and important looking papers. The perfect boarder.

"Good morning, Mr. Franks," Lizbeth and I said in unison, which made me laugh and him smile. I appreciated that he was never overly-familiar, probably because he was there on behalf of the railroad. Whenever he went out in public, he wore a dark suit and bowler hat, not the typical fashion for New Hope but certainly proper. In fact, if I had to pick one word to describe Mr. Franks, it would be *proper*.

After he departed, I said to Lizbeth, "Well, you just be careful and keep your wits about you when you're by yourself. I'm going over to talk to Mr. Chandler."

Lizbeth stared at me. "Aren't you opening the barber shop today?" The idea that I wouldn't open the barber shop on a Saturday seemed to shock her more than the news of Eddie's death.

"Yes, but later, after lunch, and then I'll stay open into the evening. It won't change when I need you here because it's Danny's half day of school. You can go home just like usual."

"If you need me, I can stay longer."

"No, that's all right. Your pa will want to pick you up when he comes into town, and I don't want you to miss the ride home with him."

She read my thoughts. "I'm safe enough, Miss Ruth. I don't want you to worry about me."

"I don't worry about you," I lied. "You've got a good head on your shoulders or I wouldn't trust you on your own here at Hart's. But you go home with your father like you always do. Life has to go on, Lizbeth, and we might as well try to keep it business as usual."

I stepped outside and down the steps, enjoying the morning sunshine that warmed my face once I was off the porch and onto the brick walk that led to the front gate. Everything in the yard looked the same. The wild strawberries I planted a few years ago by the porch steps already displayed small white blossoms. The milkweed bushes at the corners of the porch would show bright orange in just a few weeks. The big elm in the front yard had begun to leaf out. All sure signs that spring would come this year as it had every year I could remember, springtime and harvest being the cornerstones of life in Nebraska, just as the Good Book said. Nevertheless, for all that seemed familiar and common around me, I knew it would not be business as usual for a very long time. If it ever was again.

4

People, mostly men because the majority of New Hope's merchants were men, began to gather in the town's meeting and entertainment hall. We always gathered there whenever there was something to be discussed, whether it was getting our own schoolteacher and how we would pay for his services or who would be responsible for the volunteer fire department or whether a guest speaker was a good idea for the annual Decoration Day celebration. Discussions could get quite heated, the citizens of New Hope holding strong opinions about everything, but the first thing I noticed when I stepped through the hall's door was how somber the gathering was.

My friend Bathsheba Fenway stood at the back of the room, and I made my way to her side. Sheba was a woman of remarkable appearance: tall, fiery-haired and blue-eyed, with an angular face that a person might deem handsome rather than pretty. She was my age and a late arrival to New Hope from somewhere back east – she was always vague about exactly where back east – and a person knew from her speech that she possessed a fine education. Not that she showed it off, but there was a clarity to her enunciation and to the way she went about making decisions that reflected a more elevated education than the rest of us possessed. I counted her as a good friend and valued her opinion but sometimes found her a little frightening, nevertheless. Sheba was not a woman to doubt herself and that kind of self-confidence could be somewhat off-putting until a person got to know her.

"This is awful news," she said when I reached her side.

"Yes. Awful."

"Poor Mrs. Barts." Sheba is an astute business woman and her dressmaking business turned a profit almost from day one, but she has a soft heart, though she makes it a point not to display it to just anyone.

"I gave her the sad news about Eddie this morning," I said.

"Oh, Ruth." She placed a hand on my arm. "I know that was hard for you."

I nodded, remembering Mrs. Barts as I left her, head bowed, dabbing at her eyes with a handkerchief, and rocking back and forth without conscious thought of what she did. I might have responded to Sheba, but Joe Chandler, now acting his role of mayor, stood up at the front of the room and raised his voice to call the meeting to order.

As he did so, I scanned the room. Dr. Danford was there, of course, and attorney Mort Lewis and Mr. Talamine from the bank. John Bliss, owner of the restaurant that bore his name and its neighboring Music Hall, was present, although the last official town meeting had been about the slightly disreputable goings on in the aforementioned Music Hall. Bliss' dark, saturnine face didn't seem to reflect any resentful memories, however, and when his gaze caught mine, he gave a cordial nod. I saw Russ Lowe, who made the finest saddles in Nebraska, and Luther Winters, owner of the variety store that sold everything from meat to candy, and every single merchant of New Hope, even Phil Tiglioni, who must have just got home from his last freight delivery because he hadn't been in town for a few days, not since this whole sad, fearful incident centering around Eddie Barts had begun to play out. Mr. Stenton was at school and wasn't invited to the meetings, regardless, and Reverend Shulte made it a practice never to attend our town business meetings because, as he said, he didn't want anyone to think he was a merchant that peddled the Scriptures. I valued the minister's insight and good heart, but I recall being relieved he wasn't present when we discussed the women John Bliss employed at the Music

Hall. No doubt the good reverend had heard worse, but his presence would still have had a dampening effect on the conversation.

Sometimes meetings of the Merchants' Association have the din of a crowd celebrating Independence Day, but not that morning. As soon as Joe stood, the few murmurs began to subside and with his first words the room was quiet as a cemetery. Joe, young as he was compared to some of the others in the room, had a natural flair for public speech and an inherent authority about him, which was noticeable that morning as he explained about Mr. Peltier finding Eddie's body. Tom Danford spoke briefly about the assumptions he had made from the wound to Eddie's head: Eddie bending over and looking down at something and someone standing to Eddie's left killing him with a single shot to the back of his head. We sat in silence at the end of the telling. Even I, to whom the tale was not new, felt the shock of it. Something like that happening here in New Hope! It seemed that none of us could believe it.

After a moment, Joe said, "With no one to send wires for us right now, we're more cut off than I like. Yesterday, I asked Captain McGruder if we could borrow a telegrapher from the Army long enough to fill in for Eddie and train someone else for the job. The captain said he'd mention it to Major Prentiss, but he didn't think there'd be a problem with it because they have at least four men at the fort that could stand in. I expect we'll have someone manning the telegraph office by tomorrow afternoon."

"I don't want to wait for the Army now, though, not after this bad business with Eddie, so this morning I had Cap send one of his stable hands to the fort to send a wire to the county sheriff asking for his help."

There was a flutter of conversation at the news, no doubt some of it critical. The citizens of New Hope – well, really some of the men of New Hope, women being more practical in nature with less of a need to feel in charge – like to believe New Hope is their town and they don't need help from anyone to take care of it.

Joe assumed the reproach in the indistinct comments the same as I did and spoke in a stern voice. "After what Doc Danford said, it's clear this is about the murder of a boy in our town. Nothing like this has ever happened before, and we need all the help we can get. We've talked often enough about having our own constabulary and maybe we'd better talk about it again real soon, but right now that's closing the barn door after the horse got out. The truth is that there's not a one of us here that I know of who has any experience with cowardly and cold-blooded murder."

I don't know if anyone else caught it, but his words certainly chilled me with their irony, because it seemed very likely that at least one person in New Hope or its immediate vicinity, maybe even someone in the very room in which we stood, had personal experience with exactly that. I scanned the gathering again. Was it Norm from Janco's Feed and Grain? Hans Fenstermeier with his round, cherubic face and love of fine fabric? Mr. Talamine, the dignified president of the United Bank of Nebraska? The idea that one of the men in this room, many of whom I had known for more than a decade, had talked to Eddie Barts like an old friend and then murdered him just like that made my head spin. Truly, I could not take it in.

"What should we be doing then, Joe? Should we be out looking for this fella?" The question from Harold Sellers, cooper, carpenter, and undertaker, was what everyone was wondering.

Joe stood there as helpless as the rest of us at the question. I knew this group of men, knew they'd feel better if they were out *doing* something, but what, exactly? And looking for who, exactly?

"We'll let the sheriff give us direction when he gets here. Until then, as far as I can see, it's Saturday business like usual."

"Maybe the killer's long gone from here," suggested Bert Gruber. "I mean, maybe it was just a friendly stranger that beguiled Eddie so he let down his guard." Several voices muttered relieved agreement.

Why the idea of a murderous, beguiling stranger should be a comfort to anyone beat me, but I was quiet. I'm usually quiet during meetings of the Merchants' Association. Not because I'm one of only four women in the group, but because I like to think a thing through before giving an opinion.

Morton Lewis said what I thought. "Gentlemen," he paused and inclined his head in the general direction of Sheba and me, "and ladies, I don't see what difference it makes right at the moment if we think Eddie Barts' killer has already hightailed it to Omaha or he's strolling down the middle of Main Street as we speak because we don't know." I have heard Mort Lewis in the courtroom and he can get a cadence of tone and volume to his voice that is mesmerizing. That's how he addressed the room now, as if he were summing up a case. "We don't know who did this terrible crime or why and that suggests that until we do know something more, we should all be cautious, very cautious, even with each other. Keep an eye out for the unexplained and don't be afraid to ask a question now and then."

"But we're all friends here," said Fenstermeier, his German accent coming out strong because I could tell he was shaken by both the crime and by Mort's advice to be suspicious of people he knew.

No one said a word as men slowly exited. New Hope was changing already, I thought, right before my eyes. I felt a pang of alarm mixed with sadness at the realization. Usually when our meetings ended, there was considerable back-slapping among the men, laughter, old stories repeated and family news shared, what you'd expect from people who worked and lived in close proximity. Despite the silence, the way the men avoided looking at their neighbors as they headed out into the sunshine spoke a message as loud and clear as if they had shouted words into the air.

****

From the very first day the barber shop opened, it was the town gathering place. It still has its convivial moments, but when my husband was clipping and trimming and lathering, there was a different feel to the place than there is with me standing behind the chair. Part of the difference is, of course, that I am a woman, and no doubt there are many topics of conversation that the customers do not think suitable for my ears. Men sometimes believe that women are too sensitive – they would likely use the word *touchy* – to understand or enjoy some of their nonsense, and while I might argue that *sensible* or *busy* would be more accurate terms, that's neither here nor there. What I do know is that on busy Saturdays when I took Duncan his lunch, the shop buzzed as if my husband had taken up beekeeping.

That was purely because of Duncan, because of who and what he was: a joyful man of ready laughter, a man who enjoyed a good joke – but never at anyone's expense – and found humor in the commonplace. He told me once that in England he wasn't allowed to rub shoulders with what he called ordinary people because his family was high in society and had an elevated opinion of their family name. He tucked an address away at the back of a drawer – "If the time comes," he said, "you'll want to let them know," – but otherwise talked infrequently of his early life. Instead, he declared on more than one occasion, "I wasn't alive until I came to Nebraska and met you, Ruthie. It's not the air of this state that will save me, whatever the doctors say. It's you." Well, as much as I wished he was right, in the end neither I nor the dry air of the sand hills was enough to heal my husband.

I don't have Duncan's ease with laughter or his endless good nature, so while customers still gather at *Duncan's* – I have kept the name on the sign for sentiment's sake – the buzzing of the old days is long gone. Even that Saturday following the town meeting, when no doubt everyone had an opinion or comment, conversation in the shop remained subdued after I finally opened. Local farmers and cowhands and railroad men who had come in for a shave or a haircut had certainly heard about poor Eddie Barts and there was conversation about him, but it was quiet, nevertheless.

Bert Gruber, the owner of the Gooseneck Hotel, trusted himself to me despite our being business competitors because he had no wife at home to do his barbering duties. I'm being charitable about the word *competitors* because the Gooseneck has none of the refined qualities of Hart's, and Bert would never argue the fact. The clientele he sought were men that didn't especially notice things like the cleanliness of the accommodations or the civility of other people staying at the hotel.

As he waited for me to finish with the man in the chair, Bert sat at the edge of the bench along the side wall. He's a man so small that if he sat all the way back on the bench, his feet would not reach the floor, but that day it was unease that made him restless, not my bench.

"This is a bad business about young Eddie," Bert said.

"Yes," I agreed, "very bad."

"He was a likeable boy, Ruth. I fished with him many a time. Maybe if I'd gone with him this last time, he'd still be alive." I did not say, "Or you'd be dead," but I thought it.

Instead, I asked, "Did he have a favorite fishing spot, Bert?" I finished the man in the chair, pulled the cloth from his shoulders, and used the hand brush to whisk any leftover hairs from his collar. He took a quick look at himself in the mirror – it isn't only women that are vain – and with a nod of thanks placed his coins in the basket I kept on the counter under the mirror.

Not waiting for invitation, Bert came forward to settle himself in the barber chair. "He always went to the same spot for catfish, Ruth. I never could get him to believe that I might know as much about fishing as him." Bert realized that it might not be in the best of taste to sound so aggrieved about someone who had recently died and added, "Well, he knew the river, there's no denying that. You know that stand of cottonwoods right at the bend where the river shifts south?"

"No, I can't say I do." I laid a cloth over Bert's shoulders and reached for the scissors.

"Yes, you do. It's where that traveling preacher had all his baptisms last summer, remember? He set up his tent just north of those cottonwoods and then led his congregation through the stand of trees to the river. It was a sight to behold, like the old Pied Piper story my mother told me." It seemed to me that Bert was confusing his comparisons, but his words did jog my memory.

"I missed that particular parade," I said. "Missed the whole revival, in fact, but now that you mention it, I recall the area. Is that where Eddie would have gone if he promised his mother catfish for supper?"

"That's the place. He swore by it. Said there was a big old catfish that lived right there. Eddie even named him. Called him – let's see, what was it? – Tiger, I think. Yes, Tiger 'cause I recall I made a joke about seeing stripes if Eddie ever got his hook into it." Bert and I were quiet for a moment, remembering Eddie and the way he liked to tease now and then. Bert cleared his throat. "Anyway, that was his spot for catfish. He couldn't be talked out of it."

A customer entered the barber shop then, someone I had seen before but whose name escaped me. He gave me a nod and sat down to wait his turn, which brought an end to Bert's and my conversation. I finished Bert's cut, removed the cloth from Bert's shoulders, and whisked the small hand brush along his collar and neck.

"Thank you, Ruth."

"You're welcome, Bert."

"Are your rooms staying full?"

"Full enough," I replied. "You?"

"The same. Three trains a day is just about right for the number of rooms I've got."

"I wouldn't complain if the U.P. added a fourth stop; I've got the room, but I'm not complaining."

Bert licked the palms of his hands and slicked back the sides of his hair, which from my perspective did not improve his cut, but it was a habit he would never lose, and I had learned over time not to wince at the final effect.

"I've never known you to complain, Ruth. It's one of the things I admire about you." His cheeks reddened slightly with the words.

"Thank you," I said, but Bert was already outside and hurrying back to his hotel and billiards parlor and wouldn't have heard me.

I stayed busy until after the supper hour but thought about Eddie Barts and his favorite fishing spot every so often until I turned the sign on the door to closed. Tomorrow was Sunday and no doubt Eddie would be on everyone's mind so there would be a full church for the service. We had only one arriving train on Sunday, which came in the early evening, and once Danny and I were home and Sunday's dinner dishes were done, I made up my mind to take a walk out to the cottonwoods Bert mentioned and see the place for myself. Not to honor Eddie in any way – I have no illusions about the dead smiling down from above and watching what we do; wherever the dead end up, they will have more important matters on their minds than watching me take a Sunday stroll – but to set my mind at ease. Was that the last place Eddie saw on this earth? Had Eddie bent over to point out the hiding place of his favorite catfish to someone pretending to be interested? Could it have been Bert, I asked myself, horrified at the thought but unable to banish it. He would have known Eddie's likely location that day and no one, least of all Eddie, would suspect that little Bert Gruber might possess such murderous ability. The idea was sickening, but until I knew the why of it, I would no doubt continue to have all sorts of sickening thoughts about the who of it.

Sheba Fenway's dress and millinery establishment is directly across Main Street from the barber shop, and I poked my head in its front door on my way back to the boarding house that evening. Despite the front sign that announced *Dressmaking*, any discriminating person who crossed the threshold of Sheba's shop would know right off that there was more to it than bolts of calico, fashion magazines, and straw bonnets because Sheba's store always held the unmistakable odor of turpentine. Like me, Bathsheba Fenway made her own living, but while dressmaking paid the bills, it was painting she loved.

I am no expert when it comes to art, and I have never been to a museum devoted to painting, although I understand there are such places back east, but I truly can't imagine that any painter, regardless of his fame, could hold a candle to Sheba. She has a magical way with light and water, which is why I have her depiction of the Platte River at sunrise hanging in my foyer. It isn't to impress my customers, it's to lighten my spirits and remind me as I head out the door that life is worth living. I don't know how she did it, but while Sheba painted the river, she somehow also painted hope and joy into that picture. She says I'm too fanciful and that because we're friends, I'm too kind, as well, but that's not so. Anyone who can lift a person's spirits with the stroke of a paintbrush must surely be a match for any of the famous names, Rembrandt or John Constable or—well, I don't know any other famous names, but I would put my friend Sheba's paintings up against their works any time.

Sheba heard the door as I pushed it open and came through the doorway at the back of the shop.

"I'm sorry," I told her. "I didn't mean to bother you." My friend wore a scarf around her head to cover her hair and a paint spattered smock.

She waved the words away. "You're never a bother, Ruth. Are you just going home now?"

I nodded. "I couldn't bring myself to open until after lunch, what with everything that happened, but when a man wants a haircut, nothing can keep him from it."

She gave a snort that wasn't especially ladylike. "Nothing can keep a man from anything he thinks he needs at the time, no matter how inconvenient or irritating it might be, and that's the truth." She returned my half-smile with a full grin. "You know I've never had the benefit of a man like Duncan in my life, so I can be forgiven if I'm a little skeptical of the male sex." She turned serious then. "I shouldn't be talking like this, Ruth, with poor Mrs. Barts grieving her son. I'm sorry."

"I know. I found myself laughing at a joke now and then today, and right away I thought, that's not right, but that's how life goes on, isn't it? There was a time after Duncan died that I thought I'd never laugh again, but I laugh just fine now."

"That's the power of time," Sheba said. "Let's hope it's as kind to Cora Barts." After a pause, she repeated Bert Gruber's words from earlier in the afternoon, "This is a bad business, Ruth."

I pulled my shawl more tightly around my shoulders. "Yes. I'll be glad when Sheriff Bradley gets here."

"All he'll do is swear in a couple of New Hope's men as deputies and head right back to North Platte. It's what he always does."

"It's a big county, Sheba, and Sheriff Bradley has a lot of responsibility. The man can't be everywhere."

"I know," a hint of penitence in her tone, "and I'll be glad to see the man, just like you will, Ruth, but I don't hold out any hope that he can find out what happened to Eddie Barts. I think it will be up to the citizens of New Hope to uncover the answers to what happened."

I thought about Sheba's words as I made my way past the café and stepped up onto the front porch of the boarding house and through the front door. Danny had lit the lamp, which made the room cheerful and homey against the fading light of a sad day. The sound of the bell brought the boy out of The Addition.

"I'm sorry I'm so late," I said. "Are you awfully hungry? It won't take me but a minute to warm up what's left of last night's supper."

"I already did that. I was waiting for you to come home." His words touched me, made me grateful for his company and his kindness.

I had to swallow before I could find room in my throat to say, "Well, wasn't that nice of you?" I walked over and took a quick look at the book that listed the roomers' names. "I don't see any new names."

"No, ma'am. I thought maybe the last train through might drop someone off, but there weren't any new faces at the station."

I followed Danny into The Addition and had to smile at his efforts, the table was set but the pot on the stove was giving off a burnt smell that did not bode well for tonight's meal. I grabbed a heavy towel and used it to carry the pot to the table and set it on an old cast iron trivet.

"Oh." I could tell by the deflated tone of the one syllable that Danny had just realized he had left supper on the fire a bit longer than was either wise or necessary.

I looked up at him and smiled. "It's fine. There's plenty for both of us, and Othello will be thrilled to take the scrapings off our hands. Thank you for doing this."

Danny still looked and sounded annoyed with himself. "I should have paid better attention. I will next time. I promise."

At least, I thought as I went over to the sink to pump water for my hands, he'll have a next time. I recalled Mrs. Barts' face as she sat in her rocker with her hands in her lap, staring down at nothing after she got the bad news about her son, and knew she would give every last thing she possessed for just one more supper, no matter if it was burnt black to a crisp, if she could eat it with her youngest boy sitting across the table from her.

It seemed that I had no sooner fallen asleep that night than I was wide awake again, lying stiff and motionless in the way a person does when she knows something isn't right and she's afraid to twitch a muscle. Then I heard the loud and clear ring of the fire bell and knew what had awakened me. We feared fire almost as much as we feared the winds of a tornado off the prairie. I say *almost* because New Hope has a volunteer fire department to help with a fire emergency, but when the funnel cloud of a tornado rolls across the plains, there's nothing to be done but head for the cellar and pray. In that order.

I pulled a dress over my nightgown, still fumbling with the buttons as I rushed into the hallway. Danny's door remained closed, and I gave it a quick, hard rap on my way past. Knowing the boy's sleeping habits, he had probably not even heard the fire bell. There were footsteps on the stairs behind me, but I didn't stop to see which of my boarders followed me outside. Once down the walk and through the front gate, I checked the buildings in my immediate area – no fires there, thank God – and then looked north to the far end of the street to see a low burning glow of flames contrasted against the night sky.

At first, the sight was so shocking that all I could do was raise both hands to my mouth.

"Is it the telegraph office?" Silas Carpenter asked. He stopped beside me and stared right along with me.

"Yes," I said. Then, remembering, I picked up my skirts and began to run, calling over my shoulder, "Mrs. Barts lives right behind the office!"

He began to run, too, joining all the people that streamed from their stores and homes, their wooden stores and homes. We knew the danger. Just this year almost two whole blocks of Hastings were burnt to the ground. If the fire took hold, it would leap from building to building and nothing could stop it.

Russ Lowe, the head of our little fire department, was already throwing open the doors of the livery to get at the hand-drawn single-tank wagon housed there. Other men were right behind Russ, and by the time I reached the far end of town, they had the wagon in place and had added the chemicals necessary to discharge the water. New Hope purchased a modern chemical engine at great expense, and it put out a fire very effectively once it got started, but it took a while to get going, so while Russ went about his business getting the chemicals in place, the other men filled buckets and tubs from a second tank we kept filled with river water. It was a group effort and every man did his job because every man had something to lose. Every person was equal before the threat of fire.

"Where's the Barts house?" Carpenter asked.

"This way." I led him down a small alley past the post office, which shared a wall with the telegraph office and stood in the most immediate danger of being lost.

When we reached the house, both Carpenter and I stopped. The fire seemed to be localized to the inside of the telegraph office and would likely burn through into the post office, but the little house didn't look to be in any immediate danger. Still, any sensible person knew that fire had a mind of its own, and it would take only one smoldering ember landing on the house's wood roof to set the whole place ablaze. Already red-tinged bits of wood and paper floated in the night air.

"I'll go," Carpenter said. "You stay here. I'll get her," but I couldn't stay behind completely, though I knew he was right to take the lead. He tried to push open the front door, but it would hardly budge. Something or someone lay against the door on the other side and kept it from opening.

"Mrs. Barts," I cried, "it's Ruth Churchill. Mrs. Barts!" No answer. "She must have fallen," I said to Carpenter. "Maybe the shock of the fire and the bell and the noise made her heart give out. She's a frail woman."

Carpenter set his shoulder to the door and shoved gently but steadily until there was just enough room for him to get through. It was too dark for me to see anything from where I stood, but Si Carpenter slipped through the opening and after a moment, the front door opened completely. He stepped outside holding the limp body of Mrs. Barts in his arms pressed against his chest.

"Oh!" I cried. "She isn't dead, is she? Don't tell me she's dead!"

"No." The one calm syllable slowed my breathing and my panic right away. "She's not dead, Ruth, but we should get her to the doctor. She collapsed on the floor. The doc will know if it's her heart, but don't rush ahead and think the worst."

I led us back down the alley, checking for Tom Danford as soon as we reached the main street. By then, the hose was spraying soda water into the telegraph office and the glow of the fire had dimmed noticeably. Maybe we wouldn't lose the post office, after all.

Phil Tiglioni appeared next to me and then took a step toward Si Carpenter and his featherweight burden.

"What happened?" Phil asked me.

"I don't know. She was on the floor in the house. Have you seen Tom?"

Phil pointed toward the livery. "Over there with Cap, I think."

At his words, Si Carpenter moved past us in the direction of the stables, but I stayed behind long enough to ask, "Did you have any damage, Phil?" His freight company office, warehouse, and home stood to the immediate north of the telegraph office with an alley in between.

"No. The fire looks to be inside from what I could see. More chance of it burning through to the post office than jumping over to my place."

"Still, I imagine the bell gave Julia and the girls quite a start."

"They're visiting her father. I don't expect them back until Thursday."

"That was a timely visit, then," I said, and glanced across the street in time to see Mr. Carpenter crouch and as gently as if he handled something precious and fragile set Cora Barts' body on the ground. His careful action and the tenderness it displayed both surprised me and touched me deeply, and I have since thought that perhaps it was at that moment I began to love him. I can't say for sure – love can't always be pinned down – and I didn't have any time to spend on the notion just then, but from that moment on, I never thought of Si Carpenter the same way. Something inside me changed, though it would be a long while before I understood exactly what and how and why.

5

The morning after the fire was Sunday, and the citizens of New Hope are by and large a religious lot, so despite the early morning interruption, most of us showed up to sit in our usual places for the service. I wondered that Reverend Shulte did not keel right out of the pulpit from the overpowering smell of smoke that his little flock brought into the church with them, but he had an elder prop open the doors and managed to conduct the service as if the sanctuary did not smell like someone had built a raging bonfire in the middle of the center aisle.

Danny was bright-eyed, having slept through all the excitement, but I was anything but. I felt tired and lethargic because eventually when I got back home, I had a difficult time catching even an hour's sleep. I thought about the telegraph office gutted by fire and how pale and feeble Mrs. Barts looked lying on the cot in the back room of the doctor's office. I had found someone to ride out to Clayton Barts' place to let him know his mother needed him, and I sat with Mrs. Barts until Margery Danford came in to take my place. By then, the fire was out completely and except for two men assigned to keep watch in case it flared up again, everyone else had wandered home.

When I crossed the street early Sunday morning to see how Mrs. Barts fared, Margery met me at the drug store's front door. She told me Clayton had come with his oldest son and between them, they had swathed the elderly woman into quilts, loaded her into the back of a wagon, and carried her back to Clayton's farm.

"She was awake and alert, Ruth," Margery said, "but not very happy about all the fuss."

"Will she be all right?" I asked.

"She traveled fourteen hundred miles to Nebraska from Connecticut and then raised seven children in a soddy. She's a woman used to hardship. Tom says her heart isn't what it used to be, but whose is? Being with her family will do her a world of good. If I had to guess, I'd say she's too stubborn to leave this earth until she knows what happened to her Eddie."

That makes two of us, I thought, and trudged back across the street to have a second cup of coffee before church. When Danny and I went down the front walk, I looked back at Othello, seated on the top porch step and already disconsolate because the mutt knew he would have to wait a few hours for Danny's return. Without thought, I lifted my glance to the second story's front window behind which Mr. Carpenter must still be sleeping. I was already home and in bed when I finally heard him come in and climb the stairs to his room, so he was undoubtedly asleep behind the lace curtains.

In a way I could not explain, Si Carpenter had taken charge during the calamity, had spent time with Russ Lowe discussing the fire, had conferred with Doctor Danford about Mrs. Barts, and had put in time with the bucket brigade, besides. I last saw Carpenter in the dim light of very early morning as he stepped carefully into the ruined telegraph office with Joe Chandler right behind him. Mr. Carpenter wore authority naturally, but his behavior seemed more than that of a man used to being in charge. He acted like a man who had come to New Hope driven by a specific purpose known only to himself and who was ready to commandeer whatever and whomever he needed to accomplish that purpose. A man looking for answers to a question only he knew. Somehow, but I couldn't possibly see how, it seemed that the fire at the telegraph office had a part to play in the answers he sought. How else to explain his steady and serious participation in the night's activities? My other roomers, including the long-term boarder Mr. Franks, had all stood at the top of the stairs and called down questions about what was going on. Only Si Carpenter took action, and the kind of action a person might expect from a resident of New Hope, not from a man merely passing through town. I was glad to leave the troubling speculation behind, sit down at the back of the church, and let Pastor Shulte's words and the sounds of the pump organ roll over me. There are few things more freeing to the spirit than a rousing chorus of *Holy, Holy, Holy* sung in four-part harmony.

None of the congregation stayed long after the service ended but drifted home in small, worried, unusually quiet groups. Once back at the boarding house, I had Danny fill a tub with hot water for me and took a bath, tried to wash the smell of smoke from both hair and body, and then took my time with Sunday dinner. Sundays were a day of rest for just about everyone in New Hope, but more for some than others. Every retail establishment closed for the day, but Bliss' Restaurant and Music Hall opened in the evening despite a modest amount of disapproval. The only train through New Hope on Sunday was the daily four o'clock from Grand Island, and it did not usually bring much business into town. It did, however, bring a bundle of copies of the week's Grand Island *Independent*, which many of us looked forward to with the fervor of a religious revival. New Hope didn't have its own newspaper, but we considered ourselves loyal citizens of both Nebraska and the United States of America and we hungered for news of both.

The day's weather was fine, sunny but still spring-cool, perfect for a stroll, and because I was restless and worried, I set out after dinner, knowing where I was headed before I ever stepped off the front porch. Our branch of the Platte River is a comfortable walk south of New Hope and remembering Bert's conversation about Eddie's favorite fishing spot, I had an inexplicable desire to find that stand of cottonwoods. The walk was longer than I remembered, but

I'm a busy woman, not used to sitting down, and there's something bracing about a brisk walk along the river's path. I tied my shawl around my waist and swung my arms and for a few minutes felt happy again, until the trees came into view. There was little to see, of course, just a narrow branch of the river, a grassy bank, and a path that led down from the copse of cottonweed trees to the water. The line of converts following the revival preacher through the trees and down to the river to be baptized must have been quite a sight. Nothing like that now, however, just bob whites calling to each other and somewhere a lark singing its heart out. A peaceful place, even knowing Eddie Barts might have died here.

I walked as close to the river's edge as I could, picturing Eddie standing in that very spot. Although the river narrowed somewhat, the water looked darker in color than before, a spot dark and deep enough for a granddaddy catfish to take up residence. At least, Eddie thought so. Standing on the grassy edge, I felt a curious combination of sadness and anger and with a childlike petulance kicked at the tall grass. To my surprise, it was not just tips of grass that scattered into the air but something brighter and more substantial. I bent down for a closer view and picked up, of all things, a paper cigar band, mostly white with the word *Kipp* in flowing dark blue letters scrawled across an orange oval that was meant to resemble the sun. *Kipp*, the wrapper said, *The Cigar That Makes Good.* I was no expert in cigars, but this was not a design I recognized, despite the words *Hastings, Neb* that showed in small print on the wrapper. I stood staring at the small paper in the palm of my hand. Where in the world had it come from? And how did it find its way to the very bank of the river where Eddie enjoyed fishing? If Bert Gruber smoked cigars, I had never seen him with one in public, and Eddie couldn't have afforded a cigar, not even one of the very cheapest brands, filled, as I recently read, with just about anything except tobacco, including sugar, rhubarb leaves, lead, moss, and lamp black. I would check with Eddie's mother, nevertheless, because I sensed this paper cigar band could be important, even if at the time, I didn't understand why.

"Mrs. Churchill?" The words spoken out of the blue in a male voice interrupted my deep thought and caused my heart to race ahead of the other parts of my body. I clenched my fist around the small piece of paper in my hand, took a breath, and whirled quickly to face the speaker.

Silas Carpenter stood facing me on the rough footpath that followed the river. He held the reins of his handsome roan horse with one hand and let his other arm hang loosely at his side, a stance that was casual and unthreatening. A deliberate effort to set me at ease. He kept his distance, too. Another attempt not to alarm me. I appreciated the effort he took to let me know I had nothing to fear. A week ago, I wouldn't have given any of it a thought, but life was different now, more dangerous and more frightening.

"Are you out for a Sunday afternoon stroll, too, Mr. Carpenter?" I asked. "I would have thought you'd be trying to catch up on your sleep after all the excitement last night."

He didn't reply or move, and I dropped the cigar band into my pocket with a small gesture as I lifted my skirts to climb the small grassy knoll that separated the river from the path.

When I reached his side, he took a step back from me before he said, "When I left for the fort this morning, Danny said you were taking a bath. I asked him to let you know I was gone, but I guess he didn't say anything to you."

"The smell of pork chops tends to drive every other thought out of his head," I said with a small smile, "and he doesn't regain the full use of his senses for some time after the meal. He's only fifteen, you know."

"Pork chops can have that effect on a man, fifteen or fifty." The remark seemed obligatory on his part, something to say to keep the mood light, because even as he spoke his gaze moved beyond me to the river bank. "Is this where young Barts came to fish?"

"That's what Bert Gruber says. By the stand of cottonwoods where the river shifts south."

Carpenter took a leisurely look at the countryside around us. "Looks like this would be the place, then."

Watching the man and the careful way he examined our surroundings – just like Lizbeth had described, like he was "studying everything around him and trying to memorize it" – I surprised myself by asking, "What do you know, Mr. Carpenter?"

"Know?"

I felt a spurt of annoyance at his bland tone. "I may not be an educated woman, but that doesn't mean I'm stupid or slow."

"I believe you are anything but, Mrs. Churchill." My irritation did not abate.

"You called me Ruth last night, and since it is my name, I don't know why you persist in calling me Mrs. Churchill."

He didn't falter. "I don't know why, either. Not thinking straight, I guess, and I can't even use pork chops as an excuse."

The evenhanded response to my snippy and unreasonable criticism was said in all seriousness and took me aback for a moment; his teasing always came when I least expected it. Then I couldn't help but laugh out loud.

"I'm sorry," I said once I caught my breath from laughter. "I was wrong to take out my worry and bad temper on you." I grew serious. "But you know something about the fearful things that have happened in New Hope. I know you do."

"I would never harm you, Ruth, if that's what concerns you, not you or any law-abiding citizen in New Hope."

I took time to study his face, the weather-browned skin, firm mouth, and dark gray eyes that met my look without hesitation, and felt a weight I hadn't known I carried slide off my shoulders.

"I believe that's true," I said, "but I wish you'd tell me what you know about Eddie Barts and the fire last night. It doesn't take any effort to see that Eddie worked at the telegraph office, and it was the telegraph office that burned down. There's a connection I can't make sense of, but that I think you can. I'm a trustworthy woman – if that's what concerns *you* – and I keep my own counsel." From his expression, I saw that he had come to a decision.

"I'm looking for a man, Ruth, a bad man, and I believe he lives in New Hope. It's as close as I've ever been to him. I can smell him, and I'm not leaving without him."

I don't know what I expected to hear, but it surely wasn't that. It took some time to decide what to ask first, so instead of responding, I turned and began to walk with measured steps back toward town. Carpenter fell into step with me, his mount trailing behind, and remained quiet as I continued to ponder his words. I appreciated his restraint. It's a wise man that doesn't feel the need to jump into every silence.

"Did this bad man kill Eddie Barts?" I asked.

"I believe so."

"Why would he do such a thing?"

"Because Eddie sent a telegram for him."

I stopped abruptly. "That makes no sense. Eddie sent telegrams for practically everybody in New Hope at one time or another."

Mr. Carpenter reached into a pocket and handed me a piece of paper, a telegram that had been folded and refolded so many times it had started to tear at the creases. I thought someone – Si Carpenter, probably – had read and reread the telegram's few words so often that he must know them by heart. *Remember Langtry. No one lives forever.*

"Eddie Barts sent that telegram to a man named Hank Ketchum. I took it out of Ketchum's pocket myself."

I handed the paper back to Carpenter but kept walking, more slowly by then. I had the feeling the story would be longer than the walk if I didn't take smaller and more leisurely strides.

"Have you ever heard of Emmett Wolf?" Carpenter asked.

"Yes. Didn't he rob banks and trains a few years ago?"

"That and murdered people and violated women and made life in western Missouri a pure hell. He rode with Quantrill but when the war stopped, Wolf didn't. For the next seven years, he and two other men kept up their murderous activities."

"Seven years? But it's been thirteen years since the war ended. What's he been doing the last six? Could he be dead?"

"That's a good question, Ruth. What has Emmett Wolf been doing with himself these past six years? He didn't disappear overnight, but he got scarcer and scarcer, a bank robbery here, a train payroll stolen there, until finally there wasn't any word about him at all. He hasn't been sighted for a long time. The man isn't dead, though I admit I wondered about that for a while. He's just keeping low and staying out of trouble. Mostly, anyway. Until your Eddie Barts sent a telegram for him."

I was still tired from the night before, my only excuse for being so slow to understand the details of Carpenter's story. "I'm sorry. You need to speak plainer."

"I think you're a woman that always appreciates plain speech." I heard a smile in his voice.

"I do," I said. "There aren't enough hours in the day as it is, and I don't have a lot of extra time to puzzle things out."

"Emmett Wolf and the two men that rode with him may have decided it was time to take a break from bad habits, but the law and the railroad and the Payne and Williams Bank of Missouri haven't forgotten about them, and neither have I. Not by a long shot. We don't intend to let bygones be bygones." With the last words, Carpenter's voice hardened in a way that sent a chill through me. I would not want this man on my trail.

"All right," I said finally, "but how do you know Wolf sent that telegram and sent it from here, from New Hope, Nebraska?"

"An expert with the U.S. Military Telegraph Corps examined the telegram and told me where it originated. There are ways and records to trace it."

"All right," I repeated. "That may be so, but how do you know Emmett Wolf sent it? The only name on it was Langtry and he wasn't the sender."

"No. Winston Langtry was one of the two men that rode with Wolf. Four years ago, Langtry was arrested in Topeka for being part of a drunken brawl and before the liquor wore off, he bragged about his time riding with Wolf in Missouri. He said enough to make the law in Topeka suspicious that they might be holding a member of Wolf's gang in their jail, so instead of releasing him, they arranged to transfer him east to Kansas City. Missouri was hungry to get Langtry and even hungrier to get Wolf. There was never a good description of Wolf, nor of Langtry or Ketchum either, just that they were three men of average size and height. Wearing their hats low and keeping their faces covered was their trademark, and if they slipped up, they killed anyone that might be a witness against them. So for the Missouri constabulary, having Winston Langtry in custody was the first chance they had in years to track down Emmett Wolf."

I didn't interrupt, but I wanted to. I knew there was something awful coming, and I'd had enough *awful* for a while. I wanted it to be last Sunday afternoon, slow and sunny and comfortable.

"Langtry and the two Missouri deputies sent to get him were murdered on their way to Kansas City. Blown out of the saddle by two blasts from a double-barrel shotgun. It must have come quick and taken them by surprise because they were all three found right where they fell. They never stood a chance." He must have heard my quick inhale because he turned to look at me. "I'm sorry. I wouldn't tell you this except I think the person that murdered those men lives right here in New Hope."

"You'd better finish the story, then," I said with grim insistence, "because I don't know a person in New Hope capable of what you just described."

"I'd expect you to say that, and there's no reason you should believe me."

I did believe him, of course, believed him because I had seen how tenderly he carried Cora Barts. In my mind's eye, I could still see Si Carpenter crouch low, place her still form on the ground, and then without even thinking about it, reach to brush back her hair from her face. I believed him because of that one simple act.

"When the Union Pacific got wind of what happened in Missouri, they asked me to get involved, to see what I could find out about Winston Langtry to start with, and doing that eventually led me to Hank Ketchum and the telegram I showed you."

"Are you with the law, then?"

"Not exactly."

"Don't get me started again, Mr. Carpenter—"

"Si."

"All right, though I prefer Silas. It's a fine name straight out of the Bible."

"It is that. My older brother, Paul, died at Chickamauga, but there were three of us raised in a preacher's house, and my brother and I were Paul and Silas all our growing up years."

I didn't let that deflect me from saying, "That's all well and good – and I'm sorry for the loss of your brother – but it seems to me you're either working for the law or you're not. *Not exactly* is no proper answer."

"Right now, I'm working on behalf of the state of Missouri, but it's not a permanent post, only until I track down Emmett Wolf."

"Does that mean you have Hank Ketchum in custody, then?"

"No. Hank Ketchum is buried in a cemetery outside of Lincoln. It took me almost two years to track down all the men and women known to consort with Langtry, and it took even longer to make my way to Ketchum. By then, word was out that there was a fresh bounty on Wolf's head, and I wasn't the only one looking for him. I only wanted to talk to Ketchum at first. I wasn't sure he had anything important to tell me, but he tried to ambush me from an alley one night, and I had to kill him."

A second sharp inhale of breath escaped me. Si Carpenter didn't defend himself or his action, just continued, "That's when I pulled that telegram out of his pocket, and once the Telegraph Corps told me it came from New Hope, Nebraska, I had a good idea where to find Emmett Wolf."

"You can't know that for sure," I objected.

"You'd be right, Ruth – if Eddie Barts hadn't ended up dead. I figure Wolf was afraid the boy might remember who sent that telegram, and even if Eddie didn't remember, Wolf had to know that even the small telegraph offices keep detailed records and names from way back. For some reason, I believe Emmett Wolf got careless and used his hometown telegraph office. I don't know why. I'd have thought he was too shrewd and careful for that."

"It doesn't really matter, though, does it?" I considered Si's words. "Because the record of the telegram would be in whatever office he used, and any clerk might remember something about the person who sent it. Maybe New Hope was simply a convenient stop for Wolf." I felt a wave of sadness for Eddie Barts, a young fellow in the wrong job in the wrong town at the wrong time. I could have wept.

"I think you're partly right," Si Carpenter agreed. "It ended up being your Eddie Barts, but it could have been anyone. Once Wolf got wind of the fact that men were back on his trail, I imagine he began to worry about anything that might lead back to him. Somehow, he heard about Langtry and got rid of him, and that just left Ketchum. Only I got to Ketchum first and found the telegram. People saw me pull it out of the man's pocket or heard stories about it later so it wasn't any secret, and word spreads. Emmett Wolf doesn't like loose ends, never has, and that telegram was the only loose end left. So he took care of it the way he always did: killed the telegraph agent and burned down the telegraph office."

"But maybe it wasn't someone from New Hope, maybe it was a stranger, someone that got off the train, sent the telegram, and got right back on the train again." I knew I sounded desperate and stubborn, but I couldn't help myself.

"And then what? Came back to New Hope later on the very day that Eddie Barts decided to take off to go fishing and knew where Eddie's special fishing spot was and followed him there and somehow managed to get the boy off his guard and kill him? And then do you think he came back a few days after that and burned down the telegraph office? I know that's what you want to hear, Ruth, but I've asked a lot of questions about strangers being interested in Eddie Barts and nobody remembers any stranger in town asking the whereabouts of the telegraph clerk. Lizbeth let me look at the names in your book, and I checked at the Gooseneck, too, for recent strangers. I talked to the ticket agent at the station and even asked the railroad to check passenger lists on the local line for the day the telegram was sent, looking for – I don't know what – anything that seemed not right. They don't know what they're looking for and neither do I, but they're checking again for passengers this past Saturday to see if anything matches up. I've traveled the plains and the roads around New Hope looking for signs that someone had camped out recently so he could watch the goings on in town. I talked to the Army about anything their patrols or scouts might have noticed. But you know as well as I do, Ruth, that there's nothing for any of them to find."

Silas Carpenter stayed quiet, letting me think, letting me come to the realization on my own that he was right. The citizens of New Hope noticed things and remembered things. Even with three trains coming and going, we were just a little stop along the way. I had no doubt that someone would remember giving directions to Eddie Barts' favorite fishing spot to a stranger. If any of us even knew where the spot was. We talked about Eddie's playing hooky from his work, but no one ever said where he and his fishing pole disappeared to. Bert knew, of course. I pulled back from the thought – Bert again. Besides, Eddie hadn't known for sure he'd go fishing that day. *Maybe* is what he told his mother, maybe, depending on how busy he got. A person just off the train to take care of the loose end named Eddie Barts couldn't have known that in advance.

It was an awful truth, but Silas Carpenter had it right. Someone Eddie knew and trusted killed him. Someone I knew and trusted had set the telegraph office ablaze. Emmett Wolf almost certainly lived in or around New Hope, hid behind a mask and a different name. Did I cut his hair on a regular basis? Did he voice his opinion at the Merchants' Association meetings? Had he sat in the worship service and joined in prayer with the rest of the congregation and then walked out the door of the church intending to murder Eddie Barts, endanger Eddie's mother, and risk burning down the whole town, all for his own protection? I couldn't grasp the wickedness of it, and the effort it must certainly take to be that man. To be those two men, really.

"I can see you're right, Silas. I don't like it and I wish it weren't true, but you're right, and I appreciate knowing it."

We walked steadily side-by-side. The meadow larks had burst into an extravagant chorus and a small breeze had come up, making the tall grasses sway. Mother Nature dancing and singing all around and me so heartsick I couldn't appreciate the performance. Silas heard my sigh.

"I told you all this, Ruth, because I—" He hesitated. "I want you to be careful. I wouldn't want anything to happen to you. Now that you know there's a killer walking the streets of New Hope, you can protect yourself better against him."

"Thank you," I said. "That's kind of you."

"Kind." He repeated the word as if it was new to him. "Well, yes, there is that."

We had reached the main road into town, and New Hope stretched out in front of us. A valiant little place, I always thought. Civilization represented by store fronts and a steeple, a stone school, a college-educated schoolteacher, and a quick stop on the rail line. We tried so hard to do everything right, but we had been invaded by something as deadly as cholera and as frightening as a tornado.

Still, I liked the man walking next to me, trusted him and believed he might be the rescue of New Hope. Wishful thinking, perhaps, but I am by nature a hopeful person.

When we reached the southern end of Main Street, I saw a horse tied to the gate in front of Hart's and recognized it immediately as belonging to Captain Jeff McGruder. The knowledge made me close my eyes a moment in order to rally my good temper. The captain sat on the top step of the porch, not bothering to pretend that he was doing anything but stare at Silas and me as we approached.

"Well," Jeff said, rising and walking to the end of the walk. He spoke to us over the gate. "I was getting worried, Ruth, what with everything that's been happening. I wish you wouldn't go out on your own. It's a bad habit."

Berating me for my bad habits in public did not put me in charity with the man. "I appreciate your concern, but as you can see, I wasn't on my own, and I seem to have made it home all in one piece." I pushed open the gate, forcing Jeff to hop to the side to avoid being hit by it. "I thought someone notified the Army that we didn't need a telegraph clerk anymore."

"They did. We heard all about the fire at the telegraph office."

"Then if you didn't bring a substitute for the telegraph office, why are you here?"

The captain was not a man of subtleties, and over time I had learned there was no use beating around the bush with him. He was a man of action fit for military life, a good man, I believed, if somewhat frustrating, and he appreciated straight talk.

"I made the trip from the fort because I was worried about you," he repeated, using a tone that said he didn't understand why I needed to ask such an obvious question.

"Well, thank you, Jeff." I turned to look back at Silas Carpenter, who remained standing on the other side of the fence, observing Jeff and me with interest. I don't think I imagined the small upturn at the corners of his mouth. Enjoying the exchange and not pretending otherwise. "And thank you, Silas. I welcomed your company."

Si touched the brim of his hat with thumb and forefinger. "It was my pleasure, Ruth." He said my name with relish, and I knew without a doubt that he was making a point to the captain with the familiarity. I might as well have been a prize mare being neighed over by two stallions. I'm as vain as the next woman and any other time, I might have enjoyed the sensation, but between a dead boy and an unknown murderer, I was not in the mood for flirtatious rivalries. All I could do was nod once in Silas' direction, nod once again at Jeff, and march up the walk, onto the porch, and into the front door of the boarding house, not in the least tempted to look back at the two men I left standing behind me. Jeff did not follow me to my door to chide me further for being a source of worry as I thought he might, and for all I knew the two men had decided to indulge in fisticuffs in the middle of Main Street or commiserate over a beer at the billiards parlor. I was not inclined to care just then.

Danny sat in one of the stuffed chairs, eyes closed and lips moving. Not praying, despite what it looked like, but working on his poem for the school program. At the sound of the door, he stood. Othello groaned and rose from his place behind Danny's chair.

"You didn't have to watch the desk while I was gone," I said.

"I wasn't. Not exactly. First, I took a walk down to the telegraph office. It's sure gonna need a lot of work to put it back together. And then I tried to sit outside in the grass and work on my poem, but Othello kept bringing me sticks and I kept throwing them, despite myself. That's why I thought I should give it a try inside."

"Did it work better for you?"

"A little, but I'm never going to learn the whole thing. I'm just not."

I turned to face him before I went into The Addition. "Just do the best you can, Danny. No one expects any more than that."

"Mr. Stenton does."

"Mr. Stenton expects you to do your best, the same as I do. That's all."

Being too respectful to argue with me, Danny simply sent me a disbelieving look that expressed as clearly as words what he thought of my putting a good construction on Mr. Stenton's motivations.

"Anyway," I continued, "while I find something for supper, I'd like you to check the firewood supply in all the rooms and in the bath room, too. Clean out the ashes while you're at it. Mr. Carpenter is out right now, but I doubt Mr. Franks is. I think that new fellow from the bank – was his name Mulligan? - and Mr. Copco are both still having supper at the cafe, but you know enough to knock before you go in. Mrs. Livingston, who checked in yesterday, is leaving on the first train tomorrow morning, so her room can wait until tomorrow after she's gone. I'll have Lizbeth give it a good cleaning in the morning. Have I forgotten anything?"

"No, ma'am." He was gone in a rush, always happy to have something to do.

I knew school was hard on Danny. He liked to be active and busy and do strenuous, physical things, so sitting on a bench or at a desk must sometimes have felt like torture, but getting a good education was important. My own education ended with the start of the war. I had been the same age as Danny then, but unlike him, I loved going to school. That couldn't be allowed to matter. When my father left to fight, my sisters and I were needed on the farm, and that was the end of our schooling. Now girls went to college without a second thought! It seemed a wonder to me, and while it was too late for me to think about college, it wasn't for Danny. He could stop going to school when he turned sixteen, and he knew I wouldn't fuss. I told him that everyone was different and as long as he gave school a try up to his sixteenth birthday, I would accept whatever he chose to do after that. As much as I knew I would miss Danny, if the boy decided he wanted to go off to college, I'd pack his bags myself, put him on the first train east, and consider it the best money I would ever spend. For all the hold that memories can have on a person, life shouldn't be about the past, it should be about the future. Only the future.

6

Monday began like every other Monday. Danny went off to school muttering about poetry under his breath and Lizbeth showed up at the boarding house as dearly disheveled as always. After I fussed over her enough to make both of us happy, I left for the barber shop. The air still smelled of smoke, even with the telegraph office on the opposite end of the street. I opened the shop and began to move things around for no purpose except to stay busy because I didn't have a customer in sight. It wasn't until Sheba Fenway stopped by that I understood why.

"The county sheriff was on the early morning train," Sheba told me, "and Joe's called a meeting."

I untied my smock, turned the sign on the door to closed, and along with Sheba took the few steps toward Church Street.

"It was a very nice day for a walk yesterday, wasn't it?" Sheba asked.

With my mind on other matters like Sheriff Bradley's arrival and a cunning murderer on the loose in town, I didn't give the question much thought and responded with a vague, "Mmm hmmm."

"And especially nice if a person has good company along the way."

I stepped down, crossed Church Street, and then up onto the boardwalk on the other side before I turned to look at Sheba.

"All right," I said. "Spit out whatever it is you're anxious to tell me."

Sheba made the step up more gracefully than I – she does everything with an elegance that puts me to shame – and said, "It just looked to me that you and Mr. Carpenter were conversing like old friends yesterday. I've been trying to catch the church steeple at sunset. There's something about how that white cross stands out against the western sky at dusk—" she paused a moment and I knew she was reviewing the picture in her mind "—well, anyway, I was coming back home and I saw the two of you walking together. You looked happy, Ruth." Another pause. "No, not happy exactly, but comfortable and calm, in a way I've never seen you before."

My friend had an artist's eye, I reminded myself, able to capture even the smallest details of scene, so there was no use protesting her words, even if I wanted to, and I didn't want to because Sheba was right. While the topic Silas and I had discussed was not something that would ordinarily give rise to feelings of calm and comfort, I remembered very well how having the man walking right next to me gave me a feeling of—what, exactly?

"I wouldn't say comfortable, Sheba. More like safe. Si Carpenter has a way about him that makes a person feel safe. Protected." I shook my head because my words weren't quite right.

"Ah." Sheba pulled open the door to the meeting hall and gestured for me to enter ahead of her. "That's a good quality for a man to have," she said in a soft voice that only I could hear. "You could do worse."

I didn't want to pursue the topic and wouldn't have been able to, anyway, because by the time Sheba and I settled ourselves in chairs against the side wall, the room had filled up with all our fellow business owners. Even Ruby Strunk, whose modest home was situated behind Sheba's shop and doubled as both the town's laundry and bakery, was present. Ruby usually did not have much time to spare on meetings of any kind. Her husband rode the rails for the Union Pacific and was seldom home. His contribution to Ruby's life lay primarily in his regular begetting of children between railroad assignments. I couldn't have said how many offspring the Strunks had but enough to keep Ruby away from any meetings she considered a waste of time. Which was not this meeting, apparently. She tilted her head in my direction when I caught her eye, then leaned against the back wall with her arms folded across her chest.

Joe Chandler in his formal capacity as president of the group called the meeting to order and as soon as we quieted, asked Sheriff Bradley to speak. The county sheriff was a man of sparse attributes: a slight figure with thinning hair, a tiny mustache that tilted unevenly to one side, and a thin, reedy voice. Yet he was well thought of, and while I hadn't seen him in official action, I had been told by more than one person that the man could swell up like a rooster when confronted and was absolutely fearless in the pursuance of his duty. He worked out of North Platte, but his jurisdiction was county-wide. He was a man who was always busy, which might explain why he did not take the time to get a respectable haircut.

Much of what Bradley told us came as no surprise. He had met with Dr. Danford and concurred that Eddie Barts had been willfully killed by persons unknown. He had spent time with Russ Lowe and together they had determined from the presence of lamp oil splashed on what was left of the interior of the telegraph office that the fire had been deliberately set. Murder and arson, Sheriff Bradley announced, are serious crimes and while he could not say for sure that the two offenses were connected, it seemed likely that they were. Since our town hadn't had a crime more serious than knocking over an outhouse in the eleven years I had lived in New Hope, the sheriff's conclusion seemed a safe bet.

Bradley's next words, that he was "forced to take the evening train back to the county seat," were met with a noticeable shifting of postures and a low murmur of protest. On the whole, the merchants of New Hope are independent, undemanding, and amiable, but it did not sit well with the audience that the duly-elected head of county law enforcement had no intention of spending even one night in a town that had been twice victimized by serious crime.

The sheriff recognized the unhappy tone of the collective grumble in the room and held up a hand. "It can't be helped. Governor Garber arrives in North Platte tomorrow, and I have been ordered to accompany him on his travels throughout the county, but I'm leaving you in good hands. Si, will you step up here?"

To my surprise, Silas Carpenter joined the sheriff on the low dais at the front of the room.

"I've known Si Carpenter for a lot of years," Bradley told the group, "and you couldn't ask for a better man acting on your behalf. He made a name for himself in some of the roughest mining towns in Colorado, and he's not a man to back down. I've appointed Carpenter as my official deputy, and he carries the full authority of the state of Nebraska."

Sheba leaned over and whispered, "No wonder he seemed like such a safe companion, Ruth. I believe you're the best judge of people I know."

Silas said something that I missed because of Sheba's low comments and when it appeared that several listeners suddenly wanted to ask questions, he concluded with, "Right now I don't know any more than Sheriff Bradley knows. I'd like to talk to the doctor over at his office right now and the rest of you can get back to your regular work." He stepped down and exited the room without a backward glance, and that was that. Not a man to fit easily into anyone's pocket, I thought, and understood why Bradley had seen fit not to follow his normal practice of picking two or three of New Hope's men to act as deputies. Every one of New Hope's citizens was suspect, and putting the wrong man in a position of authority would be like giving the fox the key to the hen house. I stayed in my chair long enough to watch the members of the Merchants' Association, many of whom I had known for nearly half my life, walk slowly from the room, all the while knowing that one of them was a villain, a wanted criminal, and a murderer without conscience or principle. The idea made me shiver.

"Cold?" asked Sheba.

I couldn't tell Sheba why a chill had just settled between my shoulder blades – *"I'm a trustworthy woman and I keep my own counsel"* – so instead I rose and tried to smile.

"A little," I said. "For a moment, I felt a touch of winter in the air."

Instead of scoffing at my words, which were clearly not the case on such a fine April day, Sheba linked her arm in mine, and as we started back toward our respective businesses, said in a low voice, "I think I did, too, Ruth. At least, I hope that's what it was."

If I didn't think about the recent terrible things that had happened in New Hope, I could almost believe it was a Monday like any other, with the barber shop less busy than other weekdays but the boarding house busier. I never gave the why of it much thought but supposed it had to do with the general citizenry still feeling spruced enough from Sunday service not to need much trimming and shaving but the number of visitors to town increasing because the train schedule reverted to the normal three stops a day.

I noticed that Harold Sellers, our resident carpenter, had already conferred with Phil Tiglioni about the lumber Phil would need to haul to New Hope in order to get the telegraph office back to working order. I wondered who we could recruit to replace Eddie Barts. The Army might loan us someone for a while, but like a schoolteacher and a church, a town needed a telegraph operator of its own. Although I seldom used the telegraph, I missed having access to it. A person could write a letter, but there was considerable time involved in that. Without the more immediate connection to the outside world that a telegraph line supplied, New Hope took on the peculiar qualities of an island, and I didn't like the feeling.

I had spent Sunday evening poring over the *Independent* so I knew that Yellow Fever had killed a lot of people along the Mississippi River, that businesses and banks were still falling victim to the financial panic of five years earlier, and that something called a bicycle was set to replace the horse and cab, but all the news seemed far away from little New Hope, Nebraska. Our own news about the death of a young man and the purposeful ruin of the telegraph office seemed to top anything I read in the *Independent*. Maybe that's just human nature, to care the most about what happens closest to you.

It wasn't until the next day when I dressed for the funeral that I remembered the paper cigar band I discovered in the grass along the river. My Sunday conversation with Silas followed by the unexpected appearance of Jeff McGruder and then the welcome sight of the newspaper waiting for me on the kitchen table had made me forget all about that curious find. But when I put a hand into the pocket of the same skirt I wore Sunday, I felt the thin paper there and drew it out to stare at it again. Kipp cigars. Did it mean anything or was it just a scrap that had blown from someone's hand as he pulled a cigar from his pocket? Hard to tell, I thought, but could not bring myself to throw it away and instead tucked it carefully into the sugar bowl.

It had taken time for Clayton Barts to get word to his five remaining siblings about Eddie's passing. Two brothers made the trip for the funeral and Clayton was unable to track down the third brother at all. Neither of the two Barts girls could make it. One had just had a baby and the other, according to Clayton, didn't give a reason, just wired that she couldn't get there by Tuesday but would come next month to visit the grave and spend time with her mother.

"Hannah never did get along with her brothers and sister," Mrs. Barts told me when I inquired about her children. "Always had a stubborn streak a mile long," adding after a brief silence, "but she loved her little brother. Everybody loved Eddie."

Like any funeral, the service in the church was a somber affair, but the fact that Eddie's death had been intentional and wicked cast an awful pall on the proceedings. No one mentioned the murder out loud, but I knew as sure as if we were all clucking over it like chickens that we weren't thinking about much else. I was as guilty as the next person for giving more thought to the man who committed the deed than to the one who was his victim. It troubled me because I thought we should be remembering Eddie Barts, how smart he was and how he blushed every time he talked to a girl and how he had enjoyed fishing so much that he gave an old catfish its own name, but instead we sat looking sideways at the people around us, wondering if the murderer was one of our neighbors in the pew. That wicked man, whoever he was, had taken a young life, had threatened the safety of the town with a fire, and adding insult to injury now robbed Eddie's final farewell of its proper respect.

I stood behind Mrs. Barts at the cemetery, trying to do daughter duty in the absence of her own girls. Clayton's wife had her hands full with her own young children, and sons – well, sons mean well but when a mother is heart sore, it seems to me that it's often a daughter's care she craves. When Clayton stayed behind with his brothers to close the grave, I placed my hand on Mrs. Barts' arm to draw her away.

She placed her own hand over mine but did not budge, simply said, "No," with no hint of a weak heart showing in her tone. "Thank you, Ruth, but I want to see this through to the end." As people drifted past us, Cora Barts and I stood side-by-side listening to the sound that dirt makes when it falls on a coffin. I knew the sound well. She did, too.

"I know Eddie loved his fishing, "I said finally. "Did he have other pastimes he enjoyed? Did he play billiards? I don't ever recall seeing him with a beer mug in his hand."

"Oh, no. Alcohol made him sick. You wouldn't guess it to look at him—" It will take a while, I thought, for her to learn not to talk about her son as if he was still alive "—but he has an awful weak stomach. He liked his catfish, of course, but he couldn't stomach sauerkraut or anything strong like that. Oh, my, just the smell of cooking cabbage could put him off."

"So he didn't enjoy rolling a smoke, I guess, or crave the taste of a good cigar?"

"Eddie?" Even with the sounds of her sons' shovels as background, Mrs. Barts gave a small chuckle. "He tried one of his brother's cigarettes once and it turned him as green as spring grass. I don't know that he ever even smelled a cigar, let alone tried one. Not with that stomach of his. One time that I recall—", but she stopped with those words and didn't finish whatever reminiscence had come to mind. We stood in silence until her three sons finished their sad job and came to escort their mother back to the wagon that waited to return her to the farm.

Clayton stopped in front of me. "Thank you, Miz Churchill, for taking care of our mother. I heard it was you that got her out of the house the night of the fire."

"Oh, no," I said. "I led the way to the house, but it was Mr. Carpenter who went inside and got her out and got her to the doctor. You should thank him."

"The man the sheriff put in charge?"

"Yes."

"I'll make it a point to do that," he said, "though I don't know the man."

"He was at the funeral but he didn't come to the cemetery. You could probably find him at the jail."

"I'll find him. He needs to know that if he don't find the man that killed our Eddie, I'll make it my job, and I won't bother with no jail or trial or judge. My brothers and I can do all that on our own."

"Clayton, you know what Reverend Shulte would tell you: 'Vengeance is mine, I will repay, saith the Lord.'"

Clayton was a bigger, stronger version of his little brother. He had a face as hard as granite, and I doubted he had ever blushed in his life. "It weren't the preacher's brother that was killed, Miz Churchill, so I don't see where he's got much to say about it." Clayton gave me a final abrupt nod, put his hat back on, and turned away to join his waiting family.

I walked west from the cemetery, past the church, and down the alley dubbed Church Street until I was back in New Hope, Main Street right in front of me, the town's Meeting Hall to my right and the barber shop on my left. I had hours left in the afternoon, and I should open the shop. Farther down the street, the Bliss House restaurant looked busy with people coming and going and the same for Mr. Talamine's United Bank of Nebraska across the street. No doubt everyone had come back from the funeral, quietly turned his sign in the window to open, and propped open his door by way of welcome. But I just couldn't. Clayton's hard words and his mother's bent shoulders stayed with me.

Jeff McGruder sat on the bench outside the barber shop's front door and turned his head when I appeared at the end of the alley. He rose, stepped off the boardwalk, and came to stand in front of me.

"How are you, Ruth?" A kind voice and quiet words.

"A little sad, but I'm all right, Jeff."

"It's a sad time."

"Especially for Mrs. Barts," I agreed, then asked, "What are you doing in New Hope?"

"I had some Army business with your new lawman on behalf of the major, but I wanted to see you, too, to tell you I was sorry about yesterday." A surprising admission from Captain Jeff McGruder, and one I appreciated. "I know I embarrassed you and I'm sorry. I wouldn't do that for the world."

"Thank you."

"I thought you'd open up the shop so I've been waiting for you."

I shook my head. "Not any more today."

"Come sit a while, then. I warmed up the seat for you."

We sat down on the barber shop bench and wordlessly watched New Hope begin to come to life after the morning's funeral with an assortment of traffic coming and going, pedestrian and street both.

The captain spoke out of the blue, a man who had practiced his words and wanted nothing so much as to get through them. "I know you don't care for me, Ruth, not the way I care for you. You think I don't listen when you tell me that, but I do, only I'm not a man used to taking no for an answer."

"Jeff—"

"No, listen. I need to say this. I can be pig-headed, but I never meant to upset you, and yesterday, after you went inside the boarding house, Carpenter gave me some straight talk." I turned to look at the captain but let him finish his halting explanation. "He said some pretty sharp things, but what made the most sense to me was when he said it wasn't the time to be acting like a damned fool – his words – because you were upset enough by the death of young Eddie Barts and didn't need a brawl breaking out on your front porch. I can't say I take to Carpenter much, but he was right. I heard about the fire and got worried about you and then I saw you with him and I acted just like he said, like a damned fool. I don't have any right to tell you what to do." Pause, then more quietly and with less assurance, "I wish I did but I don't, and I don't think I ever will. I apologize, Ruth, not just for yesterday but for any time I acted in a way that bothered or distressed you."

By that time in a speech that had no doubt been practiced if not even written out, I was a mix of emotions: a kind of tender pity for Jeff McGruder because everything he said was right, relief that after all these months my unwelcome suitor understood I meant what I said, but most of all gratitude to Silas Carpenter for his few, well-placed words. Si was an observant man, and he must have seen something on my face that convinced him to speak as he did. It seemed out of character for him to intrude in business that wasn't his, but whatever the reason, I was grateful. Jeff McGruder was a man used to the company of men and accustomed to listening to a voice with authority. He must have heard such a tone in Si Carpenter.

"We're friends, Jeff, and we'll always be friends." My tone was gentle. "I'm sorry it won't go any further than that. You're a good man," I sent him a quick smile, "but you already have a sweetheart and a wife both, and it's the Army. You know that as well as I do."

He smiled in return, looking even more relieved than I felt, and stood up, one hand firmly placed beneath my elbow so that I stood, too.

"You may be right, Ruth. May I walk you back to the boarding house?" Without waiting for me to respond – a leopard cannot change its spots overnight, after all – he tightened his hold on my arm and propelled me off the boardwalk and across the street to the gate of the fence that enclosed the front yard of the boarding house.

"Good bye, Ruth. There's bad things happening right now, and I hope you know that if you ever need me, I'll come straight away. Don't ever hesitate to ask."

"I won't, Jeff, and I promise to let you know if I need you."

"Well, good." He was a fine-looking man. All that thick, fair hair, which I had never gotten my hands on because the fort had its own barber, gave him a strong resemblance to a photograph I had seen of General George Custer, who had so tragically lost his life two years before. Even at his most annoying, I certainly would not wish such a terrible fate for Captain Jeffrey McGruder.

"Good bye, Jeff."

"Good bye, Ruth." He swung himself up on his horse. "You'll remember your promise?"

"I'll remember."

He nodded, apparently satisfied, and started down the street in the direction of the fort, back to army life, which regardless of what he might think would always be his true love.

With my afternoon free, I had Lizbeth help me turn the bed mattresses in the boarding house rooms and take down all the curtains for a good shake. The girl is a good companion to have for spring housekeeping, the perfect combination of strong, willing, and talkative. I sent her home with an extra nickel by way of thanks and told her to stop by the variety store and pick out a treat for herself. "If you decide on lemon drops," I said, "be sure it's because *you* like lemon drops and not because those brothers of yours favor them."

The nickel pleased Lizbeth out of proportion to its worth. "You don't have to give me anything extra, Miss Ruth. You already do too much for me. I wish you wouldn't," but she held the nickel wrapped in her fist. I knew Lizbeth turned all her earnings from the boarding house over to her parents and did not get to see much of her pay, if any at all, spent on things a girl approaching womanhood would enjoy. I understood why that was, of course, having been raised poor myself, but I often wished I could do more for the girl, not for her parents or brothers or the hardscrabble farm from which her father tried to scrape a living, but for Lizbeth herself, and a nickel for lemon drops was little enough.

By early evening, all my boarders had returned to their rooms from supper, and I could hear Othello's faint barks of happiness from the backyard as he chased the sticks Danny threw. For the dog, being with Danny was close to heaven whatever activity was going on at the time, but from his exuberance, fetching sticks must be the height of canine bliss. If Danny threw all night, Othello would fetch all night and think it was the best thing that had ever happened to him. Sometimes I felt like that dog, always running, always fetching for others, though I didn't share the same level of delight for the activities as Othello.

Since Sunday, I hadn't been able to get Emmett Wolf and all the details Silas Carpenter had shared about him out of my mind, so for my own peace, I spent the last hours before bed that day seated at my kitchen table with pen and paper, putting order to my thoughts. By the time I finished, Danny was already asleep and I should have been. I folded my finished paper carefully and placed it under the sugar bowl, determined to find time the next day to share my conclusions with Si Carpenter.

Karen J. Hasley

7

The first chance I had to find our newly deputized officer of the law came when I closed the barber shop for lunch. The jail was clear on the other end of town, but it was important enough to me to talk to Silas that I warned Lizbeth I wouldn't see her for lunch and instead used the time to try to find him. Unfortunately, for all my well-laid plans and expended effort, Si Carpenter was nowhere to be found, not behind the desk at our small jail or anywhere in New Hope. The paper I wanted to share with him burned a hole in my pocket, but all I could do was renege on my earlier words to Lizbeth and return to Hart's for a quick slice of buttered bread with cheese before reopening the barber shop for the afternoon.

At closing, I tried once more to find Si at the jail, was again unsuccessful, and decided to keep an eye out for him when he returned to the boarding house, no matter how late it might be. He had told me that he scouted the area surrounding town and checked with the Army now and then, and I supposed that was what he'd been busy at all day. It was disconcerting, however, to have a lawman assigned to New Hope, if only on a temporary basis, and then not be able to find him. It seemed to defeat the purpose for having him, but I can sometimes take too narrow a view of a situation.

Mr. Carpenter returned to Hart's well after dark. Danny and my roomers were all in for the night and asleep, at least Mr. Franks was sleeping because it took only a walk down the hall in front of his room to hear his snores. The man had the low and steady rumble of an approaching thunderstorm. Sometimes, if I was in a reflective mood, I would remember how comforting it was to wake in the night and hear Duncan inhaling and exhaling next to me. I missed that and felt grateful I had slept next to my husband without needing to press a pillow over my ears.

I must have been dozing slightly because the muffled sound of the bell on the door made me jerk upright in the chair where I sat waiting. Silas was clutching the little bell to silence its jingle as he closed the door with a slow and careful push when he saw me. I had kept the lamp on the table beside me burning low so he would not think there was a person hiding and waiting for him. We would both regret it if he ended up shooting me by mistake, and I thought he was a man so relentless and so driven that in such a scenario he would be inclined to shoot without waiting for details. Perhaps I wronged him, but I didn't want the opportunity to prove or disprove my theory.

"Ruth." Surprise in his voice, and concern, too.

"I was waiting for you," I said without greeting or introduction.

"Is something wrong?"

"Of course, something's wrong," I retorted, my sleepiness replaced by urgency, "but nothing *new* is wrong, nothing that wasn't wrong yesterday. I've been thinking about our talk Sunday, and I might be able to help narrow down where you ought to look."

"You should be in bed. I'll be around all day tomorrow," but I shook my head.

"I'd rather tell you now. Did you have supper?"

"No."

"Well, come back to the kitchen and I'll heat something up for you. Then I'll show you what I'm talking about."

He followed me down the hall and into The Addition but stopped in the doorway of the kitchen.

"Sit," I said without looking at him, already busy lighting the fire under the coffee pot and scooping lard into the frying pan. It wasn't until he heard the seductive sizzle of hash heating on the stove that he finally followed orders and sat down. I poured coffee into a heavy cup and placed it next to where his hand rested on the table, set out the creamer and sugar bowl, pulled a spoon and fork from a big jar on the sideboard, and placed the utensils and a plate of savory hash in front of him. It made me smile that he stayed so quiet and respectful. Duncan would have been regaling me with stories from his day before his behind ever hit the chair, but Silas Carpenter was not Duncan Churchill, more serious and cautious than my husband ever was. Still, it felt good to have a grown man sitting at my kitchen table again. I sat down across from Si with my own cup.

"What is it you want to tell me, Ruth?" I shook my head.

"No serious talk over supper," I said, smiling. "That's a rule of the house. I was told it interferes with digestion."

"Doctor Danford's advice?"

"No, my husband's. Duncan enjoyed his supper." I smiled at the memory. "He enjoyed life, really, everything about it, but especially good food and good company."

"He was a wise man," Carpenter said, "to appreciate that he had both right in front of him." The offhand compliment – at least, that's what I think it was – surprised me, but when I looked across the table, Carpenter was intent on his food and eating with enjoyment. Already following the rules.

After I cleared the table and refilled our cups with the last of the coffee, I pulled my chair closer to his. For a moment, I felt, not uncomfortable exactly, but girlish or shy, as if I weren't a grown woman and hadn't been wed and widowed. Si didn't pull back from me as he had that time I walked up to him at the river, and I was relieved that even with the keen way he had of seeming to notice everything, he hadn't caught my foolish hesitation. I unfolded the piece of paper that I had carried about with me all day and smoothed it out in front of him.

"I've given a lot of thought to everything you told me. The truth is, Silas, I don't seem able to think about anything except Emmett Wolf walking around New Hope big as life and none of us knowing it. I don't like suspecting that every customer in my barber chair is a murderer. I don't like worrying that something awful might happen to Danny or Lizbeth as soon as they're out of my sight. It's no way to live, so I began to think about the years you mentioned, the end of the war and the years Wolf spent doing terrible things and how he slowed down and then how he seemed to vanish. I've lived in New Hope for eleven years and from what you told me, I think we can narrow down not who Emmett Wolf is but who he isn't."

Silas listened to me intently, and I could tell from his expression that he understood exactly what I was talking about. No need for further explanation, no puzzlement in his eyes, no request for additional details. His quick intellect was one of the several things I liked about him.

I pointed down at the paper. "This is a sketch I made of Main Street and the way it looks now. It seemed to me from what you said that any of the men and their establishments that were here when my mother and my sisters and I moved to town couldn't be Emmett Wolf. You said he never stopped his wicked ways after the war but was a terror for several years afterwards. So if a man was established in New Hope already when I came here as a girl in '67, then he couldn't be the man terrorizing Missouri at the same time. Does that make sense?"

"Yes." He looked down to study my drawing.

"When my mother sold the farm and bought the boarding house, New Hope was practically brand new. Rumor had the railroad coming through, but it hadn't arrived yet. That's one of the reasons my mother was able to get this house as cheap as she did. She was taking a chance that the rumors would come true and the railroad would provide boarders. When we got here, only the six I marked with an A were already here."

Si placed his finger at the end of my sketched Main Street. "Sherman, Winters, and Sellers on the north end."

"Mm-hm. The livery, the variety store, and the undertaker were built right in a row on that end because they heard that's where the tracks would be laid. They were right, too. Russ Lowe put his leather goods on the west side, more toward the center of town. Mr. Talamine set up his bank on the south end, and Bert Gruber put his billiards and hotel between Russ and Abner."

"Joe Chandler's hardware store sits between the bank and the billiards parlor, but you don't have it marked with an A. Was it built later?"

"No, but when we first came here, another man owned the hardware store. He left and the place stayed empty for a while until Joe Chandler came to New Hope two years ago and started it up again." I looked at Silas. "Doesn't it make sense that the six men who settled in New Hope right after the war and have lived here ever since can't have been running wild through Missouri killing and robbing at the same time? Or is there something I'm forgetting?"

Si studied the street map a bit longer and then looked at me. "Yes, it makes sense, and no, I don't think you're forgetting anything." He looked down again. "What about the places marked with the B?"

"Well, that was harder to remember because my mother was in charge of Hart's then, not me. I was just a girl barely grown, and more often than not thinking too much about girlish things and not enough about how the town was growing."

"There couldn't have been a lot of girlish things for you to think about in a place like New Hope. It was hardly a town then."

I said with a smile, "It doesn't take much to set a girl dreaming, Silas, even in the middle of nowhere."

At my words, the look in his eyes changed, but so briefly I would have missed it entirely if we hadn't been sitting so close. Was it sadness I saw, or regret? Or maybe I was wrong altogether. Certainly, his tone stayed the same.

"I imagine you're right. What don't you remember about the men with a B by their names?" I heard the message: let's get back to business.

"I don't remember the proper order of their coming to
New Hope," I said. "Who came first and when exactly, that
kind of thing. What I do know is that we started the
Merchants' Association in 1872 so I took a look at our
records today to see if they'd be any help. The records
weren't very good that first year, not until Mort Lewis took
over keeping track of the meetings. Mort came early in '74
because it's on the sign hanging over his door: Law Office.
Established 1874." I was conscious that I was talking a lot,
probably too much, and halted to say, "I'm sorry if I'm
confusing you, but I didn't want you to think I went at this
carelessly. I gave it a lot of thought."

"There's nothing careless about you that I can see, Ruth.
Not in who you are or in anything you do. I'm not confused."

A warmth was in his tone that almost made me color,
but I turned quickly back to the drawing on the kitchen table.

"Good. To answer your question, I put a B by any names
that were mentioned for any reason in the proceedings of the
Merchants' Association before Mort started taking the notes.
You can't miss his handwriting and besides, he's a lawyer so
he always dated and signed whatever he wrote."

"That means anyone mentioned in the early records
would have come to New Hope sometime between '72 and
'74, when the lawyer started keeping track of the meetings,"
Silas said. "Emmett Wolf was still robbing up through '74 but
less often. That's about when he started slowing down." Si
looked down again and said the names out loud as he pointed
to them on the paper. "Dr. Danford. Tiglioni at the freight
office. Fenstermeier and Janco, dry goods and feed and grain.
Four names."

"Five, if you count Mort Lewis," I said, "who were in
New Hope when Wolf was still causing trouble elsewhere."

"But not as often," Silas reminded me. "Bliss and
Chandler are the latecomers, then?"

The words made me lift my head quickly to stare at him.
"Yes," I said, "but that doesn't mean one of them is Emmett
Wolf. Wouldn't Joe Chandler be too young?"

"Not necessarily, Ruth. If Wolf was a boy when he rode with Quantrill, he might only be in his late twenties now. How old is Chandler?"

"I don't know. Not thirty yet, I'd say, but sometimes Joe has an older, care-worn look on his face, like he's gone through hard times. Of course, you could say that about anyone." I found the idea of suspecting Joe Chandler guilty of the kind of violence Silas had described unsettling. Ellie's husband and two new babies keeping him up at night. Surely not Joe. "According to Mort's Association notes, John Bliss came to his first meeting three years ago, but as I recall, he didn't come until the Merchants' Association began to get worried about the activities that were going on upstairs over the Music Hall. Then he came and from everything he said, all that was going on up there was choir practice. Mr. Bliss can be convincing when he wants to."

"Choir practice, was it?" A touch of humor in Si's voice.

"I've yet to catch any harmony drifting out those upstairs windows, but there's never been a bit of trouble. Everything's discreet and quiet, like the man himself. I always feel that John Bliss is having a good laugh at our expense and that he doesn't hold respectability nearly as dear as the rest of the Merchants' Association, but maybe I'm faulting him where no fault is due." I gave a thought to John Bliss, a man I sometimes found likeable, no matter what went on upstairs over the Music Hall. "Joe Chandler is the newest member of our little merchants' group. He bought the old hardware store and set up business there two years ago."

"It looks like there are a couple of names missing." Si's quiet comment made me look again at the sketch of New Hope.

"I didn't put Ezzie at the café or Sheba Fenway on the drawing because they're women. You sounded pretty sure that you were tracking a man."

"I am looking for a man, Ruth, I'm sure of that, so I wasn't talking about Ezzie or the dressmaker."

I squinted down at the diagram once more before I looked back at Si. "Then I don't know what you mean. I think everybody's listed here."

"What about your schoolteacher?"

I stared at Silas, flabbergasted. "Mr. Stenton?! He answered a posting we put in the Denver newspaper. He had references. How could it be Mr. Stenton?"

"Why not? I've seen him. He's average height and looks to be around thirty, even older. How long has he lived in New Hope?"

"We started the school in the fall of '75 so not quite three years." I took a deep breath and wrote *Arthur Stenton* at the bottom of the paper, then stated, "You said a couple of names were missing. Who else did I forget?"

"You have a preacher in town, too, Ruth, and I don't see that you have his name anywhere." He spoke gently – a preacher's son himself, I recalled – but there was nothing else soft or gentle about Si Carpenter at that moment. Searching his face, it seemed to me there was more at play than a man tracking down a fugitive. Something deeply personal lay behind such a long, relentless search for a bad man no one had heard a word about for the last four years.

I kept my thoughts to myself and said, "Pastor Shulte is a good man, Silas, a man of God. You don't know him."

"Do you?"

"Yes. Yes, I do. I know him by his words and his actions. Gerald Shulte came with his wife to New Hope four years ago, and they fit right in from the start. He helped me make sense of losing Duncan and feeling so – so angry and lonely about it. Duncan was already gone a whole year, but I couldn't get past his leaving me like that. I blamed Duncan as much as I blamed God, and I was just so mad about everything. It took Reverend Shulte to set me straight. He was kind to Danny, too, after the boy lost his whole family to cholera. Danny was having a hard time of it, same as I was. We were two of a kind. I can't begin to list all the kind things Gerald Shulte has done, Silas, and I will not add the reverend to this list of names. Have you been searching for a wicked man so long that you don't believe there's any good left in the world?" I surprised both of us with my fervency. Tears pricked at the back of my eyes. Gerald Shulte was the finest man I knew, and I couldn't bear the thought that he had betrayed us, betrayed me. I knew with all my heart that it simply was not true.

Silas Carpenter met my look and held it for a long time, but I couldn't read anything in his expression. In a way, it was as if he were looking at something else entirely, something only he could see. Then he placed one hand over mine where it rested on the table next to the diagram of New Hope.

"You're right that I've been looking for Emmett Wolf a long time, and maybe through the years I did start to believe there wasn't much good left in the world. But that was before I came to New Hope, Nebraska, and until I met you."

I stared at him wordlessly. What does a woman say to something like that? I couldn't think of a thing.

Si stood and reached for the paper. "Leave the preacher's name off, then. May I take this with me?"

I stood, too, and nodded. "Yes."

"Thank you for supper."

"You're welcome."

"Good night, Ruth."

"Good night, Silas."

After he was gone, I considered everything we had talked about, but it wasn't Emmett Wolf who occupied my thoughts as I lay curled up for warmth in a dark, cold bedroom on one side of a bed that was made for two. It was Silas Carpenter and how his words had touched something in my heart, had lit an ember I thought long extinguished. With the murder of Eddie Barts, I knew my life would change, but I hadn't expected this kind of change – not a change inside me. I fell asleep with the warm memory of Si Carpenter's hand resting on mine.

Danny usually took something to school with him to eat during recess, but the next day we were both up later than usual and while I probably could have found a leftover to wrap in paper and send along with him, I told him I would bring him bread and bacon later on. He felt bad about my making the trip, I could tell, and said he could live without a lunch that day, but the truth was I wanted to walk out to the school and talk to Mr. Stenton.

Si's words about our school teacher had startled me, but he was right when I thought about it. No one had bothered to confirm the written references Mr. Stenton sent to us or check that what he told us about his education and past teaching assignments were true. This sounds foolish when I put it on paper, but I don't think it dawned on any of us that a school teacher would do anything but tell the truth. We should have done more, I realized now, and yet for the past three years he seemed to be completely satisfactory. Yes, he was very strict with the children, but children often need a firm hand. None of the students really took to him, from the smallest ones to Danny's age, but they learned their reading and their arithmetic, could recite the states and their capitals, knew basic geography and came to write such a fine script that some of us adults were a little bit jealous that the children's handwriting was more legible than ours. The school's third closing program was just weeks away, and all of New Hope looked forward to it, whether a person had children in the school or not. For the previous two years, following the children's songs, recitations, and dramatic presentations, the women had served refreshments to all the attendees, and everyone, both children and adults, enjoyed the evening. Even Mr. Stenton was at ease enough to have a glass of punch and engage in congenial conversation. There were few festivities in our lives, and we appreciated any excuse to relax or celebrate. The school's closing program allowed both.

And now Silas Carpenter suggested that the man might not be a school teacher at all but a wanted fugitive, a law-breaking desperado, and a murderer! The idea was preposterous, but once Si planted the seed in my head, I couldn't weed it out. Which was why I wanted to carry a sandwich out to Danny that day. I needed to put the real Mr. Stenton up against the villain Si described and see how the school teacher fared in the comparison.

The younger children were scattered around the school yard, reminding me of ants in a recently disturbed ant hill as they ran about and shouted at each other. In my experience, children need little provocation to do either of those activities, and being released from several hours in a school room with stern-faced Mr. Stenton only increased their natural inclination. Danny sat with his back against a wall of the school and if I hadn't seen his lips moving, I might have thought he was napping, but no, he was reciting his poem to himself. I felt guilty at the sight. I wanted school to be the same pleasure for him that it had been for me, but I realized at that moment it would never be so. His was a nature made for activity and adventure and the pleasure of physical labor, not for books or lessons, and certainly not for poetry.

I made my way through the playing children and crouched next to Danny, who opened his eyes when I said his name.

"There's no use you going hungry," I said.

"You didn't need to come all the way out here. I'm not about to starve over one day without a sandwich."

I gave him a pat on the shoulder as I stood upright. "I should say not! I've seen how much you can put away at supper." He grinned. "I wanted to talk to Mr. Stenton, Danny, so it wasn't any extra trouble to bring a sandwich along with me. Is he inside?" Danny nodded as he took a hearty bite from the sandwich. "I'll see you later, then," I said and walked toward the front door of the school.

With his first-rate carpentry skills, Harold Sellers led the effort to build our school building, and all the members of the Merchants' Association contributed what they could toward its completion. In my case, it was money plain and simple because except for the ability to cut hair, there wasn't much else I could offer. John Bliss surprised everyone by ordering and donating the children's desks, beautiful things of wrought iron and cherry wood brought all the way from the Buffalo Hardware Company. It was one of the times I came very close to liking the man.

Arthur Stenton sat at his big teacher's desk in the front of the room and raised his head when I entered. I observed in passing that neither Mr. Stenton's hair nor his side burns seemed to have grown at all since the last haircut I gave him. Had he found a barber somewhere outside of New Hope? Now that I thought about it, had he joined the men to help put out the fire Saturday night? Had he been in church on Sunday? I couldn't remember either way.

The teacher was not a large man, but there was something about his gaze that turned him into one, as if he was taking your measure and like it says in the Old Testament, you were weighed in the balance and found wanting. At least, that's how he always made me feel.

"Good afternoon, Mr. Stenton," I said. He rose at my approach, never anything but proper in his words and actions.

"Good afternoon, Mrs. Churchill." He tilted his head ever so slightly waiting for me to tell him why I had invaded his school room. Of course, he would never say such a thing, but I knew that's what he thought.

"Danny left without his lunch today so I brought it."

No comment but I guessed from the teacher's expression that he considered my doing so to be spoiling the boy, an unfortunate gesture that would keep Danny from learning about actions and their consequences and ultimately ruin him as a grown man. Never mind that it was just one day and just one sandwich.

"And," I went on, "I wanted you to know that Danny is trying very hard to learn the Longfellow poem you assigned for the program, but that he's having a hard time with it. It just doesn't seem to stick. With all your teaching experience, is there any advice you could give to help him learn it?" It was the only excuse I could think of for wandering out to the school on a work day afternoon and while it wasn't exactly true – Danny was learning the poem slow but sure – it sounded believable enough to explain my visit.

"My advice is always the same, Mrs. Churchill: practice, practice, practice. Learning is nothing but repetition."

"No doubt, you're right. It seems to me that it's having to recite it in front of everyone at the closing program that makes Danny skittish. Of course, I can see that it's good for children to be able to do that, and everyone in New Hope looks forward to the program so much that I wouldn't change a thing. I'm not suggesting that." Pause. "Did you have a closing program at the school where you taught in Colorado, Mr. Stenton? Where was that again?"

"Walden." He studied me the same way he might study an arithmetic problem. "And yes, we closed the school year with a program there, too."

"Walden," I repeated. "Where did I get the idea that you came from Denver?"

"Walden is north of Denver near the Wyoming border, Mrs. Churchill."

"It's very cold up that way, isn't it?"

"Very." An impasse because I was all out of questions.

"Well, I'd better get back to the barber shop. I'll be sure Danny takes your advice. Practice and repetition." I smiled to show I had paid attention. "He's always got the Longfellow book with him, and he says it over and over whenever he has the time. Even last Thursday, with everything that was going on, I noticed him reciting it to himself." The teacher's blank look was what I had hoped for. "Last Thursday," I explained, "when they were looking for poor Eddie Barts. Danny helped out well into the night." I paused. "Did you know Eddie Barts, Mr. Stenton?"

"Only that he was the telegraph clerk."

"What happened to Eddie was a terrible thing, just terrible, and it's made all the worse because no one knows who killed him. I can hardly credit that someone in New Hope is a murderer, but that's what Deputy Carpenter thinks, that someone right here in our own little town committed the dreadful deed." I met Mr. Stenton's gaze and tried to look horrified at the thought, which wasn't all that hard because it retained a measure of shock no matter how many times I repeated the knowledge to myself.

"I agree. It was terrible, Mrs. Churchill, but I'm sure the authorities will apprehend the culprit." The man didn't sound especially shocked about Eddie or especially confident about the success of our deputy, but perhaps a person that dealt with children day in and day out learned not to show his true feelings. "And now you must allow me to ring the bell. The children have already enjoyed a longer recess than I would usually allow." His tone again chastised me for spoiling children. "And, Mrs. Churchill, while I believe education is never wasted, let me assure you that in my experience, education is not the sole indicator of a person's successful future. Danny has commendable qualities and good character that will carry him far."

I frowned at the words, glowing though they sounded, as I considered them. What was the message behind the words? That character, not college, was enough for Danny?

"That's something to think about, isn't it?" I replied. And I would think about it, which was what the teacher no doubt intended. "Good bye, Mr. Stenton."

"Good bye, Mrs. Churchill." He followed me down the center aisle between the desks to the door of the school house. I was well on the way home and could still hear the school bell clanging an end to play.

By the end of the day, I concluded that while my walk out to the school house had shown me nothing new about Mr. Stenton – could Emmett Wolf have disguised himself as a highly proper teacher of children? I supposed anything was possible but could not picture it, at all – the visit made me realize that Danny going to college was my dream and not his. I don't know what brought on the realization, Mr. Stenton's words certainly, yet something more, perhaps the look on Danny's face or the angle of his shoulders when he stood to return to the school room. Whatever the cause, somewhere between departing for the school sandwich in hand and returning to the barber shop for afternoon customers, I came to accept that Danny was not destined for more education. I brought up the subject often, and if he had not come flat out and told me of his lack of interest, it could only be because he knew that I favored college. He would not want to disappoint me. That was Danny's nature: loyal, willing to please, and tender-hearted about the ones he cared for, whether they were alive or dead. Danny would try his hardest to make my dream his. The knowledge caused a pang to my conscience. Without realizing it, I had been in danger of abusing what was most special about Danny Lake. Mr. Stenton had pegged the boy right – good character, indeed.

8

I remember the exact moment when life in New Hope as I had known and loved it for the last eleven years began to crumble. It was a Friday afternoon and Russ Lowe, my last customer of the day, stood up from the barber chair, stretched, and said, "I'll tell you something I've been wondering about." I looked at him and waited. "I've been wondering about Fenstermeier, Ruth. He don't talk like the rest of us."

"He came straight here from Germany, Russ."

"That's what he says," I heard a suspicious tone to the word *says*, "but we don't know that for sure, do we? Maybe he ain't what he says he is."

"Russ, Hans Fenstermeier came from Germany. You know that and I know that. That's why he sounds different from the rest of us. What exactly are you talking about?"

"It seems to me that what happened to Eddie Barts is something a foreigner would do, not someone upstanding from the U. S. of A. It's got foreign deviltry written all over it." Russ set his money down on the counter by the mirror, grabbed his hat from the peg on the wall, and stopped to face me before opening the door. "You mark my words, Ruth. Somebody in New Hope killed that boy, and the only one I know who doesn't fit in with the rest of us is Fenstermeier. He talks funny."

"That doesn't mean a thing." I could hear impatience and frustration in my voice. No doubt Russ could hear them, too, but he didn't back down.

"Somebody killed that boy and my money's on Fenstermeier. I already told Carpenter what I thought."

"What did he say?"

"He didn't say much, but if you haven't noticed, he ain't real sociable. Anyway, you'd best be careful around Fenstermeier and tell that boy of yours to do the same. Don't seem like the killer needed a reason to kill young Barts so I don't figure anyone's safe until Fenstermeier gets locked up."

"Russ," I said, "you be careful, too, careful about telling tales about people and saying things you can't prove. It isn't fair to Hans to have you going around saying such things." He gave a snort of disgust, unwilling to be corrected.

"Fair," he said. "I'll tell you what's not fair: Eddie Barts not living to see his twentieth birthday. That's what I call not fair." He jammed his hat on his head and closed the door behind him with more force than was necessary.

I couldn't believe what I had just heard and I didn't like it. Picking a villain based on the way he pronounced his words or because he was born in another country made no sense to me, but Russ Lowe's foolish suspicion was just the first of many mistrustful rumors that would float around town in the days and weeks to come. Even now, I can hardly believe how some people I thought I knew changed into strangers right before my eyes.

Not that I was much better. I could hardly meet a person in town without slipping a question into the conversation. When was it you first moved here, I might ask, or Where did you live before you came to New Hope, pretending to search my memory for information I knew I never had to start with. It seemed I couldn't help myself, and though at the time I thought I was pretty clever with my questions, I know now I must have been as obvious as Russ Lowe. The suspicious death of Eddie Barts had unsettled all of us, and the citizens of New Hope, Nebraska, were nervous and anxious, searching for answers in the best ways we knew how.

Most of us were, anyway, but not my friend Sheba Fenway. She is a fearless woman, I've always thought, and not one to shy away from trouble. When I stopped by her shop, she was pinning sleeves onto a man's shirt and did not look up until the job was done and her pin cushion empty.

"What do you think of all this?" I asked.

"By *all this* I take it you mean all the gossip in town about this person or the other being responsible for killing Eddie Barts."

"Yes."

Sheba shook her head, which caused several curls of fire-red hair to come loose from the casual top knot she usually wore. "Human nature is not pretty, Ruth. I have always known that to be true, but it's become especially ugly of late. If it's not the Fenstermeiers and their German accents, then it must be Cap Sherman because he's been seen wearing his old Confederate hat and anyone who can't let the war go has to be a killer." Sheba made a rude and unbecoming sound. "All foolishness." She eyed me. "And I'll tell you as a friend, Ruth, that you might consider asking fewer questions of the people you meet. It's being remarked upon."

"What?! Do you mean someone thinks I'm a murderer?"

"Ruth, even Russ Lowe who has an imagination the size of Kansas, hasn't suggested that. I'm telling you as a friend because there might be someone who doesn't appreciate you asking questions and getting answers. Someone who has a lot to hide. It might be safer for you to stop sticking your nose where it doesn't belong."

"Well, thank you very much."

"There's no use taking that tone with me. I'm talking to you as a friend. I know you, Ruth Churchill, and the problem is that you're just too honest a person. What you feel in your heart shows up on your face. That's just how you are, clear as glass, and sooner or later, you're going to get an answer to one of your questions that gives something away, something dangerous to a dangerous man. I'm staying out of this situation to the best of my ability, and you should do the same. Ask your good friend Si Carpenter if I'm not right."

I didn't have to ask Si because long after supper that same night, he knocked on the door of The Addition. He wore a serious look, and when I invited him to have a seat at the kitchen table, he stepped inside the kitchen and removed his hat but did not sit. He just looked at me with a steady, stern expression.

"Ruth," he said, "I went to talk to Arthur Stenton today and came to find out that you got there ahead of me and asked him a lot of questions."

"And if I did?" No use disagreeing with a man wearing that expression. I learned that a long time ago.

Si Carpenter sighed. "You need to stop doing that."

"I took Danny's lunch out to him and I naturally greeted Mr. Stenton while I was there and I just happened to ask him about—"

Si Carpenter interrupted my wordy excuse by kissing me firmly on the mouth, which made me not only stop talking but stop breathing, too.

Then, like he had never kissed me, he repeated, "You need to stop doing that, Ruth. You're going to find yourself in trouble."

Oh, I thought, still tasting his kiss, I'm already in more trouble than I bargained for.

"This is something for the law to handle," Silas continued, "the law and maybe the Army, but not you. It's not a game and you'll get yourself killed asking questions of the wrong person. I want you to promise me you'll keep to your own business."

"Businesses," I responded tartly. "I have two, you know."

Si almost smiled. "Yes," he said, "I know. Mind your own businesses, then, and let me handle things."

"Are you making progress, Silas? Because New Hope has become a fearful place to live. People are turning on their neighbors and bearing false witness like it was the latest fashion. Everyone looks sidewise at everyone else. I don't like what's going on in my town."

"I know. I don't like it either."

"Then—"

"Ruth." He weighted my name with solemn importance, like he planned to make a speech. Maybe he did and thought better of it because what he said was, "I am sorely tempted to kiss you again if that's what it takes to make you hush. Will you promise to stop asking questions of everyone you meet on the street?"

"I'll think about it," I said. I eyed him with equal gravity, then stepped even closer. I didn't give it a thought at the time, but later I would remember Duncan and the first time he kissed me, how he took me by surprise and swung me into his arms. But that was Duncan, a boisterous and joyful man, words that would never be used to describe Silas Carpenter. I brought Si's face down to mine and kissed him hard in return before I stepped back. "All right," I said. "I promise. But don't think that means you can tell me what to do whenever you feel like it."

He put his hat on with care before he spoke. "No, ma'am. I can assure you I would never think that. You'll remember your promise?"

"Yes."

"All right, then. Good night."

"Good night, Silas," then surprised by my own daring, I said, "I hope you got what you came for."

My words brought a smile to his face at last. "Yes, I did. More than I came for, if you want the truth." He shook his head like one would do with a vexatious but endearing child. "Not that I'm complaining." He stepped into the hall and pulled the door shut after him, leaving me standing in the middle of the kitchen. I ran a tongue over my lips. The only man I had ever kissed seriously was Duncan Churchill, and now, as if matters weren't complicated enough, in the space of one week, I had shared a walk with a man, invited him into my kitchen, cooked for him, let him rest his hand over mine, and just now kissed him. Twice. And him a man I hardly knew. I carried the lamp into my bedroom, blew out the light, and got ready for bed. I won't sleep a wink, I told myself, for thinking about Silas Carpenter and remembering my husband, but I was wrong. I fell soundly asleep before I got a single thought out. I guess asking a lot of questions takes more out of a person than I realized.

I did my best to keep my promise to Silas, but I don't think he meant I couldn't ask questions that came into a conversation naturally. Like with Ellie Chandler, Joe's wife. After an uneventful but busy weekend – New Hope filled with its usual Saturday crowd and a restful worship Sunday morning – a person could almost think it was life as usual. After a long Saturday, I usually opened the barber shop only for an hour or two on Monday and later in the afternoon. My Monday morning was spent at the bank and then at Luther Winters' Variety Store doing the week's grocery shopping.

I was talking to Millie, Luther's wife, when I saw Ellie Chandler through the store's front window. Ellie was usually as cheerful as she was pretty, but even through the smudged glass I saw that she was looking down into the street with a frown on her face. When I went over to open the door and see if there was something I could do for her to get that scowl off her face, I realized it wasn't so much a frown of displeasure as a frown of effort. Behind her she pulled a wooden wagon and nestled in that wagon were two bundled babies.

Ellie looked up when I said her name. "You have your hands full this morning," I said.

"I didn't have the heart to bother Joe. He's busy at the store. But I'm out of so many things, I just couldn't wait another day."

"Why don't you go get what you need," I suggested, "while I keep an eye on the boys? Which is which now?"

"Matthew," she said pointing to one, "and Lucas," pointing to the other. "Matthew has the pointed chin."

To my eye, both chins looked exactly the same, but all I said was, "I'll keep that in mind, Ellie, so I don't have to ask again." I made myself comfortable on the steps next to the wagon. "Go on now. I promise I won't let anything happen to New Hope's newest additions." Ellie gave me a grateful smile and went inside the store.

The babies were cute, plump, red-faced, fussy little buttons, both of them. Except for my friend Sheba, who is not especially drawn to children of any age, I, like most women of my acquaintance, am fond of babies. It's almost impossible to see one and not want to smooth back his hair or tweak a cheek or tickle a belly. Duncan had enjoyed being around children and because of his cheerful nature, children had enjoyed being around him. He and I would have welcomed a baby, but it wasn't to be, and after the consumption laid him low, it was clear we would never have a child of our own. At the time, I didn't grieve the loss of something that was only a dream, too busy grieving the loss of my flesh and blood husband, but now, looking at the two wagon-bound babies swaddled in quilts, kicking little legs and snuffling, I felt a pang of melancholy. Duncan had been a handsome man and would have fathered a handsome son. I'm not by nature a despondent woman, however, and wouldn't have time for the emotion even if I were, so by the time Ellie reappeared with her full basket, my unexpected bout of melancholy was long gone.

"Thank you, Ruth. I know I could have left them out here on their own – they can't even roll over yet, for goodness' sake – but I, well, I just couldn't."

"You could probably use some extra hands right now, Ellie. It's too bad you don't have any family nearby that could come and stay and help you get used to having two new babies in the house. Is there anybody you could ask?"

My words had an unexpected effect on Ellie Chandler because she flushed a deep rose color and looked away from me so quickly I might have had something unpleasant smudged on my face.

"I'm sorry, Ellie. I didn't mean to pry. I'm sure you and Joe don't need any help raising your boys." I was making quick conversation because something I said had embarrassed the young mother.

"Yes." Ellie sounded relieved to move the talk along, but I couldn't figure what I had said that would have brought on her noticeable change of color. "Joe's a wonderful father and so good with the boys, Ruth! He works a long day, but sometimes in the night he's the one who gets up and rocks the babies. I guess I should be ashamed to admit it, that being a mother's duty."

I snorted. "I always felt that if it takes two to make a baby, then it takes two to tend a baby. That seems fair." Ellie smiled but didn't speak. "You seem to have a good husband, Ellie, compared to some I could mention. Didn't you tell me you were newlyweds when you came to New Hope two years ago?"

"Yes. The preacher said the words in Topeka, but Joe and I didn't want to stay there. Too big for us. We weren't sure where we wanted to settle, but we liked the name New Hope when we heard it and then, when we got here and saw the town and met the people, we thought this was where we wanted to live and raise our family."

"You never said how you met Joe," I remarked in a casual tone.

"We met in Topeka. Just a chance meeting between two strangers." There was something about her tone that told me she wasn't going to volunteer any additional details.

I smiled and turned to go back inside the store to finish my shopping. "That's how it happened with Duncan and me, too," I said. "I was a lucky woman."

"I was luckier than you, Ruth," said Ellie Chandler. Her serious tone made me look back at her, but she wasn't watching me, she was looking down at the twin boys in the wagon. "Luckier than you know."

I finished my shopping, wondering what Ellie Chandler was hiding – because I knew from her tone and that deep flush of color that she was hiding something – and started on my way back to Hart's. The Chandlers were the newcomers to town, but they fit in from the start, and even as a newcomer, it was clear that Joe was suited to being mayor.

He had a way about him that suited the office, though it made it hard to guess his age. He had done wonders with the old hardware store, too. No matter how early I started my day, Joe Chandler was always up ahead of me getting the store ready for business. But now, with the mysterious death of Eddie Barts, I looked at everyone and everything with different eyes, and I couldn't help but wonder if there was something more to the story of Joe and Ellie Chandler. Had they really met in Topeka? Was there no family to help with those babies because they were two people on the run? Did Ellie Chandler know more about her husband's past than she was willing to let on? I couldn't help the wondering, but oh, how I hated it!

The week plodded along. People talked in murmurs that sometimes came to a quick halt when I showed up. I am no more high-minded than the next person, but I knew enough to recognize that gossiping about a person's neighbors wouldn't help the situation and every so often I found it necessary to say so. It didn't take long for people to get tired of that message, however, and I tried not to let it matter that many in a community which had been home to me for over a decade, people who had mourned my mother's passing and stood next to me at Duncan's grave, now shied away from me like I carried a fatal disease. Their only relief from fear was to place blame somewhere, anywhere, and never mind that their guilty party was someone they had known for years. Hans Fenstermeier because he talked different from the rest of us. Bert Gruber because he had been known to go fishing with Eddie. Cap Sherman because he fought for the Confederacy. Even my boarder Mr. Franks, that amiable man who worked for the railroad, was suspect. As a man who came and went, no one really knew anything about him, and that made him an easy target.

One evening after supper and out of the blue, Silas pushed open the front door of the boarding house and stopped next to the desk where I sat going over account books. Othello, lying flat out beside my chair, looked up and gave a half-hearted thump of his tail. The mongrel could be a good guard dog when he put his mind to it, but he had taken to Si straight off and figured there was no need to do anything more than roll over on his back and offer his belly for a rub.

Si bent and did exactly that, then straightened and said, "Come for a walk, Ruth?" His tone didn't give anything away, and I gave him a quick look. No hint of his intention there, either.

"Are you going to give me another scold?" I asked.

"No."

I remembered the kiss. "Well, that's too bad," I said. Silas Carpenter was not a man of large gestures or loud talk. He's more subtle than that, so it takes me longer to read him, but the way his smile lit up the gray of his eyes told me that for a heartbeat, he and I shared the same memory. I stood. "I'll just tell Danny I'll be gone a while," and went down the hall to the bath room where Danny was busy pumping water to fill the tank from which we drew the bathwater. Coming back, I grabbed a shawl for my shoulders and together, Silas and I stepped out onto the porch and began a leisurely walk south toward the river. The evening was pleasant with the slightest hint of warmth in the air, just enough to let a person know that summer intended to show up once more and on schedule.

"Is there something on your mind, Silas?"

"There usually is."

"Something you want to say, I mean."

"Something I need to say." Pause. "I believe I was overfamiliar the other night," I didn't need to ask which night he meant, "and I beg your pardon for my actions. I didn't mean to take advantage of you."

The last words made me laugh. "Oh, Silas, I'm way past the age when a woman can be taken advantage of. Unless she wants to be, of course."

"And did you?"

I gave the question a moment or two of thought before I said, "Yes, I believe I did. Seeing as how it was you."

"Well, I beg your pardon just the same."

"Apology accepted. Now tell me how this business with Eddie Barts is coming along."

The first topic, which for all our years seemed to make both of us a tad uncomfortable done with, he said, "Slow but steady. Your list helped."

"Good. Maybe the sooner we get this matter handled, the sooner New Hope can get back to normal. People are frightened, Silas, and I can't blame them, but I hate the way we all look at each other with suspicion."

"That's better than finding yourself alone with Emmett Wolf."

"I know you're right, but if you don't know anything that's a threat to the man, he wouldn't have reason to hurt you, would he?"

"That would be natural to think with a normal man, but Wolf's not normal. He has a streak in him that when he lets it loose makes him hurt people for no reason, makes him enjoy it. He's a man that will always do what it takes so he can walk away safe and sound."

I tried unsuccessfully to picture someone like that among the citizens of New Hope, then sighed. "I believe you because you've been after the man a long time and you must know him better than anyone else, but couldn't he have changed? Can't a man change?"

"Not Emmett Wolf."

I took a moment to measure if I should say what I thought and then, knowing this was a man I would not ever be able to hide my feelings from no matter how I tried, asked, "What harm did he do you, Silas? You've been chasing Emmett Wolf for a lot of years and not for any reward or even from a sense of duty. I don't doubt you're a man with enough pride to keep you going, but there's something else, isn't there?"

He stepped off the walking path and down the incline, then reached up a hand to steady me as I joined him at the river's edge. Constant calls of warblers had serenaded us on our walk, but their music had declined along with the sun. Two ducks floated close to the riverbank, the setting sun turning the head of one a bright, rich, and shiny green. The papa is the proud and showy one, I thought, and isn't that always the way of it? For some reason, the sight of the passing ducks brought a sharp and sudden memory of Duncan.

I wondered if I had said too much too soon to Silas and almost wished I could take the words back. It hadn't been a full two weeks and yet I had come to care a lot about Silas Carpenter's opinion of me. Care too much, probably, but I'm not a woman to hide from the obvious. I hadn't known strong feeling for a man since I closed my husband's eyes for the last time, but something about Silas Carpenter had started the blood moving in my veins almost from our first meeting. I couldn't explain it but thought he might feel the same. It would be a shame if we didn't get a chance to see this through to the end, whatever the end was destined to be. I watched the ducks drift past and waited for Silas to speak.

"In some ways, Ruth, you remind me of my sister." The words didn't seem to fit the occasion, but like that plain, brown mama duck I had just seen contentedly trailing along behind her bright mate, I was willing to follow Si's lead. At least, for a while.

"I don't recall that you mentioned a sister," I said, but with his words remembered that he had told me "there were three of us raised in a preacher's house." A brother named Paul, he said, and a third child I hadn't thought to ask about.

"No, maybe not." He picked up a small stone and skimmed it across the water. "Dorcas was the middle child, between me and Paul, and the peacemaker of the family. Kind-hearted like our mother but not above grabbing Paul or me by an ear to get our attention. Dorie was a pretty girl. I thought of her the first time I saw you, but I don't know why exactly. Her hair was so black it gleamed blue, the way a raven's wing does in the sun, and her eyes were dark like molasses. Nothing like you. You're a woman as bright and clear as sunlight."

The story wasn't about me, and he spoke the words offhand, not really thinking about what he had just said, but I was touched, nevertheless. He turned to examine my face with grave scrutiny before he said, "It's the smile. That's what it is. Dorie and you have the same smile." I met his gaze but didn't feel like smiling just then, knowing something awful was coming, something grievous and mortal. "She married a man named Pete Lindquist, a good man, a friend of mine I met in the war. He was as tow-headed as she was dark. When the war ended— But I'm getting ahead of myself. I'm not very good with words, Ruth."

"You're doing fine, and if you'd rather not say any more, that's fine, too. You don't owe me anything, Silas." For answer he placed the palm of his right hand very briefly, very gently against my cheek before continuing.

"Paul was four years older than me. When we got word he died at Chickamauga, I was sixteen, but strong and serious for my age, and I headed off to enlist. My parents were fit to be tied about that, wouldn't hear of it, so I snuck away during the night without a good bye. I regret that because when I came home to Missouri two years later, they were both gone, taken by the influenza a week apart. Dorie nursed them both and then ended up living on her own hand to mouth, not willing to move because she was waiting for me to come home. That's the kind of person she was, a girl with strong loyalties. Pete was traveling with me, not having a home of his own, and he and Dorie ended up getting married. I never saw two people more right for each other. It was like it was meant to be."

I knew that feeling and remembered thinking the same about Duncan and me, how he stepped off the train in New Hope just when I happened to be down by the station waiting for the mail to arrive, and how Duncan and I took one look at each other and that was that. We were meant to be, like Dorie and her Pete, even if Duncan's and my *meant to be* lasted only three years.

"I was eighteen then and restless. I stayed a year, but I didn't feel like I belonged anywhere, sure not with my sister and her new husband, so I just left."

"Did you say a proper good bye this time?" I asked. He nodded.

"I did. I can be hard-headed about some things, but I learned in the war how short life can be, how quick it can be taken from a man, so yes, I said my proper goodbyes, not knowing what my future held." A pause. "I was young in years, but I had seen my share of terrible things, and it didn't cross my mind that if I never saw my sister again, it would be because she was dead and not me."

"Oh," I said. I placed a hand on his arm to steady myself. "Oh, Silas, I'm so sorry. What happened?" This was the Emmett Wolf part of the story, I thought, and a selfish piece of me wished I had never started the conversation. How much grief and worry can a person carry inside her, after all?

"Emmett Wolf, Winston Langtry, and Hank Ketchum wanted Pete's stock, fifty head of prime cattle and half a dozen cow ponies he was raising for the Army so they killed him and Dorie and their little girls, too." I had to look away when Si turned to face me because I didn't think I could bear what I would see on his face. "I was gone just over four years, raising hell, working for the railroad, pushing cattle up from Texas, living in the fleshpots like the prodigal son, Ruth. And like the prodigal son, I came to my senses one day and went back to Missouri. I thought, what the hell's wrong with you, Si? – begging your pardon for my language – You've got a sister and a brother-in-law who was close as a brother and maybe by now they've got children of their own. They're the only family you got in the world; you should go home. But I waited too long. They were all dead by the time I got there."

"The little ones, too, Silas? Oh, I can't bear that!" I will not weep, I told myself, but felt at any moment that I might.

"I saw the grave markers. Emma was four, Evie two. Wolf set the house on fire and when they came rushing out the door, he picked them off like he was hunting rabbits, even the children. Left their bodies right where they fell. Men from a nearby town found them and buried them. Wolf and the others got what they came for, rounded up the stock, moved on, and laid low for a while until the next place." Silas took a breath. For all the years in between, I could see that telling the story had not gotten easier for him. How could it? "He could have taken what he wanted without killing them, Ruth, but that wasn't his way."

"How do you know for sure it was Wolf? Those years after the war were full of wicked men doing wicked things."

"He did the same in other parts of Missouri, and there were men looking for him because of it. Wolf's a man comfortable with killing little girls, but if he thought there was a chance he might get caught, he pulled back, moved on, and laid low until the hubbub died down. It was Wolf, all right. There wasn't anyone else at the time but Wolf, and it was the way he worked: make examples of a few folks so people lived in terror and wouldn't fight back, take as much as he could get, then clear out, wait a while, and do it again somewhere else." I couldn't think of anything to say and my quiet made Silas look at me. "I'm sorry. I shouldn't have told you, but–"

I placed a finger against his lips. "You hush, Silas Carpenter. There'll never be anything you can't tell me, but I wish I could make things different for you. You know, don't you, that what happened to Dorie and her family wasn't your fault?"

"I should have been there."

"You were young and on a tear. That's what young men do. It wasn't your fault," I repeated.

"A man has an obligation to his own. My father drilled that into me and my brother. Paul wouldn't have been off raising hell. He was always a better man than me and everybody knew it. He would have done his duty by Dorie and the girls."

"And that's why you've been trailing Emmett Wolf all these years," I said. "Not to bring a bad man to justice. Not to arrest him so people can live in peace and safety, but to find a way to make it right, to make up for what you see as your own sin." I felt an enormous tenderness toward him. "My dear, it was never your fault. It just wasn't."

"A man has an obligation to his own." There was no matching tenderness in Si's voice, just a ragged but implacable hatred, as unbending as iron. What I heard in him made the words Clayton Barts spoke at his brother's funeral about getting revenge for Eddie seem almost childish by comparison. Silas Carpenter had carried a burden of guilt and a quest for vengeance a long time. I felt a kinship with him because I recognized the anger and the grief in his voice, having spent too long with those same dark emotions after Duncan died. In the end, if Silas wasn't able to accept the past and move on, I doubted that catching Emmett Wolf would ease the weight he carried. Dorie and her girls, like Duncan, were dead, and nothing would bring them back.

It was nearly dark by the time he finished speaking. A slice of moon showed over the cottonwoods and the birdsong had long quieted. Si stepped back up onto the path and reached to help me up the slight embankment. We stood very close for a moment, so close I could have rested my head against his shoulder, but we didn't touch. Instead, we started the walk back toward New Hope side-by-side keeping distance between us, until I moved nearer to him and slipped my hand under his arm. At first, he didn't react, but then he pulled me closer to his side and tucked my hand more firmly under his arm. We walked like that, our breathing somehow slowing to the same rhythm, without saying another word until we spoke our quiet good-nights at the front gate of the boarding house, I going inside and Silas off on his nighttime rounds to be sure all was calm and quiet in New Hope. Later, I would hear him come in and make his way upstairs to his room for a few hours sleep. It had come to the point that I couldn't fall asleep until I heard his foot on the creaky bottom step, but I don't know when that particular habit started.

Much later, Danny off to bed, the hearth cooling, and the lamp on the front desk dimmed, I sat at my kitchen table and pictured Dorcas Carpenter Lindquist, her raven black hair streaming out behind her as she ran from her house with her husband, the two of them holding their baby girls close — were her daughters black-haired, too, I wondered, or fair like their father? – thinking they ran toward safety and instead running straight into death. My feelings that night troubled me a great deal because the emotion that plagued me wasn't sadness, which would have been natural and right, but something more hateful and more frightening: a powerful desire to see Emmett Wolf stretched out dead in front of me. I was shocked that I could hope for a man to die with such intensity and feel so satisfied about it, feel almost happy at the idea. This is what Silas Carpenter wakes up with every morning and goes to bed with every night, I thought, and how could I ever expect him to have room for anything else? Surely a man's heart had its limitations.

9

The next morning, I left a note for Lizbeth on the desk and thought I'd make an early start at the barber shop, but when I stepped outside, Si Carpenter waited for me on the other side of the gate. He sat slouched sidewise on that fine roan horse of his, one leg pulled up against the saddle horn, intent on rolling himself a cigarette. Both Silas and the horse looked ready to head out somewhere. At the sound of the front door, he looked up, saw me, and carefully placed the fresh cigarette into his shirt pocket.

"Good morning, Ruth."

One of the things I thought I would never tire of was Silas Carpenter's natural courtesy. It is a rare attribute in a man. He might have spent several years among the fleshpots, but he had been raised right and it showed in his manners.

"Good morning, Silas. You look like you're off somewhere."

"I am, but I didn't want to leave without letting you know I'd be gone for a few days." Maybe, I thought, his need to tell me his whereabouts was like me not being able to sleep until I heard his tread on the bottom step. Or maybe he had learned a hard lesson about not saying a proper good bye. Whatever the reason, I appreciated the gesture.

"Oh?"

"I'm meeting up with your friend Captain McGruder for a quick trip north."

"You and Jeffrey?" I didn't bother to hide my skeptical surprise.

"The same."

"Well, I hope you both mind your manners. The last time I left the two of you alone, I had every expectation of fisticuffs." Then, curious, I asked, "What exactly did you say to the man, Silas? He was awful humble the next time he talked to me, and I haven't seen him since."

"Do you mind about that?"

"No. He's a good man, but after five minutes in his company, I usually feel the urge to brain him with a skillet." Si laughed.

"That's what I thought by the look on your face whenever I saw you with him, but I didn't mean to intrude on anything personal."

Oh, it's much too late to worry about that, I thought, but said, "With Jeffrey McGruder, you mean? There wasn't anything personal to intrude on. He never could take no for an answer is all."

"He's got my sympathy on that. You'd be a hard woman to let go of."

I ignored the warmth of the words. "So how did you get him to understand that I didn't welcome his attentions? Goodness knows, I told him often enough, but it never seemed to sink in."

"Men talking, Ruth. It was just men talking," casual words, but he looked pleased with himself.

"Fine," I said. "Keep it to yourself, then. I'm not one to look a gift horse in the mouth, and far be it from me to interfere in the important discussions you men have – when such discussions occur, which in my experience isn't all that often. Why are the two of you going north?"

Si grinned at my words, catching my teasing tone about men and their discussions, but at my question, he sobered. "I've known Major Prentiss a long time, and he sent word there was talk about a man selling rifles to the Sioux up in Garfield County a few months ago. That's over by Fort Hartsuff, so McGruder and I want to make a quick trip and see what that's all about."

"A few months ago? Do you think Wolf had a hand in it, Silas? I don't see how he could have, considering you believe he's been living in New Hope for years."

"I don't have an answer for you, but some of the things the major passed along made me want to hear the story for myself, and McGruder needs to find out where those guns ended up and if the Sioux got their hands on any of them. It will be a quick trip, Ruth. You watch your step while I'm gone." Si kept his voice even, but I caught a touch of something in his voice that might have been worry. The guilt he carried over not being there for his sister colored his words, too, but I thought I might be the only one who would hear it.

"I will," I said. "You do the same."

He straightened in the saddle and reined his big roan into the street, starting north at a walk. Then he turned in the saddle and raised a hand in good bye before nudging his mount into an easy lope that quickly took them both out of sight.

Later in the morning, with not a customer in sight and time just crawling along, I waited for the whistle of the late morning train before closing the shop for the day. Twice a week, that particular train dropped off New Hope's mail and this was the day for it.

The post office was a sliver of space that shared a wall with the telegraph office. The recent fire hadn't done any significant damage to it, but Russ Lowe had given it a good soaking that night to be sure no stray sparks could do further damage, and the place needed to dry out before it could go back to regular use. In the meanwhile, Phil Tiglioni had volunteered the use of his freight office for mail sorting, and that's where I headed.

I remembered watching the buildings of Phil's freight company take shape six years ago. The front office with an overhang above the door held the sign: *Freight and Hauling*, written with a great many curlicues in the script. The sign was done by the previous owner of the hardware store; Joe Chandler was a more practical sort. The letters on Joe's signs were straight and solid, much like the young man himself.

Behind the front office was a large warehouse where Phil kept his freight wagon and stored the goods coming in and going out, items off the train for Phil to deliver to places not on the railroad line or goods Phil hauled in to load onto the train to fill orders from outside New Hope. The business flourished from the start, keeping him on the go and growing along with the whole county. When one day Phil returned to New Hope with a new bride, he began to find more reasons to stay close to home. No surprise there. Julia Tiglioni was the most beautiful woman I had ever seen. If I were her husband, I would have cut my wandering, too.

The Tiglionis' home sat behind the warehouse facing west. The house wasn't overly grand but it was comfortable, with a broad front porch and – unheard of anywhere else in New Hope – indoor plumbing that included a water closet. Many's the time as I trudged outside on an early winter morning to use the backyard facility when the thought of that luxury sent a stab of pure envy right through me. I'm as human as the next person, with a set of faults tailored just to me, but I can truly say that the only thing I have ever coveted with any constancy was Julia Tiglioni's water closet.

I was surprised to see Julia and not Phil when I entered the freight office. She looked up quickly when I came in and smiled.

"Hello, Ruth. Don't tell Bert I've been digging around in his mailbags. I know our postmaster doesn't like it, but I couldn't wait." She gave the open bag a little shake and envelopes tumbled out onto the counter. "I bet you're here for the same reason I am."

'Yes," I said and came in farther, leaving the door open to let in spring air. While an alley separated the freight office from the burned telegraph office, the place still smelled faintly of smoke. "Welcome home, by the way. You missed a lot of excitement."

Julia's smile dimmed. "I know. Phil told me. It's a shame about Eddie, and the fire—" She gave a slight shiver. "It was so close to the house, Ruth."

"Russ took care of it right off," I said by way of reassurance. "He's a wonder with the fire wagon. Your house was never in danger."

"Still—" Julia didn't finish the thought but began to search through the pile of letters. "Here's something for you, Ruth." I took the letter from her outstretched hand, happy at the sight of my sister Laura's handwriting.

"It's from Laura," I said.

"That's the one in Texas, isn't it?"

"Yes. I haven't seen her or my older sister, Vera Ann, since Duncan's funeral, and that's been five years now."

"It's hard being so far away from family, isn't it?" Julia's voice carried a wistful lilt. "After six years, you'd think I'd be used to it, but I'm not. My father, the judge—" Julia always said it that way: *my father, the judge*, "— just hated putting the girls and me on the train last week. He rattles around in that big house since Mother died last year, just rattles around. My brother left for school in Boston after Christmas, and that makes it all the worse for Papa." I could see her remembering her last visit.

"The judge should move to New Hope," I suggested.

"Oh, no, Ruth, he could never do that. He's a very important person in Hill City, in all of Graham County, really. Kansas would never give him up to Nebraska, but sometimes I wish— Well, that's neither here nor there. It's only two hundred miles away and with the train, that hardly takes any time at all. Phil's got a successful business here in New Hope and, of course, a wife belongs with her husband." We both must have thought of Duncan at the same time because Julia said too quickly, "Oh, look, Ruth! Here's another letter for you!"

What a welcome – and rare – occurrence, I thought, having felt unexpectedly low since watching Silas Carpenter disappear into the distance that morning. I reached for the second envelope. "It's from Vera Ann!"

"She's your older sister?"

"Yes. In Omaha." In my hand, the envelope felt stiffer than it should have. "I think there might be a photograph in here. I hope it's of her and the girls." Which made me think of the Tiglioni daughters. "Did Bella and Lucy enjoy visiting their grandfather?"

Julia smiled. "Of course, they did. The man spoils them something awful," but her tone said she didn't mind such spoiling at all. "I left them home playing on the porch and I have to get back. I just came over to see if there was anything from Papa or from my brother."

"Nothing?"

"No, nothing." She straightened her shoulders. "It's your lucky day, Ruth. Just think – getting letters from both your sisters on the same day!"

"If I'm so lucky maybe I should spend some time this afternoon at one of Mr. Bliss' poker tables."

"Ruth! The idea!" But she grinned at me. Julia Tiglioni may be the beautiful only-daughter of a prominent judge, but she's not lofty about herself and can take a joke like anyone else.

Outside, I patted the pocket where I stashed the letters and started back toward Hart's at the other end of town when I heard a man behind me call my name and turned to see Phil Tiglioni walking quickly after me.

"Morning, Ruth. Didn't mean to startle you."

"You didn't, Phil."

"Julia told me you just left, and I've been meaning to talk to you about Danny."

"What about Danny?" My tone was abrupt, but the letters were burning a hole in my pocket and I was eager to get to them.

"I could use his help, Ruth. I got some heavy orders coming in and I'm not as young as I used to be." The truth was that Phil Tiglioni had one of those faces that would look young when he was twice his age, unlined and clear, topped by a head of close-cut blonde curls just beginning to thread with gray. I never gave Phil much thought, neither liked nor disliked him except when he talked about his wife and daughters, and then the worshipful look on his face always made me like him a great deal. He had more than his share of confidence, which he must have needed to court a woman with an important father, respected family name, and enough fortune to send her on a shopping trip to Kansas City.

I remember the conversation because at the time, I had never in all my life heard of anything as extravagant as going on a trip just to buy new clothes. Duncan was dying when Phil brought Julia to New Hope as his new bride, and I was beyond weary at the time. I needed to fasten on something other than watching my husband fade away, and there was Julia Tiglioni, petite and beautiful and refined in all her ways. She was like a creature from another world, but surprisingly shy, not at all uppity for all her beauty and privilege, and easy to talk to. On one of her early days in New Hope, I asked her how she and Phil met.

"Oh," she said, blushing a little as new brides are apt to do, "Mama and I were in Kansas City to refresh our wardrobes—" If I live to be a hundred I'll never forget Julia's words, as if she assumed refreshing their wardrobes was something all women did on a regular basis "—and I stumbled on the bottom step getting off the train and there he was, right in front of me. Phil caught me before I took a tumble, and he was so solicitous! Proper in his attentions, you understand, but just so very kind. We had the briefest of conversations, but I must have let slip where Mama and I were staying while we were in Kansas City," Julia gave me a mischievous look, "and wouldn't you know, he was staying at the very same hotel!"

"That was a coincidence," I said.

"Indeed." Julia gave the word the same inflection a cat might use when you put a saucer of cream down in front of her. Satisfied. Deserving.

I recalled those details on my way home after agreeing to ask Danny if he wanted to help Mr. Tiglioni an hour before school and an hour after.

"It won't interfere with school, Ruth," Phil said, "and I'll pay him fair."

The offer made sense to me after my recent realization that Danny would not be going on to college. The boy would enjoy the physical activity of working in the warehouse, and he might learn something about running a profitable enterprise from Phil, whose freight business kept him busy and continued to thrive. In the hour after school that Danny worked at the freight company, I could close the barber shop to be sure I was at the boarding house in Danny's absence. Or maybe Lizbeth would be willing to add time to her day at Hart's. Her parents might complain, but it would be a feeble protest if I agreed to pay her more for the extra hour.

Back at Hart's, I stopped to greet Lizbeth and mention the change in hours before I went into the kitchen where I reheated the coffee and carefully slit open the precious envelopes.

Laura, the baby of the family, was happy. Oh, her letter said this and that about the ranch where she lived and the dust and the heat and her husband and her sons, but what it all boiled down to was that she was as happy as a woman living on a cattle ranch in Texas could hope to be. It sure wasn't my dream. I would miss the passing seasons and I hate dust with a passion, but Laura and I were chalk and cheese, as Duncan used to say. One day, my little sister met a fellow passing through Nebraska pushing his cattle north to the Army in Dakota Territory, and while I knew she thought highly of the man, I never dreamed that when he stopped on his way back home, she would accept his proposal without a quibble, marry him, and leave for Texas all in the space of one week. I thought it would break my mother's heart, but that was Laura. Sure of what she wanted, fearless, and always up for a lark.

I waited to open Vera Ann's letter because I wanted to savor the anticipation of a photograph, and I wasn't disappointed. Her three girls stared into the camera, solemn and big-eyed. The littlest one sat on a chair with her legs sticking out in front of her and her two older sisters stood on each side of her, each with a hand resting on the back of the chair. I knew they were brown-haired like Vera Ann, but I could see their father in their grave expressions. No smiles with these girls. Mary, named after our mother and the oldest of Vera Ann's three, was ten but wore the look of a girl much older. I could just hear Vera Ann: "A photograph is serious business. Now stand up straight. I don't want your Aunt Ruth thinking I've raised her nieces like hooligans." That was Vera Ann, serious and hard-working like Mama. She married a serious and hard-working railroad man, and they ended up in Omaha. Which was closer than Texas, but not nearly close enough.

I stared at the picture. Did they play with dolls, these nieces of mine? When the camera wasn't pointed at them, did they giggle and dream the way little girls were inclined? For just a moment, staring at their solemn faces made me want to weep. They could be Vera Ann and Laura and me twenty years ago, never dreaming our father would go off to war and not come home, not knowing that one day we would grow up and move away from each other and be connected only by letters and pictures. What a comfort it had been to stand protected and propped between my sisters the day Duncan was buried, and, oh, how I hated to see them leave!

I pulled myself up short at the memories. There was no use being maudlin about our lives. I wiped away the one tear that had managed to slip through and stood up from the table, thinking about helping Lizbeth with the cleaning and planning ham for supper. Distance aside, my sisters and I had good lives, and having the railroads back up and running after the war made it easier than ever to keep in touch. In fact, Bert announced that by Christmas, we could send packages through the U. S. Mail as well as letters. I was already planning Christmas presents.

The next few days passed without a sign of Si Carpenter, and while I told myself that the man had managed to take care of himself just fine without me hovering and fretting, I couldn't keep from sneaking periodic and quick glances out of whatever window was nearest. No one but a friend would have noticed, and Sheba Fenway was my closest friend in New Hope.

"What are you looking for, Ruth?" Sheba asked. Saturday was busier than usual, but by the end of the day, I still didn't feel like going straight back to the boarding house. Too restless to think of supper or account books or bank statements, I stopped in at Sheba's. She was finishing up the day herself, using her hands to smooth out a bright piece of satin that was stretched on her cutting table. She was intent enough on the task that I thought if I drifted over to the window and took a quick look up and down Main Street, she wouldn't notice. But I was wrong.

"Just checking the crowd. It was a busy day," I answered, taking a quick step back to her side. "I can't say that shade of green appeals to me. Who's that for?"

Ignoring my question, Sheba stood upright and gave me a narrow-eyed look. "I take it you didn't see Mr. Carpenter out there anywhere."

"Not that I recall, but I wasn't really—"

"Ruth." Sheba sounded more exasperated than anything else. "There's nothing wrong with a grown woman finding a man attractive. Your husband's been gone five years, so it would be unusual if you didn't think about a man now and then. I never knew Duncan, but from what you've told me, he was a man who loved being alive and loved being with you. Surely he wouldn't begrudge you a bit of happiness again."

"I don't think about Silas Carpenter in that way, Sheba."

"And what way would that be?" We stared at each other and began to laugh at the same time.

"Oh, all right," I said. "It's true. I think about Silas Carpenter in *that way* more often than not, and I can't help myself. I just do. There. Satisfied?"

Sheba smiled. "I like being right, so, of course, I'm satisfied." Pause. "But I'd be more satisfied if he returned your regard. Does he?"

I thought about the question a moment before replying, "Sometimes I think he could," – I chose the word carefully – "but he's a man with things on his mind other than a plain widow who runs a boarding house and cuts hair for a living on her off days."

"Oh, *plain*. Fiddlesticks! I've never known you to act coy, Ruth. Is that what you really think?"

"I know I'm not plain exactly, but there's nothing special about me, and I'm not getting any younger. I'm not you with your bright hair or pretty Ellie Chandler and surely not Julia Tiglioni – she's a beauty, isn't she? I've worked hard all my life, Sheba, first on the farm and then at the boarding house, and I know it shows."

Sheba shook her head. "Oh, lord, Ruth. I hate it when you sound so humble like that. I wish you could see yourself like other people see you, all that thick honey hair and eyes as green as springtime. You're the kindest person I've ever met, besides, and that shows on your face more than anything else. You are as far from plain as a woman could be."

I smiled at her. "And you are the best friend a woman could be." I sighed. "No, I didn't see Silas anywhere on the street, not coming or going, not anywhere, more's the pity." I turned toward the door. "I'm going home. Danny will be waiting supper, and I've got chores to keep me busy."

"Which won't keep you from thinking about our resident officer of the law in *that way*."

"You," I pointed out, "are an unmarried woman and shouldn't even know what *that way* means."

"Ha! Any woman past a certain age can figure that out. I'm not married, but I'm not dead, either." I was still laughing at the words when I reached the boarding house.

Monday morning I was explaining to Lizbeth that I wanted her to take down all the curtains from the downstairs windows and pin them outside on the line – "Let the breeze do the work for us," I told her, "and there's not a cloud in the sky to have to worry about rain" – when Tom Danford pushed open the front door just far enough to tell me that Luther Winters had called an emergency meeting of the Merchants' Association in ten minutes.

"Why would Luther Winters—" I began, but Dr. Danford was gone before I could finish my question. Joe Chandler was the head of the association, not Luther Winters, and Joe called the meetings. I gave Lizbeth final instructions about the curtains, and walked outside, through the front gate, and down the street to the Meeting Hall where people had already gathered. No Joe Chandler present, I noted, and no John Bliss, either. Sheba entered after me, and we took our usual places along the wall.

"What's this about?" she asked, then, "I don't think I like it, Ruth." I didn't like it, either.

In a few minutes, Luther Winters stood up in the front of the room and used the gavel, which was always more for show than anything else, to call the meeting to order. All talk stopped at once. All faces turned in Luther's direction. We were a restless group, on edge and worried.

"I know you're all thinking I don't have the right to call a meeting, that Joe Chandler does that, but I am the assistant mayor and you'll understand in a minute why I think it's better that Joe doesn't know about this meeting just yet." The words got everyone's attention. Luther held up an envelope in one hand.

"Thursday I got a letter from my brother in Kansas City. I've mentioned Lou to some of you before. He's lived in Kansas City a long time and he runs a newspaper there. He keeps all the back copies, so when I wrote him about what happened here in New Hope, Eddie Barts and the fire and the sheriff putting Carpenter in charge, Lou said he thought Carpenter's name was familiar." I straightened at that because Silas wasn't here to defend himself, and I wasn't about to let anything unseemly be said about him without rising to his defense. I needn't have worried.

"Si Carpenter's not a man to fool with, I'll say that, and he's stayed on the right side of the law, but what Lou said was that Carpenter's made a name for himself about one thing in particular. Lou said the man's been on the trail of Emmett Wolf for years. You remember that name, don't you? He was a terror a few years back, a robber and murderer, took that one woman off the train – well, I'll spare the ladies the details, but in his day, Emmett Wolf was the devil incarnate – and Carpenter won't rest until he finds him. That's what Lou said."

"I thought Emmett Wolf was long dead," said a man's voice. "We ain't heard a word about him for years."

"That's the thing," Luther said, "That there's the thing. The last time Lou could find anything in his back papers about Emmett Wolf was four years ago, when the man robbed the Payne and Williams Bank of Missouri of a train payroll and killed a teller in the process. So, yes, he has been quiet for four years, but Lou says, and I think he's right, that if Si Carpenter has settled into New Hope for a stay, it's because he thinks Emmett Wolf has done the same thing."

I appreciated the silence as everyone digested the information. It was a lot to take in, and I remembered how shocked I had felt when Silas first told me the story. I turned my head to find Sheba staring at me. She mouthed the words, "You knew," and I gave a short nod. Now that Si's cat was out of the bag, even if it wasn't quite the whole cat, I didn't have to pretend with her or with anyone.

"What's your conclusion then, Luther?" That question from Morton Lewis, sounding like the lawyer he was.

"I don't think it takes any special brain power to figure out that Si Carpenter expects to find Emmett Wolf right here in New Hope. My brother called Carpenter the Hound of Death in one of his articles because he's made it his mission to find Emmett Wolf, and I don't think he rightly cares if Wolf ends up dead or alive."

"Do you think this has something to do with Eddie Barts?" the question in Hans Fenstermeier's accented English.

"Well, hell, Hans," said Cap Sherman, his southern drawl more pronounced than ever, "New Hope ain't never had a murder in all its years, and I should know because I was one of the first men that settled the place. And now we got a murdered boy and a fire that somebody set to burn down the telegraph office and a man watching over the town who spent the last ten years looking for one of the worst outlaws Missouri ever had. What do you think?"

"There's no need to take that tone, Cap," Luther said. "What I think we need is a plan."

"You got one?" Cap snapped back.

"I think I do. Now, Mort, you tell me what you think about this. According to my brother, the last time anybody saw or heard Emmett Wolf was in November of 1874 so I figure anyone living in New Hope by then can't be Emmett Wolf. A man can't be in two places at once. He can't be living in New Hope and robbing the Payne and Williams Bank of Missouri at the same time."

Another silence as everyone thought about Luther's words. Heads began to nod slowly throughout the room, but because Silas and I had already had this conversation, I was way ahead of them. And I knew why Joe Chandler and John Bliss hadn't been asked to this meeting.

"I think we should be careful with this kind of thinking," said Dr. Danford. "We should wait until Carpenter's back."

"I agree." Abner Talamine, who had started the bank on the hope and rumor of a railroad, and who had sold the boarding house to my mother eleven years before, was perhaps the most respected man in town. He was a quiet sort and not one to give his opinion very often, so when he spoke, people paid attention. "You can't take back words once they're said."

"You can't take back lives once they're taken, either, by God," said Cap Sherman. A grizzled war veteran who had long ceased to need a haircut, the man still had a threatening way about him. Once I had told my mother that I thought Mr. Sherman's bark was worse than his bite and my mother said, "Think what you will, Ruthie, but take my advice and don't get too close to the man. He'd as soon take a chunk out of you as look at you." I never found him likeable, but this was the first time I could remember being frightened of him.

Mr. Talamine's dry voice continued undaunted. "No one can argue with that, Mr. Sherman, but I agree with Dr. Danford that we need to be cautious until we have all the facts and until Mr. Carpenter has returned." The slight shifting of bodies following Mr. Talamine's words seemed to indicate agreement with his words, but I thought it was half-hearted at best. People were more afraid than ever.

Luther, having lost control of the meeting, attempted to take it back. "Do we have a motion to do anything?"

"I don't need no motion to protect myself," said Cap. "We all know who the newest additions to New Hope are – Chandler and Bliss, and it sounds like they showed up here about the time Wolf dropped out of sight. Them's the two we should be watching."

"And the schoolteacher," said Phil Tiglioni. His voice was slow and thoughtful. "I don't think we should forget about that man."

Fortunately, no one mentioned that Gerald Shulte had arrived in New Hope around that same time. Maybe they just didn't remember, or maybe they had the same limitation to imagining evil in others that I had.

Thinking about the minister reminded me of this past Sunday's sermon, Easter morning and the church full of new bonnets and spring sunshine. Just about everyone in the room where I stood now had sat through yesterday's service. Reverend Shulte had reminded us again and again to love each other, to be kind to one another, to think the best of others. By the end of his sermon, I lost count of the different ways he used to say the same thing, squirming a little as I recalled how suspicious I had been of several of my neighbors. And now, here we were the very next day after Easter Sunday, without prodding or apology, thinking the worst of people we had known for years. I remembered how Eddie Barts looked stretched out on the doctor's table, and I understood that people were afraid, but what was going on here still seemed wrong.

Sheba straightened beside me and in a loud and scornful voice said, "Well, don't forget I settled in New Hope the same year as John Bliss and Arthur Stenton. Maybe you ought to be watching me, too, Cap. Good lord, people, this is ridiculous. To think I closed my shop for this foolishness!" She strode toward the door and exited without a backward glance.

"I think Miss Fenway's got the right of it," Mort Lewis said. "We don't know anything for sure and our appointed officer of the law is absent. I think it behooves us to remain calm but cautious. When Mr. Carpenter returns, Luther, you and I can go talk to him, but until then, I don't think we should be taking any action. We haven't been deputized." In response to the lawyer's advice, Cap Sherman gave a snort loud enough to be heard in the next county, but most of us nodded and proceeded slowly toward the door.

They're happy to have somewhere to lay the blame, I thought. I understood that being able to worry about only two or three men instead of every man in town made people feel safer. You could watch two or three where you couldn't watch everybody all the time. My thoughts slowed down my pace and I was at the tail end of the line leaving the Meeting Hall. As I pulled the door shut, I looked back over my shoulder to see that Luther Winters, Cap Sherman, and Phil Tiglioni had stayed behind and now huddled together, talking in low voices. I didn't know why exactly, but the sight made me uneasy. There was no reason they shouldn't talk to each other, after all, but still— Once outside, I looked from one end of Main Street to the other, as I had been doing on a regular basis since the day Silas Carpenter left for Garfield County. Now more than ever, I longed to hear his footsteps on the boarding house stairs, letting me know that he was finally home.

10

When Silas finally arrived back in New Hope, it was just in the nick of time. The day following what I considered to be an underhanded meeting of the Merchants' Association passed without incident, and if it hadn't been for the way people avoided speaking to each other about what had been discussed in the meeting, I might have taken a deep breath of relief. As it was, I didn't feel relieved at all. In the back of my mind, I could still see Luther and Phil and Cap gathered with their heads together and it worried me.

That afternoon, I crossed the street to Sheba's shop, colliding with John Bliss, of all people, leaving as I arrived,

"Mrs. Churchill." He stopped long enough to acknowledge my presence by giving the brim of his hat a light, two-fingered touch before he stepped down from the boardwalk, waited for a wagon to pass, and crossed the street.

"What did John Bliss want?" I asked Sheba when I entered the dress shop.

She scowled at me. "Hello to you, too, Ruth. We may be having a town emergency, but I see no reason why we can't attempt to maintain the courtesies."

She doesn't want to talk about John Bliss, I realized, and responded, "You're right," paused for effect, and said in an innocent voice, "Good afternoon, Sheba. Hasn't the weather been pleasant lately?" Which only made her scowl deepen before she gave a reluctant smile.

"If you must know, yesterday I shared the goings-on of the Merchants' Association with Mr. Bliss, and he simply stopped by this afternoon to thank me for doing so." She drew her brows together in disapproval, adding, "And a fine friend you are. You knew all about this Emmett Wolf business and never said a word."

"I couldn't. It wasn't my story to tell."

"No doubt the story belongs to the Hound of Death."

Her using that name almost goaded me into a sharp retort, but she didn't know about Dorie Lindquist and her husband and two little girls that would never grow up. That wasn't my story to tell, either, so I said, "No doubt," and left it at that.

Sheba sank onto a nearby stool. "I'm sorry, Ruth, for being so short-tempered. I'm still fuming about the meeting yesterday and everything's off kilter because of it."

'I know. For what it's worth, Sheba, I no more think John Bliss is a murderous outlaw than I think he's the man in the moon."

"That makes you smarter than just about everybody else in New Hope. People's opinions don't hold much store for John, and that has always riled people up." We talked about this and that but after we parted, I thought about the way Sheba had said *John* and thought maybe there was at least one person in town whose opinion mattered to the man.

Since I was already late for supper, I crossed the alley next to Sheba's dressmaking shop, passed by the bank, and stopped in the neighboring hardware store. The door still had the sign turned to open, but inside it was empty of everything except Joe standing behind a counter removing loose hinges from a wooden box and silently counting them as he did so.

He looked up when I entered and held up a finger for me to wait until he finished. "Twenty-five," he said aloud, then, "Hello, Ruth. Is there something I can help you with?"

His voice was cheerful enough that I wondered if he had heard about yesterday's meeting, but when I got closer to him, I saw that his smile was forced and frown lines seemed to have settled permanently at the corners of his mouth. He looked ten years older than he had looked the day before.

"No. I was just checking to see if there was anything I could do to help Ellie with the boys. I don't know what exactly. I saw her the other day at the grocery store, and the babies didn't look in need of a haircut just yet."

Joe smiled at my words, which was my intention. "No, they're both bald as billiard balls, but I'll tell her you offered."

"Do that." Neither of us spoke for a moment, until I added, "Well, I'd better get home before Danny tries to cook his own supper. He's at the age when he's always hungry."

"My boys seem to be at that same age," he said. I smiled, which was Joe's intention.

"If there's anything I can do," I said.

"We'll let you know, and Ruth—" I turned at the door to look back at him "—thank you." I knew the words were for more than a five-minute visit on a late Tuesday afternoon.

The house was dark and we were all in bed when I heard the front door of the boarding house open. Well, I didn't hear the door open exactly or even hear the bell on it jingle. What I heard was someone trying to muffle the sound of the bell and knew right away that it was Silas. The other boarders had all turned in to their rooms earlier and a quick peek into Danny's room told me he was asleep, as well.

I came into the hallway just as Silas gently pressed the door shut and took his hand from the bell.

"I woke you," he said when he saw me. "I'm sorry."

I stepped from the hallway into the front room. "I wasn't sleeping, Silas." I was listening for you, I almost added, but thought better of it at the last minute. "How'd your trip go?"

"McGruder and I are still on speaking terms."

I laughed. "And no black eyes, I hope."

"Not a one."

How odd it seemed to be talking like we had known each other for years instead of weeks!

"We've had a development here," I said.

"Is everybody safe?"

"Yes, but the whole town knows you're here because of Emmett Wolf."

"How in the—?"

157

I shook my head. "I'll tell you tomorrow. You look tired," but that might have been because the room was dim, with only the flame from the low-burning lamp I kept lit through the night.

"A little. Everything looked quiet when I got in so maybe a few hours sleep wouldn't hurt."

"Are you hungry?" My question brought a lopsided smile to his face, but I didn't know what it was he found amusing.

"I am hungry," he said, "but not the way you mean it, not hungry for supper. You looking like that has a way of giving a man an appetite."

I realized I stood in my night dress with the light of the lamp behind me and felt a sudden urge to take him by the hand and lead him back to my room. Danny would sleep through anything. No one except Silas Carpenter and I need ever know, and I thought that both of us could use a little comfort just then. In a way, that I even had such thoughts was a wonder because after Duncan's death, I never expected to feel that kind of longing again.

Silas must have seen my feelings in my face because he took a deliberate and deep breath before he said, "I shouldn't have said that. You go back to bed, Ruth."

Go back to bed alone, I thought, but knew it was the right thing to do for that moment. I would never be content with just the scraps left over from Si's passion and decade-long need to find Emmett Wolf. If there was a future for us – life is so full of *ifs*, I thought sadly – it wouldn't come until I was the only person Silas Carpenter needed with a passion. There wasn't room in a marriage for three people, and until the matter was resolved, Emmett Wolf would always be in the room with us.

"All right, but I'll have breakfast for you, no matter how early or late you come down. Then I can tell you what's happened here, and you can tell me what you found out in Garfield County."

"Deal," he said. He shifted his saddle bag on his shoulder and stepped around me, leaving such a distance between us that we could have set up a game of horseshoes in the space.

"Good night, Silas. I'm glad you're home."

The word took him aback and he stopped with one foot poised above the step. When was the last time he'd had a home, I wondered. How many years since he had belonged anywhere?

"Good night, Ruth."

I waited until I heard his door at the top of the stairs open and close, and then I did what he recommended: I went back to bed. Alone.

The next morning, I looked up from the griddle to see Silas in the doorway to The Addition. He hadn't made a sound, and I had the impression he might have been standing there a while. I smiled and waved a large fork at him.

"Come in and sit down. You're just in time for pancakes, sausage, and eggs, though this morning I wondered if Danny would leave any for you. It's a wonder how much a fifteen-year-old boy can eat! I never would believe it if I didn't see for myself."

Si rested his hat on the corner of the sideboard and took a chair by the table, turning to look at Danny's open door. "He must have early hours at school."

"Danny's working for Phil Tiglioni in his freight warehouse an hour before school and an hour after."

"Whose idea was that?" Something in Si's tone made me look up from stacking pancakes onto a plate.

"Phil asked. Why? Should I have said no? I didn't see how there could be any harm in it. It's right here in town, and I always know where Danny is."

"I didn't say there was any harm in it," but his tone still made me uncomfortable.

I said nothing as I busied myself putting breakfast on the table, brought over the pitcher of maple syrup and the bowl of strawberry preserves, poured Silas a cup of steaming coffee, and finally sat down across from him. When he just sat there, I reached across the table to spear two pancakes from the platter and plop them onto his plate next to the eggs and sausage already there. Then I poured a generous stream of cream into my own coffee and took a sip. He opened his mouth to speak, thought better of what he was going to say, and reached for his fork instead. The small pantomime made me smile, which he caught.

"I know the rules of the house," he said, remembering our earlier meal together. "Aren't you eating?"

"I had something with Danny." Then I volunteered, "Friday was my lucky day, Silas. I got two letters, one from each of my sisters."

"Tell me about your family," he said. The request suited me. I could talk and he could eat, which made good use of both our time. When he finished, I cleared the table and came back to sit again.

"Is it all right to talk business now?" Si asked.

"Yes. I won't count the coffee as part of the meal. Today, anyway. What did you find out at Fort Hartsuff? Was it Emmett Wolf selling those guns?"

"It's hard to say. I asked a lot of questions, but it's been almost a year and nobody remembers what the man who brought in the guns looked like, though the Army knows the Sioux got their hands on rifles somehow. There hasn't been any Indian trouble for the last three years and everyone, including most of the tribes, would like to keep it that way, so it's worrisome that a white man's been stirring up trouble with some of the younger warriors by putting guns into their hands. Nothing good can come of it, not for Nebraska or the Army or the settlers or the Indians, but it sounds like something Emmett Wolf would do without a moment's hesitation."

"We appreciate the peace," I said. "A lot of people had a frightful time for a while. Having Fort Cottonwood nearby is a comfort now, but when the Cheyenne were running wild back in the '60s, my mother and sisters and I were on the farm by ourselves, and for a while we took turns staying awake through the night and watching out the window." I remembered those times well, although I had been just a girl. Poor Mother. No wonder she sold out and moved to town. There all by herself with three girls to protect. "Does the Army expect trouble?"

"I think it's their business to expect trouble."

"I suppose you're right. You don't sound convinced that the man selling guns was Wolf."

"There's no way to know for sure. Identifying Emmett Wolf has always been the problem. One of the problems, anyway." He took a final swallow of coffee. "Now it's your turn. What's been going on in New Hope?"

I told him about the merchants' meeting and how Joe Chandler, John Bliss, and Arthur Stenton had been mentioned. "I believe Cap Sherman would have marched right out and arrested all three of them, and I think a number of men would have supported him all the way. I can hardly credit that we nearly had vigilante law in New Hope. Thank goodness for Mr. Talamine and Dr. Danford. They being older helped and people listened to them, but the mention of Emmett Wolf really stirred things up." Si looked thoughtful but stayed quiet.

"Oh, I forgot to show you something." I brought the sugar bowl to the table and pulled out the cigar band I had tucked away over three weeks ago. I hadn't thought about it until Friday when I propped my sisters' letters on the counter against the bowl. "I don't suppose it means anything," I said and proceeded to tell him where and how I had found it. "Have you ever seen a Kipp cigar?"

Silas shook his head as he fingered the white paper band with its distinctive orange sun and flowing black letters. "No. Never." He handed it back to me. "It's something to watch for."

I looked at the dishes stacked in the wash tub and sighed. I could have sat at that kitchen table all morning talking with Silas Carpenter, but I hated coming home to dirty dishes. Lizbeth would have been willing as ever to wash them, but that never seemed right to me. I paid her for boarding house chores, but my own personal cleaning was on my shoulders. In his usual way, Silas noticed the change in my mood – time for sharing over, and the tasks of the day calling. He stood.

"Thank you, Ruth."

"I'm far from the best cook in New Hope, Silas, but I believe my pancakes are passable."

"Best I've ever had." He collected his hat from where he had left it and turned in the doorway. "But I wasn't talking about the pancakes. Thank you for the company."

After he left, I thought of several responses I might have made, but at the time, I couldn't think of a thing. Silas Carpenter had a way of striking me dumb. No one, not even Duncan, had ever sounded so grateful for simple conversation.

The late morning train dropped off Mr. Parker Jones from the telegraph company, who brought with him the necessary new equipment for the remodeled telegraph office. He had a large wooden box delivered from the train straight to the new office and then walked down to Hart's to reserve a room for as many days as it would take to get the telegraph office up and running again.

"I'll take over the duties of telegraph clerk for your little town here until the company sends a replacement for young Barts. I was told they've got someone picked out. It's a terrible shame about the boy. He did good work."

"It is a shame about Eddie," I agreed as I turned the book toward him so he could sign in for his stay at the boarding house, "and we hope to have the miscreant responsible for his death locked up in jail any day now,—" I peered at his signature "—Mr. Jones." He had arrived at the boarding house the same time I came home for a bite of lunch.

"I should hope so. These are civilized times. People can't go around killing other people just because they feel like it." He hefted his suitcase and started toward the stairs.

"For an extra two bits, you can leave any clothing that needs to be washed in a pile by the door every Monday and Thursday morning," I called to his back, "and we'll return it to you the next day washed and ironed and presentable."

He waved a hand at me as he climbed the stairs to his room. "Thank you, Mrs. Churchill. By the weight of this suitcase, Mrs. Jones sent along enough changes of clothing for an army unit, and she is a woman persnickety about doing her own laundry. But I appreciate knowing the service is available."

Mr. Jones was the last boarder Hart's could take, which led me to thinking about ways to fit in another paying guest. Maybe it was time to consider expanding the boarding house. We could push out the back wall and add rooms there. I made a mental note to talk to Harold about the time and expense connected to such expansive carpentry work, checked with Lizbeth who was busy folding the clean linens Ruby had just returned, and walked back to the barber shop. Often the time immediately after a train arrived was busy with men desiring a quick shave or haircut because it wasn't only women who needed to be refreshed after an extended rail trip, but that afternoon saw only one new customer, followed by a visit from John Bliss.

He requested a shave and haircut and sat down in the chair without further comment. Once I started, however, he said, "I'm relieved to see that you don't feel being alone with me is a danger, Mrs. Churchill."

I wanted to tell him that I was the one holding the straight-edge razor but felt that was not an amiable way to continue the conversation with a man who sat with his throat bared for a shave and so said, "I don't know you well enough to say we're friends, Mr. Bliss, but Sheba Fenway is my friend, my very good friend, and if she vouches for you, then that's enough for me." He was quiet for a moment.

"And does she vouch for me?"

"She does, quite vigorously."

"Well, I'll have to remember to thank her." There was a note of surprise in his voice and something else that might have been humility, an emotion I didn't think John Bliss was very familiar with.

When I pulled the shop door shut behind me at the end of the day, I looked down to the other end of the street, what I would call the busy end, where the train depot sat. The stock pens east of the station were empty just then, but that was more and more the exception. Men brought their animals down from Dakota Territory or over from Wyoming to load into cars on the train because the East had a limitless desire for beef and the Army had a constant need for good horses. Next to the depot, Cap Sherman's livery and smithy, one of the oldest establishments in town, seemed always to be busy and right across the street from Cap was Phil Tiglioni's large business and the rebuilt telegraph office. It might have been any spring Wednesday in New Hope, Nebraska, with the sun setting and closed signs starting to show on all the small businesses that sat in a line on both sides of Main Street between the barber shop and the railroad. The United Bank of Nebraska. Joe Chandler's hardware store. Bert's Gooseneck Hotel. Hans Fenstermeier's dry goods. Lowe's leather goods. Carpentry, and groceries, and feed and grain. A fancy restaurant and a meeting hall, a post office and a jail and an honest-to-goodness working fire truck. *Civilized* Mr. Jones had said and New Hope looked civilized, at least on the outside. But there was the ominous presence of Emmett Wolf somewhere in all that civilization, and even worse, there was the memory of Monday's meeting filled with a fear that trembled on the brink of vigilante hysteria. That seemed the most uncivilized of all.

Dwelling on those serious thoughts, I turned to cross the street toward Hart's – mine was not the busy end of Main Street but as my neighboring attorney called it, the *professional* end – and from the corner of my eye saw that a few men had gathered outside Cap's livery. I stopped to stare down the street with greater care but couldn't make out individuals, only that there had to be a half dozen or so men clumped together. When they all turned at the same time and began a methodical walk down the hard-packed street in my direction, I knew something was in the works that would give an even greater lie to the idea that New Hope was a civilized community of law and order.

I reached the hardware store before the approaching men and hurried inside. "Joe," I said, slightly breathless from my rush to warn him. He stood with his back to me, stretching to place a box on a high shelf, and turned quickly.

"Is something wrong, Ruth?"

I didn't have a chance to answer because behind me Cap Sherman shouldered into the store, followed immediately by Luther, with Harold and Norm and Bert bringing up the rear. Bert met my astonished gaze and had the good sense to look sheepish, as if he knew what he was doing was wrong but couldn't help himself.

"You come with us," Cap said without greeting or explanation. He stared at Joe and Joe returned him look for look.

"Come with you where?"

"To the jail. If that poor excuse for a lawman won't lock you up, we will. We're not taking any chances with a man like you."

"A man like me," Joe repeated slowly. He had paled a little but otherwise seemed calm. "What kind of man would that be?"

"A killer. A man that didn't think twice about murdering Eddie Barts, that's always took what he wanted without a by-your-leave. You're the last man to settle here and where you come from, we never did know. There's always been something suspicious about you, Chandler. Or should I say Wolf?"

"It's Chandler. I'm not Emmett Wolf. I've never set eyes on the man in my life."

"Then where you been before you come to New Hope? And what you been up to? Answer that."

Everyone, myself included, looked at Joe, who lifted his chin a bit and stared right back but didn't speak.

"That's what I thought," Cap said. He lifted the rifle he carried and pointed it at Joe. "You been running scared for a couple of years, and then you come to New Hope and thought you'd settle right in and no one would be the wiser. Well, we ain't fools here. Carpenter come chasing Emmett Wolf and it has to be you." He waved the rifle in the direction of the door. "You can come peaceable or not. Don't make us no nevermind because either way we want you where we can keep an eye on you, jail or cemetery's all the same."

"Come on with us, Joe," said Bert, trying for a friendly tone, "just come on. Let Carpenter sort it out." Joe didn't look in much of a mood to cooperate and I don't know what would have happened if Ellie hadn't stepped from their living quarters in the back into the store proper.

"Joe?" she said, a quick glance at the gathered men and a longer look at her husband.

There was a general shuffling of feet, but Cap didn't lower his rifle and Joe said quickly, "It's nothing, El. These men got some questions for me. I'll be back in a little while." He took off the apron he wore, its pockets rattling with nails and bolts and such, and draped it over a stool. Then he came out from behind the counter and with a firm step walked through the middle of the group of men, which parted for him like the Red Sea must have done for Moses.

"Joe?" said Ellie again and got as far as where I stood.

I put a hand on her arm and said in a low voice, "Wait, Ellie. It'll be all right."

After they were all gone, she said, "What just happened, Ruth? Where are they taking my husband?"

I told her what I knew and what I was sure Cap and his posse of misguided citizens believed about Joe Chandler. The expression on her face bordered somewhere between flabbergasted and furious.

"You say Joe's been suspect for a couple of days? Well, I never heard a word about it!"

"You had the babies," I said. I remembered her husband's quiet thank you when I stopped in Monday afternoon and added, "but I believe Joe knew something was wrong. Ellie, why wouldn't Joe tell them where he was and what he was doing the years before the two of you came to New Hope? He only had to say, and I know that would have taken care of their suspicions."

Ellie Chandler took a deep breath before she said, "That's nobody's business but ours, Ruth. My husband is the best man I ever knew. He's a good husband and a good father, a good man all around, but people don't need to know all our business. We liked it here and we settled here and we're good neighbors to everybody."

"I know all that," I said. Whatever Ellie wasn't saying weighed heavy on her. She took another deep breath.

"I need to pack up the boys," she said. "I won't leave them by themselves. Will you wait and help me?"

"Of course, but help you do what?"

"We need to make a trip to the jail and clear all this up. You might as well hear it, too. Joe belongs with his family and I belong with him." I followed her back into their small home attached to the rear of the hardware store and into the bedroom with its two little cradles lined against a side wall. She lifted out one boy, wrapped him in a blanket, and handed him to me. She took the other one into her own arms.

"Which one do I have?" I asked as we walked back through the store toward the front door.

Ellie almost smiled, but clearly, she was too caught up in serious thoughts of her own to find much levity in anything.

"Matthew." I looked for the pointy chin Ellie had told me about a few days ago, but it looked no more or less pointy than his brother's chin. Mothers must have an especially discriminating eye about their children.

As we walked down the boardwalk toward the jail, a few other people came out of the storefronts and drifted in the same direction. Ahead, Phil Tiglioni crossed Main Street toward the jail. Doctor Danford and his wife trailed behind us. Mort Lewis. Hans Fenstermeier and his wife. Russ Lowe. Sheba stood in the doorway as we passed her shop but made her statement by disappearing back inside and closing the door firmly behind her. She prefers to live and let live, hates gossip, and would have been beside herself at Cap Sherman's misplaced zeal. It was better for everyone concerned that Sheba go back to sewing or painting or whatever it was that occupied her afternoon. My experience with my friend had taught me some time ago that there was little to be gained from a red-haired woman in a temper.

The jail was a small, seldom used building, with two tiny cells – one of which housed Joe Chandler by the time Ellie and I got there – and a front office area with barely enough room for a desk, chair, and upright wooden cabinet. I was disappointed not to find Silas there. He would have known exactly what to say and do to make people see sense. By then, I knew beyond a doubt that Joe Chandler was no more Emmett Wolf than I was, but what little value I might have been able to offer the situation was offset by the fact that I held a fussy baby in my arms. My experience has been that regardless of the matter in question, some men are hesitant to take a woman's advice seriously when she is jiggling a baby on her hip.

When Ellie and I stepped inside the jail, she didn't wait for an invitation to speak but said in a clear voice, every word cool and distinct. "What exactly is it that you want to know?" She spoke in the general direction of Cap Sherman but her words were for everyone thronged into the small space.

Cap, never one to be outdone by a female, spoke with a belligerent tone. "Emmett Wolf is around here some place, laying low and pretending to be someone he ain't. You showed up here out of the blue two years ago. You never talk about your past. You never said where you come from. That's the kind of slippery thing a man would do if he was trying to hide something."

Truly, if looks had the ability to slay, Cap Sherman would have dropped down dead.

"You old fool," Ellie Chandler said. I don't believe any of us thought Ellie, usually so sweet and shy, had it in her to use that tone with a person. "My husband isn't Emmett Wolf."

"He sure could be," Luther Winters said, a stubborn set to his mouth. "What was he doing before you came to New Hope? Tell us that."

From the cell where he stood, Joe said his wife's name with a cautionary tone to his voice. She looked over at him and smiled.

"It doesn't matter, Joe. Nothing matters except the two of us staying together." Then she said to the room in general, "Joe was in the Kansas Penitentiary for five years before we came here. They'll have a record of him. And before that, he was in jail in Topeka for a while. Topeka was where we met."

"Penitentiary! What was he in for?" Luther asked.

"Ellie." Joe again, his tone asking her not to say any more.

"He killed a man."

"There you are, then!" said Cap. "I knew we had a killer here."

"He killed a man to save my life. I wouldn't be standing here today if it weren't for Joe Chandler. I was near dead as it was." The hum of voices in the room ceased.

"Even in Kansas, they don't put a man in prison for saving a woman's life," said Cap, but he got quieter.

"They do if the man that got killed was the only son of an important family in town, and if the woman he tried to kill was a whore."

"Ellie," said Joe a third time, sadness and a kind of outrage in his voice.

She ignored him. "I worked at a place in Topeka called Paradise Palace. It was a whorehouse, plain and simple. I was on my own from my early years, and I never had any man be kind to me in all my life until I met Joe Chandler. He was just a cowpoke on his way through Topeka when we met. I was young and I didn't know any different life, didn't know it could be different for me, anyway, and I was always scared, besides. Felt like I was always running for my life, and then Joe came along. I never met anybody like him before, just a good, kind man. He said we could get married and start a new life somewhere. I couldn't get over the idea of being loved and having a fresh start. I still don't understand what he ever saw in me to make him love me. It was a wonder then, and it still is." Ellie shook her head with a half-smile on her face, remembering that time. I understood exactly how she felt because that's how it was with me years ago, when Duncan Churchill, that fine, handsome, generous man, who had come all the way from England, settled his affections on me, on Ruth Hart, a girl who worked in a boarding house.

"But there was a fella in Topeka who paid to torment me. What he did wasn't—" she hesitated, looking for a word "—wasn't normal, wasn't what other men paid for. I was scared of him. He carried a knife and one night he got out of hand and he cut me bad. Would have killed me, except Joe killed him instead, and that's what happened."

"I'd do it again," Joe said in a conversational tone, "to anyone that hurts my Ellie. My wife. The mother of my sons." He and Ellie just kind of smiled at each other, and I thought, what have we done to these two, exposing their private confidences like they were printed on the front page of the *Independent*? What right did we have to know their secrets? I felt ashamed, not of anything Joe and Ellie Chandler had said or done or been, but of us, the good, upright citizens of civilized New Hope, Nebraska. Then the baby – whichever one it was I held, I couldn't remember – stretched and fussed a bit, and I had to switch hips.

"The judge sentenced Joe to five years in the state penitentiary for saving my life. Five years." Disbelief in Ellie's voice at that, but a different side to the amazement she felt at being loved. "For killing a bad man to save my life. But Joe did his time, and I waited for him. There was a preacher in

Topeka named Ellicott and him and his wife took me in until I was healed, and then they found decent work for me in a hotel. Oh, it was hard work, and dirty, but that didn't matter. I saved every cent and I waited because I knew Joe Chandler was coming for me in five years." She looked around, proud. "And he kept his word. We got married and we moved around a bit doing whatever work we could find and saving our money until we came to New Hope. My, it sounded like the perfect place for two people who had spent a lot of their years without hope. We started a family and we thought we made some friends—" Her voice faded. "That's the part I guess we got wrong. Anyway, you can check with the Ellicotts in Topeka or with the penitentiary or wherever you need to, but whoever Emmett Wolf is, it sure isn't Joe Chandler. Now I've got supper waiting and I want to take my husband home." She looked at Joe. "Nothing matters, Joe, except us keeping together and raising our boys. Raising them right. We'll find another place. New Hope needs us more than we need them."

No one moved or spoke or seemed even to breathe. I elbowed past the men in front of me, walked over to where the key ring hung on the wall, took it down, and went over to Joe's cell. I unlocked the cell door and said, "Go home, Joe. I'm sorry to say your supper's bound to be cold, but Ellie'll know what to do. Doesn't she always?" I slid the baby into his arms. "This one," I added, "is going to be a big young man. He's a chunk already."

Joe smiled, like it was just two friends talking. "He is, isn't he?" He looked down. "Come on, Matthew. Mama's got supper on the table." Trust a father to recognize his baby's chin.

I watched Ellie fall in beside Joe and walk to the open door. The others inside the jail, still quiet, shifted back from the couple, and those outside on the boardwalk did the same. I don't think either of the Chandlers noticed, however, because both babies had begun to cry in earnest and two crying babies demand a lot of attention. I was surprised to see

Si Carpenter leaning against the back wall of the jail by the door and wondered how long he had been there and how much he heard. He gave Joe a respectful nod in passing, an acknowledgement that didn't surprise me. I recalled Si's words: "A man has an obligation to his own," and knew that despite being hired to uphold the law, Silas Carpenter understood and probably approved Joe's actions in Topeka. Sometimes right and wrong aren't as easy to tell apart as a person expects.

I was done with the whole sorry scene, but on my way out I stopped in front of Cap Sherman long enough to say, "And you, a man with the years and experience to know better, ought to learn to mind your own business."

Cap, with the sour temper my mother had recognized right off, snapped back, "And maybe uppity women ought to learn to—"

I never found out what Cap wanted uppity women to learn – though I had a fairly good idea – because Silas stood upright and said in a quiet but compelling voice, "Anybody plans to take the law into his hands again, he'll be the one behind bars." He reached into his shirt pocket and held up a piece of paper. "I picked up this telegram from the fort this afternoon, which confirms that Arthur Stenton is exactly who he said he was, a man that was teaching in Colorado for a decade before he came here." There was a murmur of interest. "And I've talked to people who've known John Bliss for the same number of years, so you can leave that man alone, too." Si tucked the telegram back into his pocket. "I understand why you did what you did, but it's not your place. The man I'm looking for—" Silas corrected himself "—the man the law's looking for has run out of places to hide. It won't be long now and you'll have your town back, safe and peaceful, the way you want it." He moved out of the doorway as people exited past him.

"That's good news about John Bliss and Mr. Stenton," I said in a low voice when I reached Silas.

"Yes." Pause. "That just leaves the one, Ruth. You see that, don't you?" He and I were alone then, everyone else hurrying home to their own suppers, no doubt with a little crow served up on each plate.

"Not if you mean the reverend, Silas. You go talk to him and you'll see what I mean." Silas shrugged, not wanting to argue about it. I didn't either because I knew I was right. "But I have a feeling we're missing something, something important, something that would explain everything. I just can't think what it is."

Si put a hand on my shoulder. "Well, if you do think of it, you come and tell me before you do anything else."

"I will."

"Promise?"

"I promise."

"See that you keep it. The more desperate Wolf gets, the more vicious he'll get, too. I don't want you anywhere near him." His hand tightened on my shoulder. "I want you safe, Ruth. I don't know how it happened, but—" He stopped speaking, leaned and kissed me lightly on the lips, removed his hand from my shoulder, and stepped away. "You're a woman it's a pleasure to be around. I'd like to keep it that way."

I smiled, happy with what I saw on his face and heard in his voice. Not passion just yet, but warmth and surprise and a touch of perplexity, like he was lost and couldn't quite remember the way back.

On my walk home to the boarding house, I remembered that parting moment with Silas as wholly satisfying because, as I told myself, it's a woman's duty to keep her man just a little off balance and from his expression, I was succeeding. Then I stopped in my tracks, realizing what I had just done, how I had used the words *her man* to refer to Silas Carpenter and me. Exactly how and when those feelings of belonging and ownership blossomed, I couldn't have said; Silas wasn't the only one to feel perplexed. I hadn't planned or even expected it to be so, but for all the mystery of it, *her man* was exactly what Silas had become in my life.

11

It took Mr. Jones two days to connect whatever wires he needed to connect, set up the telegraph equipment he brought, and have our telegraph office once more up and running. It felt good to be in touch with the outside world once again. I hadn't liked the feeling of living on an island in the middle of Nebraska. Every time I looked down the street that Saturday, I saw a gathering of people in from the outlying farms and ranches standing in front of the new building doing nothing but stare at it like they had never seen a telegraph office before. Evidently, I wasn't the only person that appreciated being reconnected.

Business was brisk as usual, and I was tired from a day of standing but not too tired to take a detour across the street to the hardware store. Two full days had passed since Joe Chandler had been mistakenly jailed. I left the Chandlers alone because I thought they might harbor some bad feelings toward the citizens of New Hope, which included me whether I liked it or not, and need time to recover from having their past lives announced to everyone in town. The hardware store had opened for business every morning since that awful day, but until Saturday, I had not seen much traffic going in and out. Saturday was different, however, and the few times I stepped outside the barber shop to enjoy the late April sunshine, I had noticed that the hardware store enjoyed a steady stream of customers.

When I closed the barber shop, the sign in the hardware window still read open. Joe looked up when I entered.

"Ruth," he said by way of greeting and went back to counting whatever small items were spread on the counter.

"Hello, Joe. Were you as busy as I was? It was just clip, clip, clip for me all day."

He made a final count and wrote down a number in the ledger book in front of him before he answered, "We did a solid business today, and I've got two new big orders to fill, one from Herman Kendall and the other from that new fella that bought the Delaware spread." Hearing the happy tone to Joe's voice made me feel happy myself.

"So you plan to stay in New Hope?" I asked. My question might have seemed just another intrusion into his private life, but I hoped Joe realized it came from good intentions.

"I think I've convinced Ellie we should stay. She wasn't keen on it at first, mad as a wet hen and ready to pack up everything and be gone tomorrow."

"I hope that won't happen."

"Maybe you could talk to her, Ruth. Ellie admires you highly. She'll listen to you." Joe turned and went to the doorway to call into the back, "El, someone's here to see you." Then to me, "Go on back, Ruth. She's at the stove."

The feminine touches of Ellie Chandler were everywhere: a bunch of wildflowers in a small jar in the middle of the table, a brightly crocheted afghan thrown over the back of the rocking chair that sat next to the stove, a small display of china cups stretched across a shelf on the wall. Ellie herself stood at the stove with a baby balanced on one hip, yet somehow managing to stir a pot of stew that smelled rich with beef and onion.

"Joe said I should come back," I told her, "but I can see you're busy."

She propped the stirring spoon against the pot and turned to smile at me. "With these babies, I'm always busy, Ruth, whenever and wherever you find me."

I took a breath and started in. "I was glad to hear Joe say you'd be staying in New Hope, Ellie. I worried that you'd be so mad about what happened, not that you don't have a right to be mad, that you'd want to leave as soon as you could get everything packed."

Ellie sat down at the table and moved the baby to her lap, unbuttoned her dress, and began to nurse him. She seemed to be thinking more about my words than the baby at her breast, and I supposed that with two babies, she had probably grown used to buttoning and unbuttoning and didn't give it much thought any more. I sat down across from her.

"I won't lie, Ruth. I want to leave and I've fussed at Joe about it since, but he doesn't want to go, and he fusses back at me, and that's not like him, at all."

"Can't you find it in your heart to forgive us, Ellie? I know we did wrong, but people are so frightened after what happened to Eddie Barts that they aren't acting like they know they should. Can't you at least try to forgive us?" I remembered the reverend's Easter sermon about loving each other, about being tender-hearted and forgiving each other. It was a hard task he gave us.

"Oh, Ruth." Ellie's voice was shaky. "It isn't that, and it sure isn't you. It's people knowing what I used to be that I can't stand, knowing what I used to do. I thought that was all behind me, but now that everyone knows, I can't bring myself to go out on the street." I heard anguish in her tone and I understood her feelings. Surely everyone had done things they were ashamed of, and how would a person feel if those actions were announced before a crowd of onlookers? I would hate it, I knew that.

I was quiet a long time. The baby – Matthew? Lucas? his chin was hidden against his mother – made soft slurping sounds, took a breath, and went back for seconds.

"I don't know what to say, Ellie, except we all have secrets we'd like to keep hidden and we've all done things we don't want shouted from the rooftops, but it's just because we're human. I can't speak for others, but I can tell you I don't think worse of you. I admire you."

She didn't ask the obvious but gave me a questioning look.

"You left your old life behind and you worked hard and you stayed true to Joe and now you've got two beautiful babies and a husband that loves you. There are a lot of things about you to admire. I wish you'd stay. You were right when you said that New Hope needs you more than you need it." My speech done, I stood up. "Like I said, I can't speak for anybody else, but that's how I feel. Now I have to get home. Poor Danny's not getting anything near as good as what you've got cooking."

Ellie set the baby in her lap and fastened the front of her dress before she looked at me. "Thank you, Ruth."

"You're welcome, Ellie."

I passed Joe on my way out of the store and gave a shrug in response to his questioning look, but privately I thought that if he wanted to stay in town, Ellie would find it in her to want the same. And the citizens of New Hope had better mind their manners or they'd hear about it from me. The Chandlers were two people that knew more than their fair share about unhappiness and suffering and loneliness. With time, memories of the bad things might fade, but the good things they shared – love and faithfulness and making the other person whole – had a way of going on forever.

Early Saturday night was the busiest time for baths in the back room of the boarding house, and it had long been Danny's chore. It wasn't just that he had the muscles to empty the bath tub and then fill it with more fresh hot water for the next guest, although that's certainly part of the reason Danny handled the bath tasks. Another equally important fact was that most of the people hiring a bath were men, and they did not take to having a woman around when they were in the altogether. Frankly, considering the specimens that stopped for a bath before they began a night of carousing, I preferred not to be around them, either. The odor peculiar to a man who has not bathed any part of his person for at least a full week was not one of my favorite fragrances. So Danny did it all, from collecting the money to heating the water to putting out the lavender soap and fresh towels. As reward for all his efforts, I tried to have one of his favorites for supper, and that night it was fried chicken. He was partial to the dark pieces and could make his way through drumsticks and thighs without any effort at all. Over time, I learned to enjoy the white meat.

After supper on the same Saturday I visited with Ellie Chandler, I joined Danny on the front porch where he sat on the top step tossing a stick for Othello to fetch. It remained a marvel how that dog never tired of fetching the same stick over and over, acting each time as if he had never imagined there could be so much fun in the world. Arranging my skirts, I sat down next to Danny.

"How's the poem coming?" I asked.

"All right." Toss the stick.

"There's about four weeks left before the closing program."

"I know." Pull the stick from between Othello's clenched teeth.

"Do you think you'll have it memorized by then?"

"I think so." Toss the stick again. "But Mr. Tiglioni says that poetry won't teach me to be a man." In a bid for Danny's attention, Othello dropped the retrieved stick by Danny and sat panting in front of him with a big dog grin on his face, waiting for the next throw. "He says there are better things for a man to know than poetry."

"Such as?"

"How to take care of yourself. How to put money away in the bank. How to be the best at what you do. How to make sure you get everything that's coming to you. How to hold your own with other men."

"I can't argue with Mr. Tiglioni, but you can learn all those things and still like poetry."

"Mr. Tiglioni says poetry is just words on paper that don't mean anything to anybody."

I had the sudden memory of my wedding night, Duncan next to me in bed and turning onto his side to whisper against my cheek, "I love thee to the level of every day's / Most quiet need, by sun and candlelight." There was more to it, but those are the words I remember from that night, how they stirred me, took all my nervousness away, and turned me into his arms. Since my husband's passing, I had read and reread the book of poetry he brought with him from England: *Sonnets from the Portuguese.* I would never meet their author, Mrs. Browning, because she was long dead, but I understood her as if we were sisters. I wanted to tell Danny that poetry had its place, and when a man spoke it to a woman, it held power to break down walls, but I didn't have the words a fifteen-year-old boy would understand. Another ten years and a wife of his own and he would appreciate what I had to say, but not now.

"That may be true for some people," I said, "but don't be too quick to believe everything Mr. Tiglioni says about poetry."

"He knows a lot, though, and he's seen a lot. He's been to Chicago and St. Louis."

"I'm glad you're getting along with Mr. Tiglioni."

Danny nodded. "I like him, and I'm learning a lot more from him than I ever learned from Mr. Stenton."

"But you're still planning to recite your poem at the closing program, aren't you?"

Danny hesitated before he said, "If you want me to."

"I do. It would make me proud."

"Then I will." Danny lifted his hand that held the stick. Othello's ears stood at attention and his eyes fixed on Danny's hand as the dog rose to its feet.

In the same ungainly way as Othello, I pushed myself to my feet. It had been a long and tiring day, and I had been on my feet for most of it. "Thank you," I said, resting a hand lightly on the boy's shoulder as support.

Danny looked up at me and smiled. "I'll get it right, too. I promise." He tossed the stick and Othello raced after it.

The dog would never tire of the stick game because anything Danny did was near to perfect. Love seemed to work that way.

Back inside, I felt sad, but whether it was the unexpected intimate memory of Duncan or the fact that Danny didn't have a father of his own to teach him about being a man I didn't know. Maybe neither. Maybe both.

I couldn't have repeated one word of the sermon I heard at church the next morning because I was too wrapped up in studying the minister's tones and expressions. I might tell Silas in no uncertain terms that Reverend Shulte could not possibly, under any circumstances, be Emmett Wolf, but there was a tiny part of me, no bigger than a sliver, that doubted. What better way for a sly man to hide than behind a pulpit, said a voice in my head, and so I studied the preacher as he smiled and sang, read and exhorted. After the service, he stood in the doorway wishing the file of exiting worshipers a good morning, but when I reached him, he said in a low voice, "Stay a moment, Ruth," before he spoke to the person behind me. I waited to the side, still watching. Was it possible that the smiling man in the dark suit, the one inquiring about babies and their stomach aches, about spring planting and a newly built barn was the same man who had shot down Dorie Lindquist as she fled her burning home clutching her daughters? It could not be. And yet... I recalled Eddie Barts' ruined face. Who in all of New Hope would Eddie have trusted more than the preacher?

Even as I had those thoughts, Cora Barts stopped a moment in front of the reverend. It was the first time since Eddie's death that the Barts family had attended church. All of Clayton's family had filled up a whole bench, with Cora on the very end. Clayton sat stone-faced, his sons the same, but the two women, Clayton's wife and mother, reached for their handkerchiefs every so often. I remembered those days after Duncan died, how a sight or a smell or a sound could bring tears. And sometimes there was no reason at all, only the tears. My heart went out to old Mrs. Barts. Parents did not expect to bury their children.

She walked past where I stood and stopped to speak a few courteous words. Did she really care about the weather or the newly planted garden? I doubted it, but even in grief, a person has to find something to say.

Finally, the congregation on its way home for their Sunday dinners, Reverend Shulte walked over to where I stood. Lydia started home with the children, then turned as if to come back and join us, but the minister gave her a quick shake of the head. Reading her husband's signal, his wife and the children continued their way home.

"Come in and sit down a minute, Ruth."

We sat on the very front bench, each of us turned sideways to face the other the best we could. Someday the congregation hoped to have enough money to order real church pews, the kind with a carved design on each end and a more comfortable curve to the edge of the seat, but what we had now and would likely have for a few years to come were makeshift benches with half backs and a spindly arm at each end, a practical necessity because without the arm rail, an inattentive person could get pushed right off the end of the bench. That and splinters from the seats had both been known to happen.

The minister had called the meeting and I waited for him to say what was on his mind. He was a good listener, as good as Silas Carpenter, but in a different way. Silas listened so he wouldn't miss anything important to his quest for Emmett Wolf. I always thought Reverend Shulte listened so he could figure out the best way to help you. That's how I had felt when I poured out my grief and anger to the man four years before, and I wanted it to be the truth.

"I had a visit from Mr. Carpenter yesterday, Ruth. He was asking about my years before I came here, and I understand why. New Hope's my flock, and I know when they're restless. They're restless now."

"And frightened," I said.

"Yes, and frightened. I believe you and Mr. Carpenter have become good friends." I was surprised by the observation but couldn't deny it. "When he mentions you," Pastor Shulte went on, "his voice changes. Softens. I believe there might be some feeling there, but that's not my business. Not yet, anyway." He smiled slightly. "I know from my talk with Carpenter that he has suspicions about me, and I know from what he said that you don't agree with him. I appreciate that, and I wanted you to hear from me, not from the deputy, what I told him. I wasn't always a man of the cloth, Ruth, and it took some years for me to figure out what I was meant to be. I'm not proud of a lot of my actions during those early years. There are some things I did that still shame me at the memory. I know the good Lord has forgiven and forgotten them, but I have a hard time doing the same. Then six years ago, I got led to a small Bible college in Michigan, and I graduated with a certificate that hangs on my wall today. You've seen it."

I nodded, remembering the fancy lettering and the gilt print of the certificate. Grace Seminary. Graduate of the School of Biblical Studies. An impressive document in a place of honor in the minister's study.

The pastor continued, "At first, it was just a piece of paper. I wandered for a year or two looking for a place to settle, looking for a place that felt right. Then I met Lydia, and we came to New Hope. From the start, I knew this was where God wanted us to be. I still believe that." He stood up and paced a few steps away from me before he turned back in my direction. "But what you should know is that except for that piece of paper on the wall, there's no proof for anything I just told you. The school burned down and the fire destroyed all its records, and until I met Lydia four years ago, I wasn't any place special doing anything out of the ordinary. Working here and there. Waiting to find God – well, more like waiting for Him to find me. I doubt there's a soul who'd remember me." He sat down again. "I can't prove where I was ten years ago or even five years ago, but I wanted you to

know that I am who I say I am. I'm not a murderous outlaw.
I'm not Emmett Wolf."

"Why are you telling me this?" I asked.

I don't think that's what he hoped my response would
be, but he answered in an even voice, "When I came to New
Hope, you were a woman being eaten alive by grief and
anger. I'll never forget how you listened to me, Ruth, listened
and believed what I said. I prayed for the right words, and I
watched those godly words heal you. It was a miracle, and I
needed it as much as you did. Now if I turn out to be this
man, this Emmett Wolf, you'll think everything I told you
was a lie, and it's not. Everything I've ever said about faith
and trust and hope for the future is God's truth, Ruth, and
everything I'm telling you now is the same. I just wanted you
to know that my words and my calling are true. Everybody's
got a past, but mine belongs to Gerald Shulte, not Emmet
Wolf." We sat in silence for a while, I mulling over everything
he said and him looking straight ahead at the wooden altar
with its plain, straight cross in the center. New Hope was
proud of its church in the same way it was proud of its
school. We were a civilized community. Religion, education,
law and order were all important to us.

"Thank you for telling me," I said.

At that moment, sitting in a quiet church beside a man I
held in high esteem, it was easy to believe everything he said.
I certainly wanted to believe him. But I knew that Si's stern,
gray gaze had a power of its own, and I doubted that Silas
had believed one word of the minister's story. Reverend
Shulte met my gaze with a serious one of his own and then
smiled. There was relief on his face and kindness, too. I've
done my duty, his expression said, and now it's out of my
hands. We stood at the same time.

"Thank you for listening, Ruth."

He followed me down the center aisle of the church, and
we stepped outside into a sunny Sunday afternoon. Gerald
Shulte, the man who represented the presence of God in

New Hope, looked calm and at peace with the world as we said good bye. I only wished I shared those same feelings.

That following week, now the end of April, Jeff McGruder came to say good bye. He waited for me on the bench outside the barber shop, leaning back with his shoulders against the building, eyes closed and legs splayed out in front of him. When he heard me pull the shop's door shut, he sat upright and went to rise.

"No," I said. "I'll come join you." I sat down beside him and turned to look at him. "I believe you need a haircut, Captain."

He ran the fingers of one hand through the curls that lay against his collar. "I've been on patrol up in Wyoming. Just got back last night and wanted to let Carpenter know what I found out about those guns." I didn't ask the obvious. If Silas wanted me to know, I presumed he'd tell me later. I hadn't seen much of Si Carpenter for the past few days, and the week had moved along the way it used to move along: Lizbeth rushing through the front door of the boarding house fearful she was late, me off to the barber shop, then boarding house work and supper with Danny, trying to catch up on his school and his work at the freight company. Normal life. The way it used to be. Before.

"I'm glad to see the two of you getting along," I said.

"He's a man I'd want at my back in a skirmish, I can tell you that." Pause. "I was jealous, Ruth, when I first saw the two of you together. There was something— Well it doesn't matter now, but at the time, it bothered me to see how you enjoyed his company. You do, don't you?"

"What? Enjoy being in the company of Silas Carpenter?"

"Yes."

"That's a funny way to put it, Jeff, but the answer is yes. We've become friends."

"Friends," he repeated. "Well, maybe that's all it is, but if it ends up being more, you could do worse than Carpenter. He's a man to be trusted. He'd never do you any harm."

I wondered about that, about the different kinds of harm that can come to a woman's heart, but aloud I said, "It's just friends, Jeff. He's got his hands full right now."

"Emmett Wolf. I know. We talked some about Wolf during our travels up to Garfield County." The Captain cleared his throat. "I've come to say good bye, Ruth. That's why I was waiting for you."

"Good bye for good?"

"Yes. I'm transferring to Fort McKinney in Wyoming Territory."

"Is it dangerous?" I couldn't help but think what a lure all that thick blonde hair might be to a belligerent warrior bent on revenge for the death and destruction of the recent Indian Wars, death and destruction on both sides and both sides with long memories and short tempers.

"Not like it used to be but with more to offer than Cottonwood. Fort McKinney's charged with keeping the Sioux and the Cheyenne off the warpath."

"And Major Prentiss is willing to let you go?"

"He's willing."

"Well, if it's what you want, I'm happy for you."

"Thank you." Pause. "I just want to say, Ruth, that you're the finest woman I've ever met, and I'll never forget you. You can't force a woman to care for you. Carpenter said that to me and I see now that he's right, that I was trying to force you to care for me. When a woman's made up her mind, it's best to say "yes, ma'am," and move on to something else. It's more respectful to the woman," then spoiling his fine speech he concluded, "even if she's got it all wrong." I swallowed a laugh, trying to follow his well-intentioned lead of being respectful and kind, and stood, holding out my hand.

"Good bye, Jeff. I wish you the best."

He took my hand, then surprised me by bending to kiss me. I turned my face at the last minute so that the kiss landed on my cheek. I allowed him that first – and last – liberty, but there was a limit to my generosity.

"Good bye, Ruth. With everything that's going on around here, I wouldn't feel right leaving you if you didn't have Carpenter taking care of you."

"I wouldn't say he's taking care of me," I protested.

Jeff McGruder shook his head at the continuing error of my ways, a gesture that reminded me why spending extended time in his company often sent me in search of a frying pan, smiled and said, "Yes, ma'am." He mounted his horse that waited for him at the rail, looked down at me, brandished his hat in an expansive farewell gesture, turned south, and disappeared from view. I never saw Jeff McGruder again, and while I don't mean to sound unkind or disrespectful, I will admit that I never missed him after he left. Of course, it's possible that because I'm a woman, I've got that all wrong.

When I went to drop off return letters to my sisters that Thursday, I was surprised to see Julia and Phil Tiglioni along with their little daughters standing on the train platform. Phil came over to me.

"It's the judge," he said. "We got a wire last night that he had some kind of attack. Sounds like his heart, but whatever it was, it doesn't look good. He's alive but not awake."

"I'm sorry," I said, glancing over at Julia. She had a girl by each hand but lifted a chin to me in acknowledgement of what she knew Phil had just told me and gave a weak smile.

"I left some notes for Danny about some things he could do while I'm away. He knows how to handle orders when they come in on the train, where to unload the boxes, and how to stack them and the like. There might be a couple of folks in to pick up their orders, and Danny knows how to mark it all down in the accounting book. He's a smart boy, Ruth."

"Thank you. I've always thought so, but maybe book learning isn't where he's strongest."

"It's not book learning that makes a man, it's grit and purpose."

"How long will you be gone?" I asked.

"That depends on what happens with the judge, but no doubt Julia and the girls will stay on a while. I'll stay as long as she needs me." The train whistle gave a blast. "You watch your step, Ruth, with everything that's going on in town. I don't mind telling you I'm glad to get Julia away from New Hope until Carpenter catches this outlaw Wolf, though it doesn't seem to me our deputy is moving very fast on his task."

I heard the criticism in Phil's voice and was indignant on Si's behalf. "Well, he is," I said. "Silas has it narrowed down enough to know who couldn't be Emmett Wolf, and in a small place like New Hope, that doesn't leave many who can't account for the past ten years." The thought of Gerald Shulte worried me because he was the only one I knew that fell into that category. "It'll be over soon, Phil, and we'll all be glad of it. Deputy Carpenter has been tracking Emmett Wolf a long time, so if he says he's close to discovering the man, I believe him."

"I hope you're right." The train whistle blew again, and Julia called her husband's name in a low voice. "Coming," he said.

I waved good bye to the little girls, and Bella and Lucy waved back, both curly-haired and cute as could be. They would grow into beauties like their mother. On my walk back to the barber shop, I wondered when I would see Julia again. If her father needed care, I doubted she would leave him. It always seemed to me that if for emergency's sake Julia Tiglioni had to pick between her father and her husband, Phil would be the one doing his own cooking.

After supper that first Friday in May, Silas appeared in the doorway to The Addition where I was cleaning up after the meal. He knocked lightly, and when I looked over at him, he said, "Come for a walk, Ruth?" My heart gave a little lurch from pleasure, and I smiled as I quickly untied my apron strings.

"Yes." By the end of the day, I knew I didn't look my best and tried to tuck my hair back behind its pins.

"Don't fuss, Ruth. You look pretty just like you are."

I fussed anyway, pulled out all the pins so my hair fell loose and used an old strip of ribbon from the sideboard to pull my long, unruly hair back from my face.

"There," I said. When I looked up, Silas was watching me and for just a moment I thought I saw my own yearning reflected in his eyes. Almost a hunger. I had been feeling that on and off for some time now.

He stepped back and without speaking followed me into the hallway, out the front door of the boarding house, and down through the front gate.

"I love the month of May," I said, by way of conversation. "Nature starts to show her true colors." I think the words sent both our thoughts in the same direction, toward Emmett Wolf and discovering his true colors, and I regretted my words. We turned toward the river and our usual walk along the footpath that followed it.

"I understand your friend McGruder said his goodbyes earlier this week," Silas said.

"He's off to find adventure and thinks he'll find it in Wyoming Territory. I hope he does."

"I imagine you'll miss him."

I thought Silas was looking for some kind of reassurance and decided not to give it to him that easily. I won't miss him nearly as much as I'd miss you if you left, I wanted to say, but aloud I replied, "A little. We've been friends for a few years now, and I don't hold friends cheap. And Jeff always meant well."

"I know he thought highly of you."

"In his own way. Of course, he thought highly of you, too." I couldn't keep the mischief from my voice, and Silas sent a glance in my direction. "He appreciated all the good advice you gave him. He considers you quite the expert on women, you know." By then Si knew for certain I was teasing. "It's a pity you didn't come to New Hope sooner," I went on, "because with all your good advice, Jeff and I might have made a go of it." Now I was the one looking for reassurance.

Fortunately, Silas wasn't as begrudging as I was. He stopped, turned to me, took me by the forearms, and pulled me against him. "I wanted to see the backside of that man the first time I ever heard him use your name. Any advice I gave him was intended to get him to keep his distance," Si said and kissed me, a long, rough, hungry kiss that I matched without effort. Both of us had been alone a long time, and what we felt between us could have flamed into something more if we were anywhere but in the middle of a public path along a public river. I didn't know if I was relieved or disappointed that we had to settle for kissing. After a while, when I stood encircled by his arms with my head against his chest, I decided I could be content for a while with what I heard in his voice as he whispered my name. But someday, I promised myself, when this business with Wolf is over and Silas has laid the man to rest, however it happens, we will not stop with kissing. We started walking again, hands entwined because we knew that was all that was allowed us just then.

Si started to speak, cleared his throat, and spoke again. "I wanted to tell you about Gerald Shulte. That's why I asked you for a walk."

"Hmmm," I said, "then I guess I should be grateful we got to the kissing first." I squeezed his hand. "I know about Gerald Shulte, Silas. He told me he couldn't prove where he was and what he was doing five years ago, let alone ten, that the Bible college he went to burned down, and he didn't know a person who could speak for his actions or whereabouts before he met Lydia."

"He told you all that?"

"Yes."

"Why?"

I wanted Silas to understand but didn't think I had the right words to make that happen. I tried, anyway. "I told you how he helped me after Duncan's death, but I don't think you can appreciate how bad I felt then. I wasn't myself, not the Ruth Churchill I am now. I missed my husband something fierce, didn't want to think about life without him, and couldn't understand why other women's husbands were allowed to live while mine had faded away in front of my eyes. I felt like I was trapped in a tunnel black as night. Then Reverend Shulte came to New Hope. He listened, and he cared and got me out of that dark place. I trusted him, Silas. I believed every word he said. This past Sunday he told me that after he talked to you, he got worried that if I thought he lied about his past, then maybe I'd believe he lied about everything else, too. The idea troubled him. He's a man who sets great store by the truth."

I expected to hear more about Gerald Shulte's suspicious past, but instead Silas said, "What was it about Duncan Churchill that made you love him like that?"

We stopped where we had stopped twice before and turned to face the river. It was empty of traveling water fowl, but the prairie on the other side was alive with sunset birdsong.

I didn't know what to say or how to describe the only man besides my father that I had ever loved, especially to Silas Carpenter, who stirred up feelings I thought were long dead and proved me able, even eager, to love again. I picked each word with care.

"Duncan made life easier somehow. He was so full of life, even when he was dying, always finding the good in things, and he could make me laugh with a joke or a silly song. Everything was hopeful to Duncan. I never knew a single person he didn't like or who didn't like him. And that he loved me, picked me, me, Ruth Hart in little New Hope, Nebraska, when I know he traveled all over the world and could've had any woman he wanted! Well, I just couldn't believe it. The idea of being so lucky was wondrous and made me so happy!"

Something close to a growl came from Si's throat and he turned to place both hands once more on my forearms.

Instead of pulling me to him, however, he pushed away a bit and stared into my eyes.

"Listen to me," he said. "I'll never meet Duncan Churchill, and anything I'll ever know about him will be what you tell me or what I hear from other people who knew him. I've been told the same things you just said, and I believe he was a fine man, the kind of man people are drawn to, but you weren't the lucky one." Silas spaced out those last few words with firm emphasis. "Duncan Churchill was the lucky one because you loved him and you picked him, not the other way around. Any man you'd pick should count his lucky stars."

I stared back at Silas, feeling weepy for no reason I could name. Then I reached both palms to the sides of his face and drew him down to me so I could kiss him. "Thank you," I said in a whisper, not drawing away, my lips so close to his that it seemed we shared the same breath. "Thank you for that, Silas." I kissed him once more, because you can never have too much of a good thing, and dropped my hands. "I think we should get back," I said, trying to get my heartbeat and my voice back to normal. "It's getting dark, and I didn't tell Danny I was leaving. He'll worry." I took a few steps and looked back when I realized I didn't have a companion. Silas Carpenter stood with his hands at his sides, watching me and looking like a woebegone boy suddenly denied supper, hungry and confused and surprised by the circumstance.

I held out my hand. "Come along, Silas," I said.

He straightened his shoulders and with one long stride caught up with me, taking my hand in his. We were quiet until New Hope came clearly into view, then Silas dropped my hand and said, as if nothing personal had passed between us, "Still, I don't want you to be alone with your preacher. Not for any reason. Promise?"

"I've already made you so many promises I can't keep track of them all," I said, "and you'll remember that I've managed to survive in New Hope for the last ten years without you telling me what to do."

"Ruth." His tone and expression were back to Silas Carpenter, Deputy Sheriff, tracker of men and enforcer of the law. I missed the man I had felt quiver ever so slightly as my hands moved along the back of his neck, as my mouth opened to his.

I said, "I promise. Within reason and when it's convenient," because I have never been a woman that took to being dictated to. I could tell he wasn't happy, but Silas knew me well enough by then not to argue. If we have a future together, I thought, there will be days we argue a plenty, but our feelings were too fresh for that just then. So instead of argument, we spoke chaste good-nights to each other at the front gate of the boarding house before Silas continued his patrol of the town and I went inside to finish my kitchen chores.

12

So much happened the following week that remembering the details takes concentration, let alone remembering the details in their proper order. Sometimes when life is just moving along at its regular pace, one day can seem very much like the day before or the day after. That's how the week started, but it surely wasn't how it ended.

At supper on Monday, I asked Danny how things were working out at the freight company in Phil's absence, and for the first time I could recall, Danny seemed shifty with his answers. It was so noticeable to me that I finally set down my fork, rested my elbows on the table, and looked straight at him.

"Is there something you're not telling me?" I asked.

"No, ma'am," but he had a hard time holding my gaze.

"You know," I said, "that you can always wire Mr. Tiglioni in Hill City where he's visiting his father-in-law, don't you? I mean, if there's something you're worried about—"

Danny was quick with his retort. "No, ma'am. I don't need to do that. I know what to do. Mr. Tiglioni said I'm a quick learner and that he trusts me. He told me he wasn't worried about anything, and if I wanted, I could help myself to—"

He stopped just short of saying what he could help himself to, and I prompted, "Help yourself to what?"

Danny looked uncomfortable. "Well, he said anything I want, anything I find stored there in the warehouse."

"No alcohol," I said sternly. "You're too young for that. And no tobacco, either. You're not sixteen yet, and you've got plenty of time to pick your vices. You know I won't have either of them in the house."

"Yes, ma'am."

Danny knew alcohol and tobacco were forbidden to our boarders, so my words to him couldn't have come as a surprise, but by then, I was heartily tired of all his *ma'ams* and certain he was hiding something. I could just barely remember being fifteen myself, however, and could recall keeping plenty from my mother. It's the age you start dreaming of spreading your wings, when you think there's nothing you can't do and resent anyone trying to hold you back. I almost sighed. The Danny who had collapsed against my gate five years before had been sorrowing, frightened, and lonely, and he had appreciated whatever I did for him. This strapping young man in front of me was no longer any of those things. He's nearly grown, I thought, has feelings of his own and doesn't need me the way he used to. I felt a pang of regret.

"Never mind," I said. "I didn't mean to pry."

My change of tone confused him for a moment, and then he mumbled, "That's all right," before he excused himself from the table.

I wondered briefly if he had his eye on a girl, maybe someone who came to town once a week from a local farm or the Winters girl, only fourteen but sassy and just the kind of girl to catch a young man's eye. But there wasn't much to be done about that. I couldn't stop nature from taking its course, and sooner or later Danny would learn about girls all on his own.

I was washing up the supper dishes when Silas came knocking. I smiled at him as he stood in the doorway.

"I've just finished," I said, thinking – hoping – he wanted to propose another walk, but that wasn't his intention.

"I wanted you to know that I'll be sleeping down at the jail for a while." I noticed that his saddle bag filled with his worldly goods was slung over his shoulder.

"Whatever for?" I was surprised by the announcement and felt a quick, sharp disappointment at the idea of not falling asleep to the comforting sound of him climbing the stairs.

"It'll be safer."

"You think you're in danger here at my boarding house?" The idea made no sense and my surprise sounded in my voice.

"I think my being here could put you in danger," he said. I examined his face for a hint of what he was talking about.

"Has something happened, Silas? Have you found Emmett Wolf?"

Silas gave a cautious answer. "Not exactly – to both of your questions."

"What does *not exactly* mean?" This conversation following up on my recent exchange with Danny was trying my patience.

"I'm close to being certain, so close I'd bet money on who the man is, and Wolf has got to know that. I feel pretty sure it'll stay quiet around here for the next few days, but I need a little more information, and I don't want to take a chance that if he tries something in the meanwhile, you could get caught in the crossfire. It's just better if I'm not staying here and everybody in town knows I'm not here."

"Can you tell me who—?" I began, but Silas shook his head.

"Don't ask. The less you know the better. You're a woman who finds it hard to hide her feelings." To prove his point, he said, his tone gentle, "Don't look like that, Ruth. It'll be over soon enough."

"Not soon enough for me, but you be careful."

"I will."

"Promise?"

"Within reason and when it's convenient," he said, and grinned.

Oh, that man! To use my own words against me! I had to fight the urge to march right over and kiss him squarely on the mouth. He didn't lose the grin so I think my inclination must have shown on my face.

"If I'm arears paying for the room, you can let me know what I owe," he added.

"I will certainly do that." I'll miss having you around, I wanted to tell him, miss you surprising me in the kitchen doorway, miss your good-mornings and the security of knowing you're sleeping in the room just above me.

"Well, all right, then," he said but made no move to leave.

I considered the small cell and narrow cot down at the jail. "You'll need something for the cot. I'll ask Danny to bring you one of our pillows and a couple of warm blankets. Can you think of anything else you need for your bed?"

I didn't think about the question until it was out of my mouth and at the look on his face, I felt myself turn pink. Me, Ruth Churchill, who hadn't blushed since her wedding night! But that was the effect the man had on me.

To his credit, Silas Carpenter did not say the obvious, but I could tell he was tempted. My red face must have convinced him to go gentle with me.

"No," he said. "A blanket and pillow should do it," but we were both thinking along other lines entirely.

The next day, Sheba made a quick visit to the barber shop when I was between customers. "You and Mr. Carpenter have a falling out?" she asked.

"No."

"It's just that I noticed – well, everybody's noticed – that he moved down to the jail."

"He says it's safer for him to be there."

"Mm-hmm." She nodded slowly and gave me a knowing look. "Safer for him or you?"

"Both, I guess, and not in the way you're thinking. We haven't—I mean Silas and I have never—"

Sheba smiled at that. "If that's true, then shame on both of you. You know better than anybody, Ruth Churchill, that life's too short not to take advantage of a situation when it presents itself."

Sheba Fenway was my friend, and I never pretended with her. "Silas Carpenter is a man with a single purpose, Sheba, and right now there's no place for me in it."

She lost her smile at my serious tone. "But someday there will be," the words more question than statement of fact.

"Yes," I said, "I hope so. Someday, and it can't come too soon for me." Changing the subject, I added, "Silas says that John Bliss has a past he could trace back for the last ten years, and that Mr. Bliss can't possibly be Emmett Wolf. In fact, for all Si's digging into Mr. Bliss' past, it turns out that while Mr. Bliss has walked a few narrow lines in his time, the man isn't any kind of a criminal, at all."

Sheba's face was a study in scorn. "I don't need anyone, not you or Deputy Carpenter or any person under the sun, to tell me what I already know, Ruth." She flounced – Sheba Fenway can flounce like no woman I have ever seen; it must be all that red hair – out the front door of the barber shop without closing the door. John Bliss and Sheba Fenway, I thought to myself as I pushed the door shut and stood in contemplation with one hand still on the knob. Whoever could have imagined that?

That was the same week Mr. Stenton stopped in at the end of a day for a haircut. I hadn't spoken to him since my visit to the school, and his hair, which had not seemed to have grown at all then, now definitely needed a good trim. He was a dignified man, not given to inconsequential chatter, and the two of us were quiet as he sat down in the chair and I went about my business. When he stood and placed his coins on the counter by the mirror, he gave an additional brush to the shoulders of his waistcoat for any hair I might have missed before he turned to face me.

"Mrs. Churchill, it occurs to me that your recent visit to the school was motivated by your suspicion of my character."

"Mr. Stenton," I responded, "I won't try to deceive you. It's true that I was concerned about Danny – still am, truth be told – but because you were given the responsibility of the children of New Hope, I felt an obligation to try to be sure you were who you said you were."

"That would be the responsibility of the School Board, and as I recall, you are not on the School Board."

"I can't argue with that." We eyed each other, two people who would probably never be friends or even like each other very much. But you don't have to like your barber to get a good haircut, and I supposed the same held true about teachers.

"Has Deputy Carpenter set your mind at ease?" Mr. Stenton asked.

"He has."

"I'm glad to hear it." A brief hesitation before, "About Danny, Mrs. Churchill. He's a well-mannered, helpful young man, except of late—" I waited. Maybe I wasn't the only one who had noticed a change in the boy. "I believe he's feeling his age and ready to be done with school."

"Is he ever disrespectful to you, Mr. Stenton?"

"No, never, but he's not a boy any more, and I would not suggest he continue in school at New Hope after this year."

"I know, and I agree with you. Danny's got to find his way, but I don't know how to help him do that. I don't know much about young men."

At that, Mr. Stenton smiled. "'A boy's will is the wind's will,' Mrs. Churchill, 'and the thoughts of youth are long, long thoughts.'" I smiled, too. There is no way a person would ever consider Arthur Stenton playful, but for that one moment he came close. I realized with those words that he was a better teacher than I gave him credit for and understood that he had assigned that particular poem to Danny for a reason. *Long, long thoughts* seemed to be exactly what Danny was having. It was humbling to think that Mr.

Stenton had been aware of the fact long before I ever noticed.

In the middle of that same week, I packed up supper in a basket and carried it down to the jail. I knew that Silas was seldom still, that during the day when he wasn't out on the prairie looking for signs of strangers, he was usually on the prowl through New Hope. He didn't miss much and had come to know what was normal in town and what might demand investigation. We were a normal community, I had always thought, but with matters as they were and the shadow of Emmett Wolf hanging over Main Street, every one of us appreciated seeing the figure of Silas Carpenter about town. He was a man of composure, not given to excitement, a man methodical and steady. It was a comfort to know he was on our side. I wouldn't have wanted to face him as an enemy. I doubted Silas made himself so visible because he expected Emmett Wolf to come leaping out of the alley with guns blazing. It was more his way of reassuring the citizens of New Hope that he had things under control, and we didn't need to be afraid. Although we were afraid, anyway.

I said as much when I sat down next to him on the bench outside the jail. The only time I knew for certain that I could find him was around the supper hour, when he would walk down to the Nebraska Café and then come next door to Hart's to say hello. I treasured those hellos and made sure I stayed close to the boarding house until I saw him. That night, however, I decided to deliver supper and save him the walk south.

"Good evening, Ruth," he said when he looked up and saw me. For some reason, he had been intent on the train station, as if he expected to see Wolf step onto the platform off New Hope's last train of the day.

"Good evening, Silas. I brought you supper."

"That was thoughtful." I sat down beside him and we smiled at each other, and I remember thinking at that moment, *I believe I love this man.* I was content with the knowledge. I had loved Duncan, too, with the kind of love that made me want to sing at the top of my voice and twirl down the middle of Main Street for joy. With Silas it was different, still love, but different. Not exuberant, but quiet and sure and constant, no sudden highs and lows, only a steady flame that could flare up hot to the touch when I least expected it. It was as if, I thought, love took on the character of the person you cared for.

Supper waited in the basket, but neither of us made any effort toward it.

"It's been quiet lately, hasn't it?" I asked, finally. "I wish I believed that was a good sign, but to me it feels like the time just before a thunderstorm. Brooding, sort of, or—" I searched for the word "—menacing. The wind and thunder and lightning right over the horizon, and not a thing a person can do to stop its coming. I doubt anyone will think to tell you, but while we're all worried, the citizens of New Hope are glad to have you here with us taking our side."

"I wonder."

At his serious tone, I turned to look at him. "Wonder what?"

"If my being here hasn't made things worse for the town."

"I don't see how that could be true when Eddie Barts was killed before you arrived in New Hope."

"Emmett Wolf has a way of knowing things. He's known for a long time that I was on his trail and getting closer to him every day. Maybe if that wasn't the case, Eddie Barts would still be alive."

"Oh, *maybe!*" I said. "Maybe the sun won't go down today. Maybe the grass will turn blue tomorrow. You can *maybe* yourself all you want, Silas, but a wicked man named Emmett Wolf has killed a lot of people, and there's no reason to lay Eddie's death at your own doorstep. Wolf killed him, not you. Sometimes I think he must be a man so used to killing to get what he wants that even if he could get it another way, he wouldn't. Who knows if someone else wouldn't have been next? It seems to me from the little I know that the man finds pleasure in taking a life. You're right to stay on his trail, but I wish——"

I stopped and Silas asked in a quiet voice, "Wish what?"

"I wish," I answered, equally as quiet, "you could be content to let the law take its course with him because I fear you have your own plans for Wolf that have nothing to do with the law and a trial. Most of all, though, I wish you could learn to be at peace with yourself."

"Peace," Silas repeated. He laid one hand over mine on the bench between us. "I never knew what it was, Ruth. Too much war and wild living and these last years staying on Wolf's trail, but the first time I saw you, I remember thinking, here's a woman who's good for a man's soul. That's what you mean by peace, I think." I love a preacher's son, I thought, and I should get used to the power his words have over me.

I wanted to lay my head against his shoulder and sit like that until the moon rose, but instead, I said, "Something like that. Now come inside and have your supper. It's no doubt cold, but I'm not taking the blame for it. You're a grown man that preferred talking to eating." Silas stood and stretched without speaking while I rose and pushed open the jail door. Once he followed me inside, I went to close the door, but Silas stopped me.

"Better leave it open or you'll have the whole town talking about you being alone with me." I was unloading the basket onto the desktop but stopped long enough to shake my head at the man's innocence.

"Oh, lord, Silas, I can tell you've never lived in a small town before. If you think there's a person in New Hope that isn't already talking about the time you and I spend together, our afternoon walks and conversations on the porch steps and the like, you need to think again. I wouldn't be surprised if we were already old news."

He laughed at that, then sat down and started in on his supper while I went into the back to straighten his cot and add a second blanket at its foot. He was still eating when I returned so I went to stand in the doorway of the jail and look west across the street at Norm's feed and grain store and the Fenstermeiers' dry goods business, both closed for the day, all the merchants of New Hope enjoying their families and their suppers. It looked so commonplace that I had to sigh. How could anything as ordinary as New Hope contain the wickedness that was Emmett Wolf?

I heard Si rise and felt him come up behind me to look out at the street same as I before he put a hand on each of my shoulders. I could feel my skin grow warm under his touch. For so brief a moment I might have imagined it – but I didn't – I felt his lips on the back of my neck, a gesture so intimate I had to close my eyes for the pleasure of it. Then he stepped away and reached for the empty basket.

"I'll walk you back before it gets dark," he said, as if the moment hadn't happened.

I can't recall what we talked about as we meandered south along the boardwalk toward the boarding house. This and that. Certainly nothing about how his touch had the power to stir me or how I hated having him sleeping on the other side of town from me. Nothing like that. Just this and that.

We walked past Bliss House, the restaurant's supper crowd done. Through the front windows, I could see the girls that served the meals scurrying from table to table getting everything ready for the morning. Rumor said John Bliss was a fair man and paid his restaurant help well. I might have repeated the compliment to Sheba, but no doubt she would have reminded me that she didn't need anyone to tell her what she already knew.

The Meeting and Entertainment Hall next door to Bliss' establishments was dark and empty. In just a few weeks, we would all gather there for the school's closing program. That made me think of Danny, and I mentioned my concerns about the boy to Silas.

"Do you think it's just growing pains?" I asked. "I know a boy Danny's age could use a man around, but I'm not sure Phil Tiglioni's the right man for the job." We stepped down from the boardwalk into the alley that lay between the Meeting Hall and the barber shop, the alley we politely called Church Street because it led back to the church and the Shultes' house, but before Silas could answer my question, there was the startling crack of a gunshot and a corner of the barber shop seemed to break into a hundred pieces. I stood stunned, but Silas shoved me to the ground and threw himself over me just as a second shot sounded. The bullet kicked up dust next to where we lay and skittered down the alley. Just the two shots and then it was still.

We lay that way for what seemed like a long time, Silas shielding me with his body, keeping us both motionless. All I heard was his quick breathing above me. Finally, he asked softly, "Ruth, are you all right?"

"Yes," I said in a shaky voice. Both of us heard a third shot, farther away and down the alley directly across from us, the continuation of Church Street in the opposite direction from where we lay.

"That's where Ruby Strunk lives, Silas! Down the end of the alley where he must have run. You need to see if he's hurt Ruby." Neither of us needed to give the *he* a name.

"I don't like to leave you." Si had rolled off me and now crouched with a hand extended to help me sit.

"You need to make sure Ruby's all right," I repeated. "I'm fine, and I'll wait right here for you. Be careful. He might be waiting for you at the end of the alley." Because I wasn't the one the shooter had aimed for. I wasn't the one who had dogged his trail for the last ten years. I wasn't the Hound of Death.

Silas left without another word, moving kitty-corner across the street until he stood under the overhang at the front of the bank. As soon as he slid around the corner into the alley, he disappeared from sight. I waited for the sound of more gunshots, but none came. Instead, doors began to open. I could see Joe Chandler silhouetted against the back light of the hardware store. Sheba's door opened, too, and I saw her step outside and look around. Silas and I had been easy to sight as we stepped off the boardwalk, no one else around and nothing behind us but a prairie sky dimming at the end of a bright spring day with just enough light to make us good targets.

"Mrs. Churchill?" a man said. I had been concentrating so hard on listening for Silas that the voice and the figure standing in the entrance to the alley gave me a start. I must have given an audible gasp because he said, "It's John Bliss, Ruth." I exhaled the breath I was holding as he stepped into the alley.

"Someone took a shot at Silas and me," I said, "and maybe a shot at Ruby Strunk, too. I'm fine, but I don't know about Ruby."

Bliss came closer and crouched next to me. "You don't look fine to me," he said. I stared at him blankly for a moment and then all of a sudden, though it must have happened with that first shot, I felt something warm and sticky running down the side of my face. I put up a hand to my cheek and then squinted at my bloody palm.

"Oh," I said, 'I believe you're right."

"I'm going to get Dr. Danford. You stay right here." I barely heard him, listening as I was for the thuds of Si's footsteps against the hard-packed dirt of the street. What, I thought suddenly, if Emmett Wolf had a knife? What if, when Silas turned the corner of the alley, Wolf was in the shadows and before Silas even knew it, the outlaw had found his mark? What if Silas lay bleeding to death in the middle of the alley right across the street while I sat here like a sack of wheat doing nothing? It did not bear thinking. I shifted to my hands and knees just as Bliss returned with the doctor. Each man put a hand to one of my arms and helped me stand. Dr. Danford took my chin between his thumb and forefinger and turned my face to try to get a better look at the damage.

"John," I said, ignoring the doctor's efforts, "Silas has been gone too long. He went down the alley on the other side toward Ruby's place. I think something happened to him." Bliss sent Dr. Danford a quick look, got a nod in response, and left without a word. "You watch your step," I called after him. 'Everybody's got a gun back there." If anything happened to that man, I had the feeling I'd hear about it from Sheba.

"It's too dark to see much, Ruth," Tom Danford said, "but it looks like you picked up some splinters, and we should get them out as soon as we can."

"I told Silas I'd wait right here for him."

"Mr. Bliss will tell your Silas where you are, and you know as well as I that he wouldn't want you to sit bleeding in an alley when the doctor's office is right around the corner. He's a sensible man and he thinks the world of you."

There, I thought, if that doesn't prove my point that everyone in New Hope was well aware of what was going on between Silas and me without either of us needing to say a word.

I sat on the edge of the examining table in the room behind the pharmacy, the same room and the same table where Eddie Barts' body had been laid out, and tried not to fidget as the doctor got out a big magnifying glass and examined the side of my face. I wasn't paying much attention to his actions because I was listening for the sound of the front door opening and Si's voice. Above anything else, that's what I needed to hear for my peace of mind. Doctor Danford said something that because of my inattention to the matter at hand I had to ask him to repeat.

"I said this will take a while because you caught a lot of little splinters and I need to get each one out. We can't chance infection. There's just the one big one—" he lifted my hand to a splinter that felt as big as a tree trunk lodged by my temple at the edge of my scalp "—but it's a doozey. The alcohol is going to sting like all get-out, but it's the best way to be sure everything heals clean and neat. Do you understand what I've told you?"

"Of course, I understand. Not a single one of the splinters reached my brain, Tom," but I wasn't really taking in his words. No bell on the front door sounding. No Silas

Carpenter, safe and sound and all in one piece, waiting for me in the front of the pharmacy. Talk about splinters and alcohol didn't hold a lot of meaning for me just then.

Margery, who stood next to her husband, reached for one of my hands as Doctor Danford sighed and picked up his tweezers and the bottle of alcohol. "Steady on now, Ruth," he said.

Before he started picking wood out of my face, however, I turned to Margery. "I appreciate you being here, Margery, but I'd feel a lot better if I knew someone was out front watching for Silas. He'll worry if he steps inside and there's nobody to tell him I'm all right. I can hold my own here." She sent a quick inquiring glance to the doctor, who made a shooing motion with one hand.

"Go ahead," he said. "She's not a woman to reason with right now."

Of course, Dr. Danford was right to warn me. Even the little tugs he made hurt like blazes, and the alcohol stung so bad it brought tears to my eyes, but after the first time he asked, "Do you want to take a break?" and I replied, "No, I want it done with," he didn't bother to ask again.

When he was finished, I said with a touch of embarrassment, "I think I might be sick to my stomach, Tom," and he handed me a basin. I didn't need to use it after all, but that's how Silas Carpenter found me – sitting on the edge of the doctor's examining table, no doubt with one side of my face white as a sheet and the other covered with gauze and the blood from a multitude of small pricks beginning to soak through, all the while clutching a basin in my lap like it was my dearest possession.

Still, at the first moment Silas appeared in the doorway, none of that was important. It was like I had been holding my breath all that time and could finally let it out. Alive. The word repeated in my head. What did a few splinters matter?

Silas said my name like a question, and Dr. Danford turned from where he was washing his hands to say, "Some splinters is all, but it was hell getting them all out. As long as there's no infection, she should be fine. The big one just missed her eye, thank God, or we'd be having a different conversation." He turned toward Silas. "Did you get him?"

Silas wasn't looking at the doctor when he answered, he was looking at me. "No." The tight fury I heard in his voice was reflected on his face. What a disappointment to be at the heels of the man he had chased for so many years and then lose him! No wonder he was angry.

"Is Ruby all right?" I asked. I didn't sound like myself, too shaky and weak, and I repeated the question with more firmness.

"Yes. She stepped out her front door when she heard the first shots. He tethered a horse at her washtub and when she called out, he took a quick shot at her. To scare her back inside, I think. He's not a man to miss what he aims for."

"He missed you," I said, "so don't credit him for more skill than he's got. Did Ruby get a look at him?"

"No. It was dark and being shot at scared the hell out of the poor woman and all her children, besides. I couldn't get much out of her. She went back inside, pushed a chair against the door, and wouldn't come out until she was convinced I was who I said I was. It took a while."

"I'm sorry," I said.

Silas stepped into the room and put two fingers very lightly against the bandage on my face. "No," he said. "I'm sorry. I wouldn't have you hurt for the world. You know that, don't you, Ruth?"

Tom Danford said, "You come see me first thing in the morning, Ruth," and slid out of the room without another word, closing the door quietly behind him.

"I do know that, Silas, and it's not as bad as it looks."

He bent to kiss me very gently on the lips. "Well, it looks pretty bad, whatever you say. I don't like seeing you like this."

I took hold of his arm. "Everything heals with time, heads and hearts both. Now help me off this table, would you, please? I want to go home." I was still a little woozy on my feet and had to hold onto him tightly for a moment until I got my balance.

"I could carry you back."

"I should say not!" I said, horrified at the idea. "Because of a few splinters?" We stood very close and I gave him a searching glance. "You still look angry, Silas. It wasn't your fault Wolf got away."

"Emmett Wolf has gotten away before. I've learned patience dealing with him, and I know I'll win in the end. He's a worried man because I'm closer now than I've ever been, and I won't stop until I have him. He should be worried, too, worried more than ever, because he could've killed you, Ruth, and I won't have it." It was probably being treated like one of Sheba's pincushions for the last hour that weakened me and allowed tears. His tone more than his words was what affected me. Under the grim resolve in his voice, I heard tenderness and something else he probably wasn't fully aware of just yet, though I heard it loud and clear, being more familiar with love than Silas Carpenter. He used his thumb to wipe away a tear from my good cheek before he said, so low I almost missed it, "A man has an obligation to his own." Then, as if his voice and his words had not told me what I wanted to hear, had not set my heart racing, he added, "Come on, Ruth. Let's get you home." That was frosting on the cake, I thought as I took his arm. *Home.*

13

We crossed Main Street slowly. I could see the figures of people standing on the boardwalk outside their establishments, watching, and knew they were concerned more about the threat of violence to their own families than they were about me. I understood their feelings. We seldom heard gunfire within the city limits of New Hope. Once in a while a cowpoke over at the Music Hall shot off his revolver for no reason except high spirits – spirits in more than one sense – but John Bliss didn't brook that kind of rowdiness and always managed to squelch both noise and noise maker. Rifle shots aimed at people were unheard of. And frightening.

Sheba waited in front of the gate to the boarding house. "Is she all right?" she asked Silas.

"I'm right here, Sheba," I said. "My hearing and my ability to speak are just fine."

She sent Silas a quick grin before giving her attention to me. "Which is more than I can say about your face. Even in the dark, you look awful."

"Well, thank you. I can always count on my friends to make me feel better." After that heavy dose of bad temper, I said in a milder tone, "One of the shots you heard kicked up some splinters from the corner of the barber shop, but Tom cleaned me up and says I'll live to a ripe old age."

"Do you need me?" Sheba gave a sideways look at Silas. "No, I guess not, but you make sure she rests for a while, Mr. Carpenter. Don't let her reach for a broom or a ledger book." With a direct look at me, Sheba pronounced, "Rest, Ruth."

"I will," I said, then, "By the way, it's likely you'll see John Bliss before I do, so be sure to thank him for his help on my behalf." Sheba wanted to give me a tart reply but contented herself with, "I'll do that," before she went back to her shop.

Inside the boarding house, Danny and the boarders were huddled together in the foyer. They all turned in the direction of the front door when we entered.

"Everyone's fine." I spoke first to head off any inquiries. "We had some shooting, as I know you heard, and I got a few splinters in my face, but the shooter has long departed, and we are all safe in the hands of Deputy Carpenter. You can do what you please, return to your rooms or go for a stroll, whatever you choose." Mr. Jones, the telegraph man, raised his eyebrows at that, but no one commented aloud as they turned toward the stairs and their rooms, speaking to each other in low voices as they did so.

Only Danny remained. "You're all right, then," he said, looking a lot younger than fifteen just then.

"I am. Dr. Danford cleaned out all the splinters."

"Good." The boy shifted his stance from one foot to the other. "I was worried. I didn't know what to do."

"It looks like you managed to keep all our boarders quiet and calm, and that was good thinking, wasn't it, Silas?"

"Yes." He watched Danny with an objective gaze, but I didn't know exactly what he was looking for. "Maybe you could go and turn down the covers on Ruth's bed."

"I have no intention of going to bed this early," I retorted. "Danny, if you'd please pull the rocking chair out here by the fireplace and then make me a cup of hot tea, I would like to sit for a while."

Danny, who had once been as eager as a puppy to do whatever I asked, turned his attention to Silas to get his nod of approval before following up on my request. I'll have to get used to that, I thought. Boys of a certain age get their approval more from men than women. I already missed the youngster Danny had been but thought that with Si Carpenter, he would have a good example to follow.

Once situated in the rocking chair and awaiting my tea, I said to Silas, "I'm fine now. I can see you've got things you want to do."

He paced between the windows on each side of the front door, not looking out but deep in thought about something. At my words, he looked over at me.

"I don't like leaving you."

"Silas, I was never the target. You know that as well as I do. I'm safe as can be, and I can see how restless you are to be doing something, though what you can think to do at this late hour, I can't imagine."

"I need to take a look at a couple spots in town that would make good hiding places, even if it appears our man is long gone by now. Then I need to make a trip to the fort."

"Tonight?" I was dismayed at the idea.

"Yes. I need to send a telegram."

"Mr. Jones is right upstairs."

"I don't want to take a chance with the man's life."

Oh." I mulled his words a moment. "You're going to send a telegram using the name of someone in New Hope that Mr. Jones will recognize."

"Yes."

I knew better than to ask anything more because Silas wouldn't tell me anything more, for the same reason he would ride all the way to the fort to send a telegram when we had a perfectly good working telegraph office in New Hope.

"I don't like it," I said. "Evil is most active at night, and you'll be out in it." I didn't know if I was talking about the night or the evil. Probably both.

"I'll be careful."

"Because," I went on as if he hadn't spoken, "you're not on your own any more. It's not just you at risk. There's two of us now, Silas, you and me. Do you understand?"

"I never meant for that to happen."

That wasn't quite the response I wanted to hear, but I was suddenly tired, and my face had begun a steady ache that

I thought would keep me awake regardless of any weariness I felt.

"The world is full of things we never meant to happen but that happen, anyway, usually in spite of our intentions and not because of them. I'm just reminding you that your well-being is tied up with mine, whether you like it or not."

He came to stand behind the chair and dropped a kiss on the top of my head. "I know," he said. "I never met a woman more deserving of happiness than you, and I don't want to be the one to bring more grief into your life."

"Too late for that," I murmured. "Now you'd better go. And watch your step, Silas Carpenter. The road to the fort is pretty open but still—" Danny came in from The Addition holding a mug of tea with both hands.

"I'll be careful." To Danny, "You watch out for Ruth. Make sure she has what she needs."

"Yes, sir."

I thanked Danny for the tea, and when I looked up from my first sip, Silas was already gone.

I slept on and off in the chair all night and rose at my usual time to put breakfast on the table, but Danny was at the stove ahead of me. He was not an early riser, and the sight surprised me.

"Did you get any sleep?" I asked.

"Yes." He pushed the bacon around in the pan and reached for the coffee pot. "If you sit down at the table, I'll pour you some coffee." I didn't need a second invitation. I like my morning coffee and felt the need for it, especially just then. My face hurt from the doctor's probing and my back hurt from sleeping in the rocking chair. Age is creeping up on me, I thought, and decided Sheba was right – life was too short not to take advantage of a situation when it presented itself. I wondered if Silas was back from the fort yet. I wondered if he was safe.

"Have you seen Silas this morning?" I asked. Danny nodded.

"He stopped in for a few minutes while you were sleeping. Said he was going to get some sleep at the jail."

We ate breakfast together, but Danny ate most of it himself while I watched him. All I wanted was my coffee and not much else. My stomach hadn't settled from Dr. Danford's work with his tweezers, and the memory of it still made me queasy.

"Are you still managing at the warehouse all right without Mr. Tiglioni being there?"

Danny nodded, swallowed, and said, "It's not hard work. Someone came all the way from Stapleton to pick up a special order yesterday, and I knew exactly what to do."

"Special order? That sounds interesting. Do you know what it was?" I was flabbergasted to see Danny's brown face turn rosy at my question. Had someone ordered girlie pictures? Indecent magazines? What else would make a young man blush like that? If I didn't know better, I might have guessed a guilty conscience of some sort, but that made no sense. Someone picking up an order from the warehouse wouldn't lend itself to blushing. I was curious but tired, too, and felt a quick sympathy for Danny having to answer embarrassing questions from a female. Boys liked their privacy. I knew that much."

"Well, never mind," I said, rising from the table. "I'm going to put on a fresh shirtwaist before I go see Dr. Danford. I'll leave a note for Lizbeth so she knows I'm at the barber shop." He looked up at me, his normal color returned. "How's the poem coming?" I asked. For just a moment, I could tell Danny didn't know what poem I meant, and that bothered me more than his blush. He was so caught up in other thoughts, whatever they were, that the poem had slipped his mind.

"I've got it down." He answered so quickly that I almost thought I had imagined the momentary blank look in his eyes.

"Good." I paused. "You know," I said, "that it doesn't matter to me what you do in school or in life, for that matter, as long as you do it honestly and the best you can. You understand that, don't you, Danny?"

"I do," but he looked briefly unhappy with the question. I'll ask Silas to talk to him, I told myself, but as it turned out, I didn't need to do that to get my answers.

Doctor Danford cleaned my face with lye soap before he reapplied alcohol, and I was relieved that it didn't hurt anything like the night before.

"The little spots are already healing," he told me, "but I want to keep an eye on that gash along your hairline. That was a mean one. We should keep that covered with a bandage for a while longer."

"Thank you, Tom," I said. "You do good work with a tweezers."

He laughed. "It's a skill I hope I don't have to use again for a while. Margery and I – well, everybody in town was relieved it wasn't worse. There isn't one of us who doesn't think highly of you."

I fingered the gash at my temple and replied, "Thank you, but I know of one person who doesn't hold me in much regard."

"You weren't the target."

"I know, but it didn't matter to him if I was in the cross hairs."

"That says something about the man, doesn't it?" Tom Danford asked. "It's hard to believe it's somebody we know, maybe somebody I've given care to in my time."

"And maybe somebody whose hair I cut," I said, "but I think we'll know soon enough now."

"If I were him, I'd be worried. There was a look on Carpenter's face last night that made me glad he wasn't on my trail."

"Silas has a sad reason in his past for being so fierce about Emmett Wolf," I said.

"He may have a hundred reasons, Ruth, but last night it wasn't anything from his past that put that look on his face. It was all about the here and now, all about you, I'd say."

"Past and present can get mixed up, though, can't they?" I asked, not bothering to deny Tom's words. "Memory can confuse you sometimes, so you don't always know why you feel what you feel or do what you do."

"Sometimes," the doctor agreed, "but there wasn't any confusion in Mr. Carpenter last night. It was you he had eyes for. I think you've got a good man there, Ruth. I'm happy for you." Throughout the morning, the passing recollection of the doctor's words made me happy, too.

I forgot that Lizbeth hadn't seen me since before the alley run-in last evening, and her wide eyes and open mouth when I walked through the front door of the boarding house were almost comical.

"Oh, Miss Ruth, whatever happened to you?" I wrestled with what to tell her and then finally decided on the truth. It's easier to remember afterwards. I worried the girl would be frightened, but far from it. Lizbeth was indignant more than anything.

"The idea that someone would try to hurt you! I can't get over it!" She was a pig-tailed, freckled avenging fury on my behalf.

"And that's why I worry about you," I said as sternly as I could manage. It's hard to be stern with Lizbeth, whatever the cause. "There are wicked people in this world, Lizbeth."

"I know about wicked people, and I can take care of myself. You don't need to worry about me." The look she gave me was older than her years, but in a lighter tone, she added, "I'm not the one who looks like she was in a fight with a porcupine, Miss Ruth."

Vanity at her words made me put a quick hand to my cheek in dismay, but then I had to laugh. Lizbeth was right. As often as I had harped at her to be careful, I was the one with a bandage on my face.

A stream of people flowed by the shop through the afternoon, well-wishers with a hint of curiosity. Silas stopped in, too, asked for a haircut and waited his turn. He would be my last customer of the day, I decided. The ruckus from the night before followed by sleeping in a chair had left me wearied.

Silas sat down, let me drape the cloth over his shoulders, and then met my eyes in the mirror. "You look tired," he said.

"I am, but you came in with two ears and I promise you'll leave with the same number. I'll be careful."

"You know that's not what I meant."

I started snipping. "I know. Did you send your telegram?"

"Yes, but no answer yet. Major Prentiss told me he'd have somebody ride it over as soon as it comes."

"And you think the answer will make a difference?"

"It'll be the nail in Emmett Wolf's coffin." The phrase bothered me, but I didn't let it show. It wasn't my search and Wolf wasn't my quarry. "I'm glad to see that big bandage is gone. The doc must think your face is healing like he wants it to." Changing the subject. Maybe I had let some of my worry show, despite good intentions.

"I'll be right as rain before you know it." He stood and might have touched me, thought better of it, and instead reached past me to place his money on the counter.

"Thank you." He looked around at the empty seats. "Are you going home now?"

"As soon as I clean up." He went and turned the sign on the door to closed while I busied myself with end of the day tasks, then stood with his hands in his pockets, watching out the window and waiting patiently. Duncan was not a patient man, I recalled, too much to see, too much to do, too many people to meet, as if he knew his time was limited for discovering all that life had to offer. But Silas was the opposite, a patient, steady man, able to wait as long as it took. Wait for Emmett Wolf, and maybe wait for me, too. Not that he would have needed to be on my trail for ten years. Ten days would have been more than enough.

I stopped at the corner of the barber shop before we crossed the street and fingered the gouge in the wood. The bullet had ripped off part of the corner and plowed along the side of the building. It was hard to believe that something the size of a bullet could make such a deep groove in solid, heavy boards. It could have been Si that bore its mark, I thought, and without thinking I tucked my hand under his arm.

"It was a near thing," I said. Si gave a light touch to my wounded cheek.

"It'll be over soon." He had said that same thing to me just the day before.

"When you get your telegram?"

"That should do it." We heard the whistle of the late afternoon train, the last one of the day, just as we reached the gate to my front yard. "I need to go," he said. The train whistle had caught his attention in a curious way.

"Good night, Silas. I'll see you tomorrow," but I said the last words like a question.

"Try to keep me away." He gave me a light, brotherly kiss on my good cheek. "Good night, Ruth."

After supper that night, I sat out back with Danny and Othello for a while enjoying the night sky. We were a week away from the full moon and the visible half-moon above us was brilliant and white. It was like the old days with Danny, him sharing this and that from his day and me listening and making a comment every so often so he knew I was paying attention. We had been good company for each other for five years, but I could see both of us had changed. I thought about Silas Carpenter more and more, and Danny had ideas for his future, too, some of them far-fetched but fifteen is an age for fanciful dreams.

Finally, I yawned and stood. "I'm going to bed," I said.

"I think I'll stay out here with Othello a while longer." Danny lay back on the sparse grass that grew at the rear of the boarding house with an arm thrown over the big, black dog stretched out beside him.

"Good night, Danny."

He didn't look away from the night sky with its white moon and sweep of diamond stars when he replied, "Good night, Ruth."

I felt weepy that night, but not in a bad way. If I was reading the signs right, Danny would head off on his own one day soon, and Silas would be done with Emmett Wolf, and I would once more be a wife sleeping with a husband at her side. It's comfortable living in the past and finding your consolation in memories, but life wasn't meant to be comfortable. It was meant to be lived.

In the morning, I was almost myself again. Though my cheek still felt tender to the touch, the tiny piercings had begun to heal in earnest. The most serious spot by my temple was healing, too, but Dr. Danford told me he was afraid it would scar. I just shrugged. When I remembered how close the bullet had come to both Silas and me, and when I ran my finger along the rough groove cut along the barber shop wall, being concerned about a small scar over my eye seemed foolish and frivolous.

The day was a perfect May day, warm, sunny, breezy, and beautiful, the kind of day to turn a person restless. I shooed away my last customer from the barber shop and stepped out into the afternoon sunshine. Sheba had her shop door open and when I peeked inside, she was wielding a broom with ruthless vigor, her hair pulled back under a bandanna. She looked up at me when I said her name from the doorway.

"Sometimes I can't help myself," she said. "When the place begs for a good cleaning, I can usually resist, but not today. The sun and the breeze are both against me. I should be finishing Mrs. Talamine's traveling dress, and I want to capture the way the sun sets the rooftops ablaze, but look at me! Cleaning!" She sounded more disgusted than proud of herself, but she didn't stop sweeping for a single moment. I knew the feeling. Lizbeth did a fine job with the boarders' rooms, but lately, seated at the kitchen table with a morning cup of coffee in my hands, I had noticed that the kitchen and Danny's and my rooms needed the same springtime attention

Sheba was giving her shop. Bright sunshine through a window has a way of showing you things you'd rather not see.

"Don't let me interrupt an artist at work," I said with a grin and walked down to Hart's at a brisk pace. Sheba was right. I could throw open the windows in The Addition to the breeze, clean out the oven, scrub the floor, turn the mattresses, and do the chores that spring cleaning demanded but that I never had the heart to ask Lizbeth to do on her own. Since she had taken to staying later while Danny put in his extra hour at the freight warehouse, however, I thought that between the two of us, we might get some of those jobs done.

Sometimes I wonder how things might have turned out if that Friday in May hadn't been so warm and sunny, if Sheba Fenway hadn't thrown her door open for all the world to see her sweeping, if I hadn't felt so improved from my run-in with a side wall of splinters...if...if...if... I know wondering does no good, that all those things happened and because they happened, they had their own set of consequences, but I wonder about the why of things just the same. Like Sheba said about cleaning that afternoon: "Sometimes I can't help myself."

Lizbeth and I started in my room, gave the blankets, pillows, and small bedside rug a hearty shake outside, dusted the head board and the bureau, turned the mattress, put fresh linens on the bed, and washed down my bedroom floor. It was a satisfying experience, but I felt a little guilty that we had started with my room and not Danny's.

"Can you stay long enough to help me turn Danny's mattress?" I asked the girl. "I know it's past time for you to go home."

"I can stay as long as you need me," she said, but I worried about her going home later than usual.

"I can do what's left to be done except for turning the mattress," I told her. "That takes two sets of hands."

She pulled the linens off Danny's bed and then we each took a side of the mattress and hefted it up and over. As we did so, a light object fell onto the floor, followed by a second soft thud.

"What is that?" Lizbeth asked and bent to pick up what had fallen. "Oh. Oh, dear." She stared for a minute as if trying to make sense of what she held in her hand and then looked at me. "I know it's against boarding house rules, Miss Ruth, but maybe Danny discovered he enjoys a good cigar. Some men do. My pa likes a good one now and again when he can afford it. Danny didn't mean any harm."

She was a kind-hearted girl, and I knew she was worried about my being angry with Danny, but it wasn't his breaking the rules that made my stomach give a roll. I put out a hand and she placed both cigars onto my palm. I stared the same as Lizbeth had done but for a different reason because the two cigars, uncut and unsmoked, were wrapped with a white paper band adorned with a bright orange oval and dark blue script that spelled out the words *Kipp. The Cigar That Makes Good.* The exact same cigar band I had found on the bank of the river where Eddie Barts liked to fish.

I tried to smile. "I need you to do something for me, Lizbeth."

"Yes, ma'am," her eager tone willing to do anything if the crisis had passed and all was forgiven.

"I'm going to go down to the warehouse and talk to Danny." I interrupted her first word with, "I'm not angry, Lizbeth, not at all, but I want to talk to him about this." I nodded toward the cigars I held. "Will you go get Mr. Carpenter, tell him how we found the cigars and that I went to talk to Danny at the warehouse?"

"It's not a crime to smoke a cigar, is it?" Lizbeth's voice shook a little.

Even with the shock I felt, I had to smile. "No, it's not a crime, and I'm not going to have Danny arrested. Everything is fine, and I'm not angry. Just do what I ask. Keep looking until you find Deputy Carpenter. You may have to go a few places until you run him to ground, but you keep looking until you give him my message. Then, I want you to go straight home."

"But we haven't finished here." She looked at the unmade bed.

"I'll finish it later. You helped me with the mattress, and that's the part I have a hard time doing on my own. Go on now and do what I asked. Promise me you'll go straight home without stopping or talking to anyone after you find Silas."

"Yes, I promise." Lizbeth heard the serious, almost panicky tone in my voice and her face paled, making the brown dots of freckles across the bridge of her nose stand out in contrast. She looked at me with a troubled expression that made me want to give her a hug, but I didn't want to take the time for it.

Instead, I gave her a smile that was as reassuring as I could manage under the circumstances. "Good girl. I'm counting on you."

After she left, I took another long look at the cigars, remembered some of the recent conversations Danny and I had shared, and felt a dark and terrible suspicion begin to spread through me, the way a spill of ink broadens on a carpet, slow and unstoppable. It can't be true, I told myself. It's another suspicion you'll be ashamed of later. But I found my steps picking up speed as I started for the freight office, hurrying past Sheba's shop and the bank and the hardware store, everything closed up tight by then, walking on the edge of running past the Gooseneck Hotel and the Dry Goods Emporium and Norm Janco's feed and grain store, then skirts up and all out racing across a side alley and past the post office and the new telegraph office. I stopped at the front door of Phil's freight business, breathing hard, and shook the knob, but the door was locked. Of course, locked. The Tiglionis were two hundred miles away, weren't they? I took a long breath and then a second breath, not sure why I felt so anxious. Danny had worked at the freight office every afternoon for the past two weeks and had come home every day safe, fit, and hungry. Why should today be any different? I knew I was panicked and that panic bred unreasoning behavior – look at the good citizens of New Hope arresting young Joe Chandler – so I took a few additional breaths before walking down the alley that separated the freight and telegraph offices. I could see the Tiglionis' handsome house where it sat behind the warehouse dark and empty. Knowing everyone was gone made me calmer still. I'll find Danny working in the warehouse, I told myself, and get him to answer some questions, and then Silas will come and he'll know what to do. Silas Carpenter was a man who always knew what to do, a level-headed and composed man. I wished he were there with me just then, wished I had controlled my fears long enough to find him and show him the cigars, wished I was back at the boarding house beating carpets and curtains and bemoaning winter's dust.

But as much as I might wish it, I wasn't at the boarding house. I was at the rear double doors of the warehouse, which unlike the front office door pushed open easily. It would, I told myself, if Danny was working inside. I stepped into the warehouse. It was nothing but a big empty space filled with rows of stacked crates and big wooden barrels. Every so often a lit lamp or lantern sat atop a barrel to give modest light to that particular part of the warehouse. Overall, the place looked dim and empty.

I went in farther, getting worried all over again. Danny should be here. We hadn't passed on my hasty walk north, which we should have done if Danny was done for the day. But then he wasn't done for the day, not if he left lamps burning. He would never do that with all the wood and paper about. Danny must be here, working in a back corner somewhere, lost in his *long, long thoughts*, maybe smoking one of those fancy Kipp cigars. The idea of the boy working with a big cigar lolling from his mouth made me smile in spite of myself. Had his first few puffs made him sick? I was told that a cigar could have that effect on a young man when he tried it for the first time.

"Danny?"

I stopped midway into the warehouse to listen for any sounds that indicated Danny was there. Nothing. Two more steps.

"Danny?"

I clutched the Kipp cigars in my hand a little more tightly. What would I say to him about them? What did I need to know for sure? What was I afraid to know for sure?

"Danny?"

And then, from behind me, a low, friendly, familiar voice said, "He's not here, Ruth."

14

I gasped from being startled and turned, saw who it was, took a second, calmer breath, and said, "I can see that, Phil, but he should be. He's late for supper." He doesn't know about the cigars, I thought. He doesn't know what I know, and I can bluff as good as he can.

"When did you get home?" I asked, walking forward a few steps. "Are Julia and the girls home, too? How's the judge?"

Phil Tiglioni watched me with a slight smile on his ever-youthful face. A handsome man with a beautiful family. An upstanding citizen, business owner, and important member of New Hope's Merchants' Association.

"Oh, I've been home a day or two now. Not Julia and the girls, though. She wouldn't hear of leaving the judge." His voice held a slightly bitter edge I had never noticed before. "My wife is devoted to her father."

"Well, that's a good thing, I think, but not my business. Where's Danny?"

"I imagine he's on a pick-up. There's one showing in the log I left for him."

"Pick up from where?"

"Arnold's mill. I watched him leave and figured I had a little time to get over here for some supplies I need. I figure Danny'll be gone a little while yet. He's a boy careful about his work. You did a good job with him, Ruth."

"Thank you, but I can't take the credit. It was his parents that set him on the right track. If he'll be a while, then I'd better get home and put his plate of supper in the oven to keep warm." Phil stood between me and the warehouse doors and did not move when I stepped toward him.

"What's that you got in your hand, Ruth?" he asked. In one way and one way only he was a man like Silas Carpenter because those clear eyes of his did not miss anything. I had tried to slip the cigars into my pocket, but he caught the gesture.

"I found these under Danny's mattress," I said. I brought out the cigars and held them open-handed so he could see what they were. He doesn't know what I know, I told myself again. He can't. To him, they're just cigars. "If I'm not mistaken, you gave him these."

"I did. Kept a few back from a special order. Cigar smoking appeals to boys. Makes them feel like men." *Boys. Them.* He had tempted Eddie Barts with cigars, too, the devil!

"Well, I could dispute that if I had time. I've noticed that spitting on the floor makes boys feel like men, too, but I can tell you that neither spitting nor cigars is likely to endear him to any female."

Phil laughed. "No, you're right. Julia won't have either in the house. Is that why you're here, to give Danny a scold for the cigars? He didn't steal them, Ruth. I told him he could take a couple if he wanted. They were a gift."

I moved to the side, determined to slide past him as he talked, but he moved, too, like we were chess pieces on a board, until he stood between me and the door again.

"We have boarding house rules," I said. "No alcohol and no tobacco on the premises. I was doing some spring house cleaning and when I found these under Danny's mattress, I guess I was just so shocked I wanted to come right down here and see what he had to say for himself."

Phil Tiglioni's gaze was fastened on my face so intently that I didn't believe it possible anyone could watch with that kind of deep concentration and still hear what was being said.

"I'm afraid you'll have to hold your scold 'til the boy's back." For a moment, I heard something threatening in the words. Had he hurt Danny? Was the boy floating in the river?

Would it be Danny's body laid out on Dr. Danford's table? The fear made me reckless.

"If it was ordinary times, I could wait as easy as the next woman," I said, "but with what happened to poor Eddie Barts, I don't like it when Danny's out of my sight too long." Phil smiled again, and I knew then that he wasn't going to let me pass him without a struggle, that for a reason I didn't understand, he suspected I knew more than I said.

I shifted once more to the side, and he took a long step forward until he stood right in front of me, so close I could smell his breath when he spoke. A touch of alcohol there but nothing overpowering. Phil placed the tips of his fingers on my cheek.

"What happened here? You look like you had a run-in with a porcupine." I felt a spurt of anger mixed with fear at his playfulness – I am not a mouse to your cat, I thought – and willed myself calm.

"Just an accident," I said. "Hardly worth a mention, really." He didn't take his hand away, and we stood close that way for what seemed an eternity, his palm against my cheek and me stiff with fear and anger and outrage. Then I thought, what would I do and how would I act if Phil Tiglioni was who he said he was, Julia's husband and Bella's and Lucy's father?

I batted at his hand. "You're too familiar, Phil. What's the matter with you? I hate to think what Julia would say if she saw us like this."

He let his arm drop to his side but didn't back up. "You're right, of course, Ruth. I forgot myself, and I beg your pardon."

"Julia's a wonderful woman," I said. I had seen his look soften at the mention of his wife and wanted to pursue talking about her. His smile gained warmth, too, no longer at my expense but a smile that came from happy memories.

"She is that, and you don't know the half of it. I remember the first time I saw her stepping off the train. I had never seen a woman like her before, so elegant and beautiful.

And then she smiled right at me – me! – and she let me court her and she said yes to marrying me. That was like nothing I ever thought possible, Ruth. I felt like the luckiest man in the world." For a moment, for one perverse moment, I saw myself in him. It was a shock but that was exactly how I felt about Duncan from the day he arrived in New Hope. Could they both be love? Were Phil Tiglioni and I so much alike, then?

"And the girls look just like their mother," I said.

"They do. Sometimes I stop by their room to watch them sleep, and I can see Julia in their little faces." Did Pete Lindquist stand in the doorway and watch his Evie and Emma sleep, too, I wondered. Did he see Dorie in their faces?

Phil stood with his arms loose at his side, smiling a little at the memory of his daughters, and I made a sudden lunge toward the door, fast but not fast enough to keep his right hand from landing a flat-palmed blow to my chest that sent me backwards stumbling to my knees.

"Well, I must be right about you, Ruth. I wondered, but I couldn't be sure. I thought keeping Danny around might help me figure out what you and Carpenter knew, but that didn't work. Always thought you were a woman I could read a mile away, but I see I was wrong. You sure had me going." He sounded surprised.

I stood, gasping a little for breath, and said in a strangled voice, "How dare you manhandle me like that, Phil?! I have no idea what you're talking about, but your behavior made me uncomfortable from the start. I believe you've been drinking, but I won't mention it to Julia if you promise it won't happen again. Now I'd like to go home." Because of where his forceful shove had pushed me, he no longer stood between me and the door. Now or never, Ruth, I thought. I couldn't outrun him or outmaneuver him so instead I lifted my chin and took two firm and deliberate steps past him, a woman shocked and outraged by the behavior of a friend's husband and showing nothing else. Not suspicion. Not horror. Not fear so deep that at any moment I expected to start trembling nonstop with terror. Though I felt all those things deep inside, I was determined not to show them.

Phil put a hand on my arm, and when I tried to jerk loose, he said my name with a sigh and then, "I can't let you go." I know I wasn't myself just then, but I would have sworn I heard a touch of affection in the words, affection and a true regret. He looked right into my eyes, willing me to agree with him. "You understand why, don't you? You know too much, same as Carpenter. He'll get word that I haven't been in Hill City for days, not that Julia's missed me, being so wrapped up in the judge." That same bitter tone to his voice as before. "I have a good life in New Hope, Ruth, better than I ever knew before, and I can't let either of you ruin it."

"It's too late for that, Wolf."

Both Phil and I turned our heads at the same time to see Silas Carpenter standing in the open doorway. In one hand he grasped a pistol aimed at Phil, and with his other hand, he held a short-barreled rifle low against his thigh. In a fluid motion that took me by surprise, Phil yanked me against his chest, one arm tight across my ribs. I could feel the unyielding bore of a revolver pressed into my side. Maybe I would have acted differently if I had known he carried a gun on him. I hadn't seen it, but if I had, I might have been more inclined to keep my distance. The problem was that he was still Phil Tiglioni to me. Owner of the freight company, Julia's husband, and the father of two cute little girls.

"If you move one more time, Ruth, I'll be forced to kill you," he said to me, and to Silas, "You'd better tell her I mean it, Carpenter. You understand that better than anybody. It won't bother me to pull the trigger, and you know what'll happen then. Poor Ruth will end up with all her insides on the floor. Not a pretty sight for such a pretty woman."

"If you do that," I said, "Silas will kill you, and what will anyone have gained?" Except with Wolf dead, maybe Silas would be able to find a measure of peace, though I had hoped to share that peace with him.

"Stay still, Ruth," Silas said without looking at me.

Tiglioni – I supposed he would always be Phil Tiglioni to me, whatever happened – jerked his arm against me with such force that I made a small sound of protest. "Yes, stay still, Ruth. This is between men."

"If it's between men like you say," Silas said, "then you should let Ruth go. It's not her fight."

"Not my fight, either," Phil said. "Hell, you're the one who wouldn't let it go. *Hound of Death* the papers called you. You couldn't let me live in peace. What did I ever do to you?" Si didn't answer. "Times were different after the war, Carpenter. You know that. Everybody ran wild. But I got a family and a business and a standing in the community now, and I like it. A man can't go back and change the past, but these last few years I hardly bothered anybody. Just a bank now and then and only when I needed the money."

"Except for Eddie Barts," Si said. "Except for selling guns to the Sioux to use against homesteaders."

"I felt bad about Eddie, I did, but I heard you found my telegram on that fool Hank Ketchum, and I knew you'd track it here. What else could I do? And those guns? People think this freight business makes a lot more money than it does, though it gives me the freedom to be gone for days on end with no one the wiser. I needed that freedom because from the day we got married, I told myself my wife would never do without. Julia deserves a fine house and beautiful clothes and anything she wants. Hell, she's never known anything different than that all her life. Then the girls came along, and she wanted the best for them, too, so I got the money any way I could to keep my Julia happy."

"But always at other people's expense," Silas said, careful not to let any blame or accusation show in his tone. Phil heard it, nevertheless.

"I don't give a damn about other people, just Julia." Phil paused and with a suddenly sly tone to his voice said, "You understand that, don't you, Carpenter? I watched you and Mrs. Churchill here," he shoved the revolver into my side with enough force to make me give a sudden whimper of pain that I feared might distract Silas. I needn't have worried. Si hadn't looked at me once since showing up on the scene, and he didn't look at me then. All his attention was on Wolf. I didn't blame him, either. Silas was closer to his quarry now than he had ever been in his life, and the knowledge of it must be consuming his every thought.

"You wouldn't want anything to happen to her, would you?"

"No."

"I thought so. I could see how it was. You can't hide much in a small town."

Except you being Emmett Wolf all these years, I thought. I couldn't believe it, even as I stood held against him with his arm pressed across my ribs like an iron bar and in his other hand a gun aimed and cocked to send a bullet in my one side and out the other. It still felt like it couldn't be true.

"You ruined the life I had here, Carpenter, and I can't get it back so why shouldn't I return the favor and blow a hole right through the middle of Mrs. Churchill? Even if you manage to kill me, you'll always know she'd be alive except for you. That's a hell of a memory for a man to carry the rest of his life."

"What do you want, Wolf?" Silas, cool and steady and still without looking at me. He watched the other man without once shifting his glance away.

"Will you beg for her?" Whatever I expected, it wasn't that question, with its slight touch of merriment and what sounded like honest curiosity. "Will you beg me not to kill her? I'd do it for Julia if the situation was different. And maybe if you do that real pretty, I won't kill her. Maybe I'll just kill you. Will you get down on your knees and beg for her?"

Silas never hesitated. "I will," he said. He might have been agreeing to have a beer with a friend. "Tell me what you want me to do."

"First, set down your guns real careful." I realized with dismay that bordered on despair that Emmett Wolf had found a way to use me against Silas, and that Silas was going to do what he said. For me. He was going to try to buy time from a man who had stolen other people's God-given time without a second thought, people like Si's Dorie and her family. For me. And in the end, Wolf would kill us both. How could he not? All three of us in that warehouse must know it. I wanted to tell Si not to do what he was doing, but I didn't. It wasn't my place. As wrong as it seemed because I might die in the exchange, Wolf was right. This was a fight between these two men.

Si crouched slowly, held up the rifle so Wolf could keep it in sight, placed it on the ground, and followed suit with his revolver. When he had put both weapons on the floor, he stood, arms loose at his side, and waited.

"I want you to get down on your knees and beg me not to kill Ruth. I want to see it. I want to hear you say it."

"All right," Si said. Then in a friendly way, he asked, "Do you plan to keep your word and let her go when I do? Just curious."

"Maybe I will, just for the hell of it. I always liked Ruth." He spoke about me as if I wasn't there, as if he wasn't pressing my ribs back with enough force that I couldn't take a full breath. "She brought presents for my girls when they were born. Pretty little dresses that made Julia smile. Julia likes Ruth, too, so maybe I'll do exactly what I said and send Mrs. Churchill on her way home free and clear. But I can tell you this, Carpenter, she won't live to see tomorrow if you don't do what I tell you, and that's a guarantee you can take to the United Bank of Nebraska."

Silas gave Emmett Wolf a long look and then I believe it was his intention to drop to his knees just as Wolf commanded except exactly at that moment we all heard the jingle of harness and the creak of wheels as a wagon pulled up outside the open double doors of the warehouse.

"Mr. Tiglioni?" Danny's voice.

Everything happened fast then, though the telling of it will make what occurred seem as long as one of Reverend Shulte's sermons. Danny's voice startled Wolf enough to make him shift his gaze outside. I felt the gun shift away, too, no longer pressed against me but now pointed toward the open doorway of the warehouse. I was freed just enough to jab my right elbow back sharp and hard into Wolf's ribs. He gave a grunt at the impact and tried to bring the barrel of his pistol back against me, but his grasp across my ribs loosened as he tried to adjust his aim. That gave me the time I needed to grab hold of his gun arm with both hands, drag it down, and clamp my teeth hard into the soft flesh of his wrist. I gave him as fierce a bite as I could, and his pistol clattered to the floor. Wolf gave a ferocious curse and tried to shake me off, but by then Silas was on top of him and we all tumbled to the floor. I rolled away and dragged myself behind a barrel. A fight between men, Wolf had said. Now he had a chance to know what that really meant.

Wolf's gun skittered in the direction of the barrel where I landed, and as the two men rolled wildly on the warehouse floor, grunting, arms flailing, fists thudding with the awful sound of flesh on flesh, I crawled on all fours to get the pistol. I rose unsteadily to my feet with the gun in my hand just as Silas connected a hard fist to the side of Wolf's head and sent the man backwards against a stack of boxes. I think I remembered before Silas, though he was not far behind me, that it was in that general area where Silas had laid down his own guns.

"Silas!" I cried. "Here!" He reached up with his left hand and caught the gun I tossed just as the outlaw rose holding Si's pistol. I saw it with my own eyes, but I still couldn't say exactly how it happened, just that with the smoothest, fastest motion I have ever seen, Silas flipped the gun into his other hand, his gun hand, and without taking aim shot Emmet Wolf before that man was able to get off a single shot. The sound of Si's gunshot echoed in the warehouse. He's killed that bad man, I thought, but realized almost at once that I was wrong.

Emmett Wolf gave a scream of pain, an awful sound that echoed like the gunshot, and fell to his knees, clutching his wrist to his chest. Blood gushed from his arm and soaked onto his shirt. For a moment, I couldn't drag my gaze away from the sight of protruding bone and all that blood, but then I came to my senses. I had to go for the doctor. When I started toward the warehouse door, I saw Danny standing there with a look on his face as he stared at Phil Tiglioni that was equal parts shock and confusion. I said Danny's name and, when the boy didn't look at me, said it again, louder and in a tone firm enough to get his attention.

"Hurry and get Dr. Danford," I told Danny, surprised I sounded as normal as I did after what just happened. The boy opened his mouth to speak, but I cut off whatever he was about to say. "Go get Dr. Danford. Right. Now. We'll talk about this later." Danny gulped, nodded, and took off at a run.

I went to stand next to Silas and wanted to take his hand in mine, but I stopped when I saw the look on his face as he stared at Emmett Wolf. Wolf saw the look, too.

Still using his good hand to hold his broken, bleeding arm against his chest, he said to Silas, "You can kill me, Carpenter." Wolf was the one begging now. "I can see you want to. You can end it right here, and no one needs to know. Ruth won't tell. They'll hang me so why wait for that?" He took a deep, shaky breath; the pain of his shattered arm must have been excruciating. "Be done with it, man. Why let the state of Missouri do what you've waited ten years for?" There wasn't any taunt in Wolf's voice, and I guessed that what he dreaded more than anything was seeing the look on his wife's face when she found out who she had been married to all these years. To this day, I believe that was the only thing Emmett Wolf ever feared in all his life.

I thought that Wolf was right, that in the end he would die by the rope, and I thought he was right about Silas, too.

For ten years, Si had lived and breathed nothing but Emmett Wolf, and here was his chance – at last, at last – to put paid on his relentless quest. Wolf was right about me, as well. Whatever Silas chose to do, I would support him and say nothing. Hadn't I lost someone I loved and then spent the next years in misery bred by sorrow and anger? In my own way, I understood about grief and guilt and chasing peace.

As if Wolf hadn't spoken, Silas turned to me. The look in his eyes almost made my knees buckle.

"Are you all right, Ruth?"

"Yes." The word came out a whisper. I knew he wasn't going to kill Emmett Wolf – for that moment I would have sworn he wasn't thinking about Emmett Wolf, at all – and it was like someone had lifted a heavy load off my heart.

"You kept a cool head. That was good."

"I didn't feel very cool. Not inside," I admitted.

"Still—" We looked at each other a moment before Silas smiled at me.

Who was this man standing in front of me, I wondered, that could fight like a wild animal and shoot like an army sharp-shooter and then give me a smile sweet enough to sprinkle on shortcake?

"Will you do something for me?" Silas asked. Wolf might not have been there at all.

"You know I'll do anything you ask."

"That'll make good conversation later," he said, "but right now, I need you to go over to the jail and unlock the cell door. Leave the keys on the desk so I can pick them up on my way through. Then I want you to go home and stay inside and wait for me. However long it takes, you wait for me. Will you do that?"

"Yes."

"Promise?"

For a second, one corner of Si's mouth twitched, and I knew we were both thinking the same words - *within reason and when it's convenient* - but I restrained myself. It didn't seem like the time or place for levity. Instead, I nodded.

"Yes," I said. "I promise," and left through the warehouse doors to do as Si asked.

What surprised me most was that it was still daylight outside, a warm late-afternoon in May like any other. What had taken place just now inside the freight company warehouse had seemed to go on for hours, but I knew from my own memories that fear and darkness seemed to last forever when you were living through them.

I crossed the street to the jail and, my tasks there finished, stepped back outside just in time to see Danny and Dr. Danford hurrying down the side alley by the freight office. The whistle of the departing late afternoon train sounded and passengers took a final stretch on the platform. Rays of the setting sun caught the roof of the Gooseneck Hotel on fire – Sheba should try to paint that sometime, I thought. How normal New Hope seemed again!

My thoughts were all a jumble, my feelings even worse as I walked south toward Hart's. What should I make of all that happened these past weeks? I harbored some awful suspicions about some of my friends, but I learned to look at Arthur Stenton kindlier and with greater appreciation. I lost what little respect I held for Cap Sherman, but my regard for the Chandlers increased the more I found out about them. Because Emmett Wolf came to New Hope, so did Silas Carpenter. Darkness and light lived side-by-side. Was that what life was all about? What love was all about? When I pushed open the gate, Othello rose from his place on the porch, realized I wasn't Danny, gave a mournful little whine, and lay back down with his chin on his paws to wait for his boy. Light and darkness, love and grief were all mixed up in my head and my heart just then, but I knew eventually I'd make sense of it all. Just as soon as Silas came home.

15

I'm good at waiting. Many's the night I sat by Duncan's bed holding his hand in mine until pale morning light showed faintly behind the curtains of our bedroom window. If Silas wanted me to wait, then that's what I planned to do.

Because I had lied to Phil about Danny's supper growing cold, I thought my first task was to get something edible on the stove and then onto the table. Once in a while as I busied myself in the kitchen, someone would stick his head in the front door of the boarding house and call my name. It was always the same question: "Is it true about Phil?" And I always gave the same answer before I went back to pork chops in the frying pan. No elaboration or explanation, just, "Yes, I'm afraid so."

I was just completing the cleaning Lizbeth and I had left undone in Danny's room, when I heard the boy come in through the back door at the end of the hallway. I went out to meet him. When he saw me, he licked his lips and said, "I got to get something off my conscience."

"All right."

"I'm sorry about the cigars. I know you said no tobacco on the premises, and I know I was wrong to have them. I'm awful sorry, Ruth." The hang dog expression on his face would have put Othello to shame.

"You're forgiven." I didn't say, if you hadn't tucked those cigars under your mattress, Emmett Wolf would still be trying to kill Silas, but I thought that was likely true. There was no use letting Danny think that on some occasions the end justified the means, however. That was hardly what I wanted him to learn from the experience.

Danny told me that Silas had wired the fort for support, and that the Army was going to take Phil Tiglioni – the boy never called him anything but Phil, regardless of the outlaw's true identity – into its custody that same night, shattered forearm or not. I understood that Silas wanted the man out of his sight as soon as possible but couldn't help wincing a little at the thought of riding in the back of a wagon with a recently-splintered bone. Later, someone told me that when Wolf was taken from the jail, his feet were shackled and his wrists bound and he moaned a little with pain. I didn't go out to look and I don't feel I missed anything because of it.

All my boarders trickled in following their suppers at the café, and I heard them discussing the day's events as they went upstairs to their rooms. When the sun had fully set and everyone was in safe and sound, when Danny said his good night and went to bed, and Silas still hadn't appeared, I took Duncan's book of poetry and went out to wait in one of the stuffed chairs that gave the boarding house such a welcoming appearance. I turned the lamp on the table up so I could read. *"I love thee to the level of every day's most quiet need, by sun and candlelight."* The line always caught at my throat and did again that night. By lamplight, too, I thought, and for the first time the words did not cause a tide of grief for Duncan to well up inside me. I was comfortable with that and thought Duncan would have been comfortable with it, too. It was life he loved, not memories of life. When my eyelids grew heavy, I put the book in my lap and lay my head against the back of the chair. I didn't think I slept, but I must have because I was awakened by the sound of Silas saying my name. He could have whispered it, and I would still have heard.

When I rose, he lifted both hands toward me, palms up, like he was waiting for something to drop into them from above, and I went into his arms. We stood like that a long time, pressed close together. He pulled me even closer, though I didn't think that was possible, and kissed me, and we spent a long time doing that, too. Finally, breathless but in a good way, I pulled back and said my first words, which made him laugh under his breath.

"Are you hungry?" I asked.

"Couldn't you tell?"

"For supper, I meant. I kept something warm for you."

He wanted to give a teasing response to that, too, but looked at my face and thought better of it. "I could eat something," he said.

As soon as Silas sat down at the kitchen table, I put a plate of supper in front of him and then stopped behind him long enough to rest both my hands on his shoulders. He wouldn't see thirty again, but he was still a solid, muscled man. I remembered him rolling around on the warehouse floor with Emmett Wolf and was grateful for the strength I felt under my hands.

Silas patted the seat of the chair to his left. "Come and sit down so I can look at you."

I did as he asked and ignoring my own house rules said with a touch of shyness, "You didn't look at me once there in the warehouse. I thought at the time it was because you were as close to Wolf as you had ever been, and you couldn't think of much else." He put down his fork to look at me as I rushed on, "I understand that, Silas. I can't imagine what it must have been like for you to finally catch up with the man after all these years!"

He put his left hand over mine on the table. "Is that what you think, Ruth?" I nodded, struck dumb by the look on his face. "I didn't look at you," he went on, "because I thought if I did, I wouldn't be able to control myself. I knew that man and I knew what he was capable of and the idea that he might hurt you—" Silas used the word *hurt* because I didn't think he could get out the word *kill* just then "— was enough to make me wild. I didn't want to see the expression on your face. I didn't want to see the fear in your eyes. I just couldn't look at you." He raised my hand to his lips and kissed it. "Emmett Wolf didn't matter just then. Only keeping you safe mattered."

"Oh," I said and took a shaky breath. He smiled a little, placed my hand gently back on the table – I was reminded of the night he rescued Cora Barts from the fire and placed her frail body so carefully, so tenderly on the ground, the night I started to love him – and went back to his supper. I got up, brought him cake and coffee, and sat down beside him again. There was a lot I wanted to know and even more I wanted to say, but it isn't wise to interrupt a hungry man at his meal, not if you want his full attention.

When he pushed away his empty plate, I asked, "Is Wolf gone now?"

"Yes. The Army came for him. They'll make sure he gets back to Missouri for trial."

"Will you go to the trial?" Silas thought about the question and then shook his head.

"No, I don't think so. I believe I've spent enough of my life on the man. I don't want to give him any more of it." The words sent a flash of joy through me.

"What will you do now? I mean, what are your plans?"

"I guess I'll stay on until Bradley tells me I'm not deputized any more. Then, I don't know. Maybe the railroad has more work for me." Silas eyed me as he added, "Joe Chandler came by the jail tonight to ask if I'd consider an offer from New Hope to be its permanent marshal. For a fair wage, of course."

"Preacher, teacher, keeper of the peace," I said, thinking out loud. "That sounds good and the order seems right. Are you considering the offer?"

"I am." We looked at each other, and this time I reached for his hand.

"You know what I'd like?" I asked. Silas shook his head. "I'd like you to stay the night."

"Tonight?"

"Yes."

"Here?"

"Yes."

"Well—"

"There's clean linens on my bed," I said, as if it was that temptation and not the offer of my person that would convince him to stay.

Silas scowled and said, "That's not proper for a decent woman like yourself. We ought to be married first."

Another woman might have found the scowl off-putting, if not downright insulting, but I knew this man, this preacher's son.

"You've never asked me," I pointed out in a reasonable tone.

"Will you?"

"Yes." And that was that.

"We should wait until the preacher says the words." Silas had a stubborn set to his mouth I thought I would probably see now and then in the future and decided it wouldn't hurt to figure out a way past it now. I stood and, sending the table back with a scrape, squeezed myself onto his lap.

With both my arms around his neck, I whispered, "He can say the words tomorrow. We'll say ours tonight. You and I could both be dead, Silas. It's pure foolishness for you to go back to a single cot in a cold jail cell." I kissed him long and hard.

"But Danny—" Si's voice sounded like someone was strangling him, but I didn't think my arms were wound that tightly around his neck.

"Danny slept through the fire alarm," I said and kissed Silas again. I felt him struggle with the right and wrong of things, but one thing led to another, as it tends to do in those situations, and I got my way, after all.

Later, when I woke in the night, I could feel the steady rise and fall of Si's chest under me, but I didn't think he was sleeping. His right arm was draped over me, but his left hand was behind his head. He lay stretched out on his back and I knew he was thinking, maybe remembering. I rearranged myself, felt his arm tighten a little around me, and started thinking, too, remembering that dark time in the warehouse. Silas Carpenter would have begged for me at the feet of a man he hated. I was willing to die for him in a fight I had no part of. Surely that was enough to start a life together.

Thinking of that made me lift myself off his chest and say, "Oh, Silas, what about Julia? Who will tell Julia?" Just then, warm in the arms of the man I loved, the idea of Julia Tiglioni was enough to make me weep. Si must have heard the sadness in my voice because he kissed the top of my head and drew me back down.

"Hush, Ruth."

I lifted up on one elbow again and tried to see Si's face in the moonlight that came through the lace curtains. "But—"

"Major Prentiss said he's acquainted with a judge in Graham County who's a friend of Julia Tiglioni's father. He said he'd wire the man to go over first thing tomorrow – no, today – and tell Julia about her husband. The major said the man wouldn't like it, but that he had known the family a long time and would see the need for it."

"So she'll know before the newspapers get hold of the story?" I pursued. "I wouldn't want her to find out that way." I tried to imagine what it would be like to open to the front page and see your husband's name in bold, black letters, and then read about what he was and what he did and what his future held. The idea made me shiver.

"A friend of the family will tell her before that happens. I promise."

"All right, then." I laid back down, then lifted myself a final time to kiss him. "Thank you, Silas." Which was all it took for one thing to lead once more to another. Not that I minded.

I didn't open the barber shop the next day, even though a sunny Saturday meant a good supply of customers and revenue. Instead, when Silas and I woke early that morning, my husband-to-be swung both feet onto the floor and said in a firm and satisfied tone, "Today is our wedding day." He looked over his shoulder where I still lay, drowsy and contented, and added, "Isn't it?"

For some reason the plaintive tone in his voice started me giggling. I rolled and buried my face in the pillow trying to squelch the laughter, but it was no use. I felt so joyful.

Silas hadn't moved from where he sat at the edge of the bed, but I recognized a certain look in his eyes, which made his next words disappointing. "You won't tempt me to dishonorable behavior, Ruth, not again."

"Not until we're legal, you mean?" I gave him a big, broad wink, which surprised him enough to turn his face a little pink. He was a difficult man to shock, that Silas Carpenter, because he had been a lot of shocking places and had seen a lot of shocking things, but a respectable woman winking at him from his bed might have been a first.

"Never mind," I said, taking pity on him. "Yes, indeed, today is our wedding day."

Silas snuck out of The Addition with his clothes draped over his arm like he was a robber sneaking off with the family treasure, hoping no one saw him, which made me laugh again. As if half of New Hope didn't have the deed done weeks ago. My new husband had a lot to learn about living in a small town.

With Silas headed for the bath room to pour a hot bath for himself, I took my leisure getting dressed, pulled my hair back with a ribbon, and walked down to Sheba's dress shop. A woman I didn't recognize was with Sheba when I pushed open the door so I made a few slow circuits of the shop, fingered satins that glowed in the sunlight, admired dimity stripes, and waited until Sheba's customer left.

"That was shocking news about Phil Tiglioni," Sheba said as soon as we were alone, and then at the sight of my face stopped speaking for a long while. "Well," she said at last. "Well."

"Reverend Shulte doesn't know it yet, but he's marrying Silas and me this afternoon, and I wondered if you'd stand up with me and be my witness."

"Of course, I will." Sheba Fenway isn't like me. She doesn't wear her heart on her sleeve and I've never seen her cry, but she walked over to me and gave me a long hug. "I'd be honored, Ruth," she said. "Nothing would make me happier."

Once home, I told Danny, "No school today," and sent him with a note to the Shultes' house. I heated water on the stove, gave myself a stand-up bath in the kitchen, and put on my best dress, a soft wool of sunshine yellow with tiny blue rosebuds embroidered along the hem and the collar. In the mirror, I didn't see my cheek with all its speckled pinpricks or my unruly hair. All I saw was a woman so happy she glowed. This feeling won't last forever, I told myself, because life isn't all sunshine and rosebuds. There will be hard times and arguments and maybe more grief, but I'm joyful today, this one day, and that's enough for me.

From the bedroom doorway, Silas said, "I'm going down to the jail for a clean shirt."

I turned and smiled. "You do that, but don't you dare be late for the wedding."

He took a long step toward me and gathered me up for a kiss. "No, ma'am. It was my idea, after all."

Sheba and Danny and I walked to the church right after lunch. Si was there already, talking to Gerald Shulte. Or more exactly, the reverend was talking to Silas, and Silas was listening and nodding. For a minute, he looked as young as Danny. He's getting directions on marriage, I thought, and approved the effort. I knew that marriage might take some getting used to for a man who had been on his own as long as Silas had.

Afterwards, vows spoken and blessings given, we all paused outside the church for a little while to chat – about the future, though, not the past. Finally, Silas turned to me, extended a hand, and asked, "Come for a walk, Ruth?" Oh, how I loved the sound of those words!

"Yes," I said, "always."

We had a long walk, punctuated by conversation only the two of us should know and fueled by a great deal of kissing. Then, as the day faded, we slowly made our way back home.

****

New Hope never saw Julia Tiglioni again. Her brother came to town, emptied the house and the freight office, and arranged with Mr. Talamine at the bank to sell off the buildings and property. He left without saying a word to anyone except the banker. The big house with its indoor plumbing eventually sold to a rich rancher whose wife didn't take well to country living. The bank found another owner for the freight business, too. The railroad added another stop and more stock pens. Our little town kept growing and growing.

Emmett Wolf never stood trial. He had a terrible end, but I knew it was his choice, and perhaps it spared Julia and her girls the grief and notoriety a trial would have brought. Shackled and waiting on the train platform for the incoming train that would carry him to Kansas City, he somehow managed to escape the grasp of his captors and throw himself under the approaching engine. He died instantly, nearly cut in half, so I heard, but I silenced the speaker telling the story and left the room. I don't know why hearing about Wolf's death affected me so deeply, but my husband found me later and knew enough to hold me tight against him until I was able to bear what I heard without weeping.

When our first child was due, I realized something would have to change. "The barber shop will have to go," I told Silas, "but I've decided to keep you and the boarding house."

"In that order?"

"Yes," I said, "though as you know, I've had the boarding house considerably longer." The shop's new owner kept the sign, so it's still *Duncan's*, but seeing the name over the door no longer makes my heart ache. The fellow isn't a bad barber, but he could use more practice. I have seen men walking around town with some shameful sideburns.

We added on to the back of The Addition at the birth of our second child, our golden-haired Dorie, a happy little girl all giggles and kisses and the apple of her father's eye. Then we quickly had a third child, another son. I think that at my age, we may be done with children, but I don't know that for sure. If it turns out to be the case, it won't be for lack of trying. Silas and I may be older, but one thing still leads to another more often than not.

Danny is in the United States Army at Camp Sheridan, Wyoming, soon to be renamed Fort Yellowstone. "It's colder here than it ever was in Nebraska," he wrote in his last letter; I heard the satisfaction in his words. Danny has never outgrown his love for action and adventure – for cigars, either. At his last school program in New Hope, he recited his poem and got it perfect start to finish. Bless Mr. Stenton, still a difficult man and a fine teacher. He knew what he was doing when he assigned those verses. Danny isn't a boy any longer, but he'll always be possessed of *long, long thoughts*.

Othello is buried behind the boardinghouse, and Sheba and Lizbeth – well, I love them both, but their stories aren't for me to tell.

With the slow but steady expansion of New Hope, Nebraska, the town has grown busier and noisier. Silas works with two deputies of his own now. The railroad can be a good thing, bringing in business and businesses, but it drops off scoundrels and ruffians and other assorted bad men, too. Larger stock pens invite more ranchers and cowboys to load their cattle onto the trains at New Hope, and after the loading, there's a lot of cash burning holes in pockets. Sometimes New Hope's reputable business establishments benefit from those heavy pockets, but other times the money goes toward alcohol and gambling and crime. Like the United States itself, we're a community on the move, though I'm not always sure in what direction.

For Silas, keeping the peace is seldom peaceful. I lost one husband, and sometimes on a rowdy Saturday night when I haven't seen Silas for hours, I fear losing him, as well. I never let Silas know, but I have times when worry for him is like a sharp blade thrust into my breast piercing through bone all the way to my heart. The moment can be so sudden and feel so sharp that I can't catch my breath. Then I have to slow down and remember the lesson I learned the day Emmett Wolf was caught. Light and darkness, love and grief will always live side-by-side. Sometimes they share the very same place in a person's heart.

Memories are safe. Living isn't. Living is risky and uncomfortable and messy and fearful, joyous and burdensome, tedious and tender, annoying and hopeful, unpredictable and passionate. Living is all those things and more. I spent a long time grieving for the past, and I know what I'm talking about. I may still feel the pangs of worry and fear, but if I've learned one thing, it's this – life's not for dwelling on memories. It's for making them.

If you enjoyed *What We Carry With Us*, don't stop here. Karen's books are all available at Amazon.com, in the Kindle Store, and at BarnesandNoble.com. You're sure to find more to enjoy. Her writing has been described as "satisfying" and her research as "flawless"* so there's no way you can go wrong.

The Laramie Series by Karen J. Hasley
Lily's Sister
Waiting for Hope
Where Home Is
Circled Heart
Gold Mountain
Smiling at Heaven

The Penwarrens by Karen J. Hasley
Claire, After All
Listening to Abby
Jubilee Rose

Stand-alone novels by Karen J. Hasley
The Dangerous Thaw of Etta Capstone
Magnificent Farewell

~ Remarkable Women. Unforgettable Stories. ~
All in Historical Settings

*Akron Beacon Journal, 2010

Made in the USA
Monee, IL
08 January 2023

24786572R00146